CLOSER THAN YOU THINK

A MAGS MUNROE STORY

JEAN GRAINGER

To Diarmuid,
Ni neart gur cur le cheile

Go deo

CHAPTER 1

'Mam!' Kate's high-pitched screech startles me awake. It's so loud I expect to find her in the room with me, but she's not, and her next shriek comes from downstairs in the hall. 'Mam, come quick!'

'What is it?' I yell back, grabbing my phone from the bedside locker to check the time. Eight thirty. Well, blast it anyway. The bed is empty – Kieran must have gone to work early – and I've slept through my alarm.

Another wail, and I hear the almost out-of-control panic in her voice. 'Mam, you have to come now! Rollo's escaped and he's got into Boomerang's field!'

Not this again. I scramble out of bed and pull on my Garda uniform, buttoning my shirt as I rush downstairs. 'OK, love, calm down. I'll sort it out.' My poor daughter is terror-struck. 'Where's Ellie? Who let Rollo out?' By the wide-open front door, I cram my bare feet into my boots. I haven't had time to find socks, I'm already running late for work, and I need this like a hole in the head, especially as I'll have to drop the girls to school if Kieran's gone already.

'Ellie went with Dad – she's got a school trip, and the bus was going at eight – and Rollo wanted a wee, and Ellie left the gate open, and I couldn't go after him 'cause Ellie will kill me if I lose Frankie in Boomerang's field – we'd never find her!'

Frankie is this tiny pygmy hamster, no bigger than my thumb, and called Frankie Velcro because of her extraordinary ability to cling to any fabric, her only trick. Right now the inch-long creature is glued to Kate's school jumper.

'OK, pet, don't worry. You just put Frankie in her cage and get ready for school. We're going as soon as I get back.' I belt down the drive through the misty October rain, thinking for the eightieth time how I do not wish to be a pet owner. But somehow this house went from one with no pets to one with a dog, a pygmy hamster and a frilled lizard in the space of six months.

Rollo was the first of the animal kingdom to arrive. He's a Jack Russell that Kieran found in a builder's yard three months ago. He had never been chipped and had no collar, and nobody claimed him. I was for rehoming him, to which fifteen-year-old Ellie replied, 'Is that like sending him to a farm? Because we know there's no farm. We know that they kill dogs that have no homes.' Upon which Kate burst into tears and clung to the ball of fleas. Kieran had always wanted a dog, and I'd always refused, but this one I wasn't going to win.

Frankie Velcro came next. He or she – we've no idea – was a gift from a boy called Goosey who is besotted with Ellie. Goosey, despite his nickname, breeds not ducks but rodents of all descriptions: rats, mice, hamsters, guinea pigs, you name it. And though he's a sweet lad with a kind heart, he smells accordingly. I cannot understand his passion. I intensely dislike all rodents and can't for the life of me figure out why people buy traps and poison and all sorts to keep some rodents out and then actively buy other ones to put in their houses. It's bewildering.

Thankfully Goosey's love is unrequited, because Ellie has her eye on a boy called Shane, who everyone calls Carrot, a name that also puzzles me because you'd think a Carrot would have bright-red hair, but he doesn't; he's dark and brooding and very thin. He manages to exude tortured artist despite the fact that his parents have a huge house and he goes to St Colm's, the private school. He's the type teenage girls are suckers for.

And then there's Knickers... Yes, you heard that right. Knickers, as in underwear, is the name of the frilled lizard – it's short for Frilly Knickers. Kate, who is twelve, thought this was hilarious. She won him in a raffle, which It think might even be illegal, and he's always escaping his purpose-built enclosure in the utility room and hiding – deliberately, I'm convinced – to scare me witless. What kind of a psycho-lunatic offers a huge lizard as a prize to a child is a whole other matter. Someone who wants to get rid of it obviously, but anyway, here we are. Mammy, nil. Kieran and the girls, three.

I reach the road. Boomerang Butler's field borders our garden, and Rollo has squeezed through the hawthorn hedge and is sitting on the other side of the gate watching the sheep with interest as they rush around in a blind panic as if he's the big bad wolf and not a stubby little terrier with arthritis in his hips.

'Rollo! Get back here!' I hiss in my sternest voice, but he only looks over his shoulder at me with terrified eyes, as if I'm about to take a pike to him. He loves Kieran and the girls, but the ridiculous animal cringes and whimpers every time he sees me, as if I secretly kick him whenever we're alone. I have never harmed an animal in my life, I couldn't, but this eejit deliberately sets out to make me look like a monster. Suffice to say we don't get along.

The gate is padlocked and covered in barbed wire, but Boomerang has threatened to shoot Rollo if he gets into his field again, so I have no choice but to climb over and physically pick up the cowering dog and climb back again before Boomerang can appear with his shotgun.

Boomerang Butler is not my biggest fan. He is a conspiracy theorist with odious political views on immigrants, gay people, Travellers – basically anyone not a middle-aged white Irishman. He made a big hoo-ha a few years back about moving to Australia, getting out of this damp kip of a country for once and for all, that it was going to the dogs anyway. He was going to make it big Down Under. He had connections in the farming business there, and he'd make his fortune while the rest of us suckers would be rusting away here. He threw a big party in the pub, 'so long, losers' kind of vibe, and none of us were sorry to see him go. Except I knew he'd be back in a couple of days, and sure enough, he was. Hence the nickname.

He claimed it was that he realised he couldn't leave his poor elderly mother, the woman he'd not spoken to for five years and who had no time for him whatsoever, but the reality was he had no visa due to a conviction in his twenties for Grevious Bodily Harm and he was turned around at the airport. I knew this would happen, of course, knowing his record, but it would have been unprofessional to say it. Being Ballycarrick, the truth got out – not from me or any of my officers, I hasten to add. Kieran asked me afterwards if I was aware that Boomerang could never gain entry to the USA or Australia with a criminal conviction, and I said I did. He looked at me then. 'You're a dark horse, Mags Munroe. I'm glad I'm with you and not against you.'

Maybe it was my undisguised lack of surprise at seeing him back again, but Boomerang is now convinced I ratted him out to immigration, which I didn't. He can't touch me obviously, so he's trying to find reasons to shoot poor Rollo now. I mean, if that animal knew the lengths I go to, to save his life, you'd think he'd look less like one of those medieval martyrs you see in oil paintings, all pained and put upon.

Once back on the safe side of the gate, I lug Rollo into the house, his eyes rolling in terror, and fill his bowl with dog nuts. I notice I've ripped a hole in my sleeve on the barbed wire, and I run upstairs to change my shirt and put on some socks while Kate waits with her schoolbag in the hall. At least she's no longer wearing Frankie Velcro like a brooch.

The sock drawer in our bedroom is the communal family sock drawer, bursting with single socks. I know, don't judge me, but who on earth has time to pair socks? I certainly don't. Nobody in my family cares too much about pairing them anyway; I can't remember the last time Kieran wore matching socks. I rummage frantically until I find a black one with no pattern or holes, best for work, and then a suitable comrade.

When I whip open the wardrobe to find a fresh shirt, I scream shrilly as Knickers bursts out and scarpers across the room on his hind legs, mouth wide open and flaring the yellow frill around his scaly neck like a miniature dinosaur. That lizard is the Houdini of the animal kingdom.

'Kate,' I yell, my heart pounding. 'Kate! Can you come up here please, love? Knickers is out again!'

I wonder if Knickers feels about me like I feel about Rollo. Right now he's probably thinking, *I've never done anything to that woman in all my life, I try my best to keep out of her way, and yet every time she sees me, she acts like I'm coming at her with an axe.*

But I can't help it. Of all the animals in the house, I can't bear Knickers the most. He's huge, and his knobbly head and creepy stare freak me out.

I drive through Ballycarrick to drop Kate at the community school, one minute spare to the bell. She hugs me and kisses my cheek as she leaves the car, and I realise what a great girl she is. Kate doesn't care if her friends see her being affectionate with me or Kieran. She's such a sweet kid. Then it's back up Main Street to the station, waving to Tatiana as she sweeps autumn leaves from the steps of the Samovar. I turn right, then pull in around the back of the Garda station, mentally going through the agenda for today as I climb the steps to the back door and come in past the toilets and the broom cupboard.

I love my job. I work with great people, and the locals here in Ballycarrick are overwhelmingly nice people. We have the occasional criminal, oddball or creep, but generally people are great and know we are there to help, not harass them.

But as I look through the glass door of the public office to see what awaits me, I sigh inwardly. Two people I could have done without.

One of them is our latest recruit, Zoë O'Donoghue. I am trying to be reasonable and fair, and she's ambitious and determined to be a good police officer, but she is lounging behind the public desk, taking a selfie on her phone. An actual *selfie* in her uniform. And she's making a dopey face that she imagines is sultry and sexy but makes her look like a constipated duck.

I'm trying to like her, but honest to God, she'd test the patience of a saint. She keeps referring to herself as a Gen Z, as if being born in a specific decade bestowed talents and virtues on that entire generation that the rest of us are sadly lacking. She's forever going on about influencers and looking piteously at me, since I clearly remember when dinosaurs even bigger than Knickers roamed the land and therefore have not an iota of a clue about anything, *like, actually important*. She's just a kid, and she's impressionable and not half as confident as she tries to appear, so I do my best to give her the benefit of the doubt most of the time. But sometimes it's not that easy.

The other occupant of the public office is Oscar O'Leary, a devout Catholic with particular devotion to St Gertrude, the patron saint of cats. He is sitting on the bench by the water cooler, reading the parish bulletin. Zoë is ignoring him, but to be fair to her, he has no doubt insisted on waiting to complain to me personally about whatever is troubling him today – and I suspect I know what that is.

Oscar's faith and the Church are his whole life, and he is determined to save the souls of Ballycarrick from the blandishments of Satan, so I knew as soon as I saw the broomstick poster on the pillar and the cars parked outside the newly occupied Lodge that sooner or later he'd be in.

As I open the internal door, Zoë glances up. Her eyelashes look suspiciously long, even though I've already explained that false eyelashes are a no-go for a member of the gardaí.

'Slay queen,' she murmurs as I pass.

I stop in my tracks. 'What was that?' I ask. I happen to know what this particular piece of modern jargon means, as my daughters are forever saying how this or that slays, or such and such is a 'slayful queen'. But this is a professional environment, and I am her boss. Allowing her to blur the chain of command so early on in her career won't help her.

She giggles. 'It just means you are a slayful queen, y'know? Like a boss?' Her voice goes up at the end of her sentences like she's from California, and she also says everything in that sort of forced way, as if the very action of forming words and getting them out causes her mild pain. 'It's giving…rural vibes but on-point feminism in a man's world… It's giving…Margot Robbie as Barbie…'

'Right.' I force a smile and turn to Oscar. 'Oscar, how can we help?'

Oscar, a short man with a monk-like ring of silver hair around his bald scalp, has already closed his magazine, and he rises to his feet. 'Today is the feast day of St Teresa of Avila,' he announces by way of greeting.

'Is it really? I never heard of St Teresa of Avila, I don't think?' I know I'm inviting an explanation, but despite his foibles, he is at heart a kind old man, so a bit of kindness back is no harm.

Oscar is lonely. He never married but lived with his mother until she died a few years ago, and since then his time has been spent arranging novenas and pilgrimages and special prayer services, and poor old Father Doyle is tormented from him. Our parish priest is eighty-three and exhausted, but there is nobody to replace him, it would seem, so he keeps going. But he could definitely do without having Oscar haunting him.

'She was very interesting herself, a marvellous woman, but what was more fascinating was that she died on the 4th of October 1582. That was the night the world changed from the Julian to the Gregorian calendar, so as the clock struck midnight, it became the 15th of October and ten days disappeared forever.'

'Well, Oscar, isn't every day a school day? I never knew that.' I give him a smile.

He looks proud of himself. 'It's amazing how many saints get forgotten, Sergeant Munroe, and I do like to remind people about them. But that's not why I'm here today. I need to talk to you urgently about a matter of law.'

'Righto, Oscar, why don't you come with me?'

I don't bring everyone into my private office, but I can do without Zoë's interjections on this one. Whatever about me, Oscar would be better able to converse with an alien than Zoë. Showing him in, I close my door and indicate for him to take the seat facing my desk.

'Fire away,' I say, sitting down on my own chair opposite him.

'Well, Sergeant Munroe.' He rests his gnarled hands on his knees. 'I'm here to tell you that there are evil Satanists come among us who are intent on leading the souls of Ballycarrick straight down the primrose path in through the gates of hell.'

'Could you be a little more specific, Oscar?' I see on my calendar, displayed on the computer screen in front of me, that I have a meeting in half an hour, so I'll need to get to the point of this quickly.

'Sergeant, don't tell me you haven't noticed that there is black magic being practised right in the heart of our community, drawing in every man, woman and child?' His ears are pink at the tips, and he exudes indignation out of every pore. 'Surely you cannot be blind to the evil that has come among us, Sergeant?'

He's clearly ready to go on like this all day, so I decide to help things along. 'Do you mean the couple in the Lodge?'

He slaps his knees, triumphant. 'See, you know exactly who I'm talking about.'

'And what do you want me to do about them, Oscar?'

'I want you to go down there and stop them from doing what they're doing, leading people astray with their dark...' He is reluctant to use the word 'wizardry', but I know that's what he wants to say.

Oscar is a sweet old fella really and means no harm, but I can see how Neil Jacobson and Minnie Melodie, a very eccentric couple who recently turned up here from the North of England, are like a red rag to a bull to him. The thing is, Neil is a warlock and Minnie, his partner, is a witch – a white witch, as she told me when I stopped her last week to gently explain that even those with supernatural powers are still obliged to tax their vehicles and that she needs to get an Irish driving licence.

Within a few days of arriving, they were running a nice trade in channelling the spirits of the dear departed. Everyone in the place is abuzz with how Minnie told them Auntie Eileen was unhappy about the new ring road being built on the site of her old house, or Uncle

Mikey wants them to trim that overhanging branch because otherwise it's going to fall and kill someone. Also, apparently Neil the warlock is great at cleansing auras, and he healed the wart on Louise Heffernan's thumb that was playing havoc with her golf swing. I don't hold much with it myself, but my best friend, Sharon, has been to see Minnie three times. She's convinced her mother 'comes through' and says lovely things to her. Sharon's mother died last year. They had a problematic relationship, which was why she spent most of her time as a kid in our house, and I think she's got some unfinished business there, so to speak, so whatever helps her is fine by me. Neil and Minnie seem a benevolent kind of a pair, harmless, if a little slow to pay their motor tax.

'They're not breaking any law, though, Oscar,' I explain to the old man kindly.

He scowls, his face creasing all over like a wizened apple. 'But it's an evil in our community, Sergeant Munroe. I told Foxy Clancy in no uncertain terms that selling the Lodge to those people was flying in the face of all we hold dear in this community, and that on his own conscience be it if something terrible happens, but do you know what he did, Sergeant?'

'I don't, Oscar.'

'Laughed into my face, actually laughed. As if his eternal soul was a laughing matter.'

'Right,' I say noncommittally. I assume Foxy Clancy has the same attitude to his soul as any other estate agent.

'I've been warning everyone I see, and I've tried a novena to St Michael the Archangel, known for his strength in casting out demons, and I have of course spoken at length to Father Doyle...'

I bet you have, I think, my heart going out to the poor priest.

'But – and I don't mean to sound disparaging, Sergeant – but Father Doyle is elderly, and I'm not sure he really grasps the seriousness of this. And so as a last resort, I've come to you.'

Gee, thanks, Oscar.

'Though maybe you won't want to help me,' he adds darkly, 'seeing as your husband did all that work for them.'

The Gate Lodge is a kind of Tudor-style cottage that sits inside the gates of Ballycarrick Castle, and it's very old and the roof was in bad shape when Neil and Minnie bought it, despite Foxy telling them it was good for another twenty years. And so they contacted Kieran, who is a roofer, to look at it. He came home shaking his head. 'That Clancy is some eejit Mags. That roof is a danger. I offered to patch it for them, but they want me to replace it before they move in. It's good for me, but it will set them back twenty grand at least.'

'The afterlife business must be booming so. What are they like?' I asked.

'Nice, and very impressed when I told them I was married to the most important woman in the town.'

'Oh, very funny, ha, ha.'

'And your man told me I had a lovely aura, and your woman offered me a free tarot card reading. I nearly agreed for the craic, but the room where they do the magic had no windows in it – it's kind of in the middle of the house – and it was painted black with weird crimson symbols, so I made my excuses and left.'

Kieran is a small bit claustrophobic. It's one reason he enjoys being a roofer, because he's outside all the time.

'My husband's work is completely separate from my work, Oscar,' I answer firmly.

'I'm glad to hear it,' he shoots back. 'But as his wife, you should remind him of his moral duty to the souls of Ballycarrick.'

As Mam would say, there isn't a horse high enough for Oscar O'Leary once he is on a roll. I'm beginning to revise my opinion of him as a generally harmless old man; his latest battle with Satan seems to be souring him.

I'm listening to a podcast on intelligent conflict resolution at the moment. Most assume being a police officer is all about arresting people and taking them to court and all of that, but it really isn't. It's mostly trying to get people to see things from another's point of view, trying to calm things down before they escalate. I'm not afraid of conflict and I'll go after wrongdoing without compunction – the law is the law, and I'm duty-bound to uphold it – but in a small town in

Ireland, it's much more carrot and a lot less stick that gets the job done.

On the other hand, I don't want to give Oscar the slightest hope. If he thinks there's even a slim chance that I'll do anything about the warlock and the witch, I'll never be shot of him; he's like a dog with a bone.

'Oscar, the thing is, they are not breaking any law, so I have no right to stop them going about their business. People go to them of their own free will, and if it's not for you, then don't go. But you can't really stop people doing what they want with their own money if it's not illegal, y'know?' I glance up at the clock. 'So if that's everything…' I stand and hope he gets the hint that this conversation is over.

'But it's not everything, Sergeant!' His nostrils flare, and a dark flush rises up his neck. 'That man is a self-confessed murderer.'

'And who did he murder, do you think?' I ask, keeping my voice neutral. There are no unsolved murders in this area, and nobody has reported anyone missing. Oscar needs to be careful. Making false allegations about something so serious could land him in a lot of trouble.

'He killed a man in England,' he hisses at me.

'Do you have proof of that, Oscar? Because I'd have to caution you that making unfounded claims like that is in fact illegal.'

'It's not unfounded. Desmond Dunne fully agrees with me. He tore down their poster from outside the Lodge – it had all kinds of occult symbols on it.' Oscar shudders and crosses himself. 'And that Jacobson fellow came out and said Desmond needed to let him clean his aura, and Desmond made the sign of the cross and shouted at him to stay back, and then Jacobson said there was a man back in England who refused to have his aura cleansed and he was dead of a brain tumour within the year.'

Oscar looks at me triumphantly, as if he has just produced irrefutable proof of the man's murderous tendencies, Perry Mason style.

I make a mental note to remind Desmond that harassment of a legal business by defacing their signage is a crime. I don't care much for Desmond Dunne; he is a self-righteous bully. I've never known him to be interested in religion, but I can just see him loving an excuse to pick on poor mild-mannered Neil Jacobson and eccentric Minnie. And if Oscar's associating with the likes of Desmond, then no wonder the old man is so aggressive today instead of just his usual sweet if irritating self. 'But what has that man's brain tumour got to do with anything, Oscar?'

'Isn't it obvious?' He puffs up like a balloon, the indignation inflating him. 'The man in England stood up to him, so Jacobson took against him and put a hex on him and murdered him!'

I try to keep a straight face. If willing someone dead was a crime, there wouldn't be a spare bed in any prison in the country.

'Well, even if that were the case, Oscar, that would be out of our jurisdiction, having happened in another country,' is the best I can do.

'But what's to stop him taking a set against a person here? And he knows I'm onto him, so what if he curses me?' Oscar asks angrily. 'And if I'm found dead, what will you say then, Sergeant? That you weren't warned?'

Honestly, don't believe all those programmes on the telly that show cops fighting organised crime and drug cartels day in, day out. It's mostly this nonsense.

'Well, until he actually does something illegal, commits an actual crime, with his own hands rather than the power of his mind, then I can't do a thing to him. Now I'm sorry, Oscar, I've a meeting, so I'll have to let you go.'

'I'm telling you, that pair are evil! You'll find out soon enough.' He is still ranting as I usher him out, and I have a feeling I've not heard the end of this, that's for sure. Especially if Desmond Dunne has got himself involved.

The other members of my team are arriving in the door for the ten o'clock weekly briefing. It requires them to come in off shift if necessary; they can take time in lieu. And while it's a big ask, I've found it really works because we are all up to speed in terms of what's going on. Delia, Nicola, Darren and Michael are a great team. They really are a remarkable group of young people, and I trust them completely.

Zoë has her feet up behind the desk, using her phone to arrange her hair.

'Staff meeting, Zoë,' I say through gritted teeth.

'Totes.' She clicks one more pouting snap of herself before putting her phone away.

Give me strength.

CHAPTER 2

'Right, Oscar O'Leary is very upset about having a witch and a warlock come to town, but I've explained there's nothing we can do about it –'

'Them two are a pair of liars, so he needn't worry,' says Delia sharply, which surprises me. Delia is a member of the Travelling community, and she would be the first person to say some or other relative of hers – of which she has hundreds – has 'the sight'. 'People will soon realise they're only chancers.'

Before I can respond, Zoë chips in. 'I think, you know, if someone wants to identify as a white witch, we have to, like, respect that?'

I am astonished at her confidence. When I was a young guard, I barely said a word. Seen and not heard for the first two years at least was the unwritten rule, but nobody told Zoë that.

'She's no more a witch than the man on the moon – would you cop on to yourself?' snaps Delia.

'Rude. The idea there is no such thing as magic is a colonial construct…and to deny this woman the right to identify as what she believes herself to be –'

'I wonder what a witch's pronouns are? Thee and thou?' Darren murmurs to Michael, who chuckles, and Zoë sighs and rolls her eyes as if putting up with Neanderthals like us is such a chore.

Last week our new recruit wrote a group email to all the members of the station, demanding that we all put 'she/her' or 'he/him' pronouns 'as appropriate' on the end of all communications, which was so high-handed, I was flabbergasted. It's not wrong for one of my team to send a group email, but generally I'm the one to do it, not the most junior member of staff, and certainly not about policy. I debated going out to the front office and losing the plot with her, but instead I took a deep breath and replied to all, stating that if such a protocol was to be implemented, it would be done across the force and decided at a management level, not introduced in our local Garda station by some indulged brat barely out of Templemore Garda College with a superiority complex and a sense of entitlement the size of Belgium. (I deleted that last bit.) Then, wait for this, she came into my office and 'explained' why it was critical we follow her protocol.

She's not transgender, she tells me she doesn't know anyone who *is* transgender, no member of our station is transgender, and yet apparently us all clarifying to each other our preferred pronouns is vital to what she calls 'modern, empathetic communications'.

I don't tell her about Donnie Keohane, a man who lives quietly out the Tuam road – he mends bikes – and who was born Caroline Keohane. Caroline became Donnie one summer when he was about fifteen, and while it caused a bit of a flutter at the time, Donnie has been himself now for years and everyone just accepts it. Sometimes you can trust people to make the right decisions based on innate human decency and you don't need to mandate every little thing. She'll learn that as time goes on. But you can't put an old head on young shoulders.

'Like, this is exactly what I'm talking about when I say we need to educate ourselves, Sergeant? When we know better, we do better, right?' she says now, waving her hand at Darren and Michael, who are both trying not to laugh. Nicola and Delia are staring at the ceiling. 'So I think it would be helpful if I hold an LGBTQI awareness medita-tion with everyone soon? Like, at the end of next week's briefing, when everyone is here? It's so, so important for LGBTQI people to feel totally safe?'

She's young. I try to be patient. Like every town in Ireland, we have all sorts of people here. 'Keeping *every* citizen safe, regardless of anything else, is our priority, Zoë. And any marginalised groups such as the LGBTQI community are given extra protection in the event of deeming it necessary, and An Garda Síochána provides very well for that in initial and ongoing in-service training –'

'With respect, yeah, that's reductive? I don't think, like, a bunch of old cis-gendered men can really, y'know, hold space for that? Like where are the drag queens in this narrative, where are the trans people, the nonbinary? Like, we need to totally, like, hear their story?'

I've had enough. 'Zoë, if you want to stay working in this station past your probation period, the first people you need to treat with respect are your superiors and colleagues. To assume that senior-ranking officers to you, which I will point out is everyone in An Garda Síochána, are somehow incapable or negligent in their duties is a serious accusation and one not befitting a new recruit.' I leave the words hanging in the air as I glare at her. She goes pink but mercifully stays silent.

But I really object to this generation feeling like they have the monopoly on empathy and kindness, and the rest of us are just belting people over the head with sticks till some Gen Z kid shows us the error of our ways. Gearoid, Kieran's gay brother, has a nonbinary friend, an actor and a singer, and they're lovely. It's hard to remember to use 'they' rather than 'she', but we're trying and we get it right most of the time, and they are fine with that. They can see there's no animosity, that we're not dead-naming them or whatever it is – it just takes a bit of getting used to. If it makes people happier and feel more accepted in their communities to identify as whatever they feel is more appropriate for them, well, more power to them. But I am the boss of this station, and I will not have some entitled little upstart who is in the job a wet week calling the shots. I will *not* have it.

'Now, back to the *actual* issues we are facing,' I continue, satisfied that order has been restored. 'Oscar also told me that Desmond

Dunne tore down Neil and Minnie's poster from their gate, so I intend to speak to him about that and remind him harassment is a crime.'

'I'll come with you if you want me, Sarge,' says Delia. She knows Dunne is a hard man to deal with. We were there at his house a couple of weeks ago because he and his wife were fighting again.

Desmond's wife, Maeve, is never done telling anyone who'll listen what a worthless excuse for a man her husband is, and he is regularly to be found in the Samovar with his cronies making nasty jokes about 'the ball and chain'.

Honestly, why they don't just get a divorce, I've no idea. They clearly hate each other. Their daughters, Emily and Sarah, got away to university in Dublin the second they could and rarely come home, and I don't blame them. The Dunnes generally confine their acrimony to verbal insults, sometimes at volume and sometimes in public, but on the Friday before last, she threw a heavy flowerpot at him and knocked him out cold. They live next door to Bertie the butcher, so it was he who went and checked what was going on when he heard the racket and then called us. Bertie usually tries to keep out of my way since the 'dogging' incident, but he was scared Maeve had murdered Desmond or that if Desmond regained consciousness, he would murder her.

When Delia and I arrived to investigate, there he was, sitting on the floor of the kitchen with a nasty-looking cut over one eye, but he was alive if a bit stunned. Maeve was desperate to show us a bruise on her wrist that she said he'd given her. Those two are not the usual case, to be fair. Most domestics we go to are some man beating his wife, but I swear with the Dunnes, it's 'one of them, two of them', as my mother says. And you wouldn't mind, but Desmond was engaged to some other girl back in the day and Maeve was like a dog with a bone, according to Mam, wouldn't rest till she saw the other girl off and had Desmond to herself. Some people are just so strange.

Anyway, we spoke to both of them, explained that assault is a very serious charge and that they'd find themselves up in court if they couldn't control their tempers. Immediately they went back to blaming each other with 'he said, she said', but Delia cut them off.

'We don't care who started it, but the judge will finish it if you're not careful, so let this be a lesson to you both.'

I had to suppress a smile. Delia can be quite ferocious when she needs to be – she's brilliant like that – and for the millionth time, I felt glad I'd gone in to bat for her. Talking of marginalised groups, she is the first Traveller woman I've ever known to join the force, and despite experiencing some pushback, and frankly some racism, she has stuck it out and now nobody would dare speak down to her. She's earned her stripes, several times over. Even the odious Duckie Cassidy, the detective inspector from Galway who would make your skin crawl, gives her a wide berth these days.

'Thanks, Delia,' I say, 'but I'll be fine. It's just for a chat. I won't be arresting him unless he keeps on harassing our local magicians.'

Zoë makes a small noise. She's dying to tell me our English couple self-identify as occult figures, not magicians, but somehow she manages to keep her mouth shut, and I carry on.

'The public meeting on the subject of the new housing development has been rescheduled for next Tuesday – it descended into chaos that last time. Derry tells me there are a group of far-right activists, an anti-immigrant group, who have been targeting these sorts of meetings all over the country, saying all the housing is intended for immigrants. I have not received anything to confirm that, but either way, it's causing disruption, so we'll need to be vigilant.'

Derry is the former school principal and chairperson of the community association, a rock of common sense, but even he hadn't been able to stop the meeting turning into a total free-for-all with roaring and shouting, and eventually he'd had no choice but to abandon it altogether.

People in Ballycarrick are vulnerable to being wound up at the moment; they're so worried about the rising numbers of people in the town. It's not just refugees and people seeking international protection – them too, of course – but it's all the people who are priced out of the housing market closer to Galway. Lots more of them are working from home since Covid, and so the developers are marketing their new housing estates as perfect for those who don't need to commute every day. The houses cost eye-watering amounts of money, so it means all rural house prices are soaring, and interest rates too, while banks are still slow to lend money since the economic crash. Young Irish people especially are being priced out of the market, and it's a very difficult situation because the blame is being laid at the feet of immigrants, which isn't fair or right, but it's easy to see why people feel as they do.

The trouble in Ballycarrick is that the resources needed for this huge influx of people just aren't in place. We don't have enough doctors, schools, public transport, policing, infrastructure... You name it, we don't have enough of it. As a country with surplus running in the billions each year, it's unfathomable how so many of our basic public systems are so under-resourced.

And as people's frustrations grow, they tend to take it out on those they perceive as somehow being favoured over the locals and 'having everything given to them', in this case the Ukrainians and other refugees who are being put up in emergency accommodation. It's a tricky one, involving yet more marginalised groups.

'There was graffiti on the gable end of the big house where the Ukrainian women are staying,' Nicola reads from her notes. 'One of the residents came in to report it yesterday, said people have been hanging around and they feel threatened.'

'The council was to look into CCTV up there. Can you chase them up on that, Nicola, please? Face to face would be best.'

I'm not surprised the women feel threatened. Last year they were the target of a nasty attack, but I'm happy to say, that time the right-wing extremists were seen off by some unlikely defenders, Irish Travellers. Themselves marginalised, they stuck up for the women and children in the old house, and then Jerome McGovern and his nephews drove all the way to Ukraine with supplies and brought one woman's husband back here to recuperate after an injury sustained during the conflict.

Zoë pipes up. 'I was thinking maybe some group activity for the whole village, maybe some breathwork – it promotes peace. Maybe Neil could lead it with an aura cleanse...'

'And take Zoë with you when you go, Nicola.' I share a small smile with Delia. 'I'm meeting with the Tidy Towns this afternoon,' I continue, 'and I heard there's a big row going on about painting or something, and I wonder if any of you know anything more about it.'

'Well, there was a deputation went up to Phillip O'Flaherty Motors last Thursday – Elsie Flanagan, Lavinia, Joanna Burke,' explains Darren Carney. 'You know yourself, the usual suspects, demanding that he paint his garage, said it was an eyesore and that he was the reason the whole town was in disgrace and that Dromahane were laughing at us.'

'And that went down like a fart in a lift, I suppose?' I ask.

Darren grins. 'He put the run on them, wouldn't even hear them out, and apparently told Lavinia that it was more in her line to pay her bills and that she owed him for four new tyres on the Range Rover since January.'

I chuckle. Lavinia Moran is notorious for outstanding bills around the town, despite swanning about in a huge car and living in a mansion by Ballycarrick standards. Bertie refuses to run an account for them in the butcher's like he does for everyone else, and despite that, she'll be in there, talking loudly about going skiing in Gstaad while insisting on organic meat to prepare something nutritious and delicious in her perfect home for her perfect family. She was in the *Western People* a few years ago, showcasing her house, and has been dining out on it since, but the Morans are very slow to pay their bills. Some people have no shame.

'Yes, and she and Elsie Flanagan were wearing the ears off poor Father Doyle after Mass on Sunday, demanding to know why Dromahane Tidy Towns got the lottery money for a paint job on the town hall and not Ballycarrick,' adds Nicola.

'So it's going to be paintbrushes at dawn, is it?' I sigh.

The Tidy Towns had started out as a nice idea, a friendly national competition between towns and villages to clean the place up a bit, plant a few flowers, that sort of thing, but somehow it has turned into a barely concealed murderous rivalry between Ballycarrick and the next town over. Dromahane won the national award for the last two years, and Ballycarrick has never won it, which is driving some of the people here up the walls. They beat us in the hurling too, which added salt to the wound. The whole town was in mourning for a week after the match.

'Yes, they were telling Father Doyle that the local authorities don't care if the place goes to rack and ruin, and asking him in his position as moral guardian of the town to write a letter to the lottery about it, demanding Ballycarrick get their fair share of money.'

I shake my head, bewildered. 'What possible influence could that poor priest have over who gets lottery money?'

It's bad and anti-feminist and all the rest, but those women need a job; they'd have less time to be mithering the rest of us over nonsense. The place looks fine. The houses and gardens are well maintained, and the shops take great pride in their façades. Mam ran the committee for funding Christmas lights and all the decorating of the shops at various times of the year for the trader's association, so they always looked well. And we are not a show village; we are a busy working town full of ordinary people trying to get by.

Again there's a small noise from Zoë, probably to interject about the separation of Church and State or something, but again she supresses it. As a reward, I include her in my next question, looking at each of my team in turn around the table. 'Now, is there anything else?'

Of course she jumps in immediately. 'OK, peeps, just an idea. But you know how there's all these fake text messages going around? I read about this police unit in America, and within the unit, they have a word they use that only members of the unit know, and if they use that word or symbol in a message to the group, or over the radio or whatever, then whatever the message actually says, it means they're in danger or a bad situation. So I was thinking we could use something like that, and the word could be "Sarge", and in messages we could use the woman cop emoji? Or even just so we'd know it was a genuine text from one of us, and not someone pranking us? We could keep it secret so only we know it?'

Before I have time to dismiss it as another of her hare-brained ideas, I see the others look interested.

'Good idea,' says Darren. 'I got a text last week from someone claiming a car was on fire. Wasted twenty minutes driving around till I saw the Carmodys laughing like donkeys up on the bypass.'

'Clever. I'm in,' adds Michael. 'If it doesn't have Sergeant Munroe's emoji, we'll assume its fake.'

A smiling thumbs-up from Delia and another from Nicola.

Seems I'm outnumbered, and maybe it's not the maddest idea the girl has come up with.

'Good idea, Zoë,' I say. To be fair to her, she is desperate to be a good officer, even if her approach is more bonkers than I'd like. 'Sarge with the woman cop emoji it is.'

CHAPTER 3

*K*ieran is out on Tuesday evenings now, which is both good and bad.

It's good because I finish early on Tuesdays, Ellie has training for camogie until six, Kate does Irish dancing, and they both go to my mother's for their dinner afterwards because they're watching a show where people turn rubbish into fashion or something. I don't ask.

Mam and the girls have a great relationship, and they're always watching something together. It's not beyond the bounds of possibility to find any one of the three of them head down in the wheelie bin these days extracting silver foil or cardboard boxes for the next design. But that's this season's idea. Over the years they've got into gardening and making QR codes – that was particularly bizarre – and then there's the annual stalwart: *Strictly Come Dancing*. They get so worked up about people's paso dobles and Charlestons, it makes me laugh. It's lovely to see, though. Mam adores them and they her, and they have a connection far beyond me.

So Tuesday afternoons are for myself. And I love the peace and quiet.

Then what's the downside of Kieran being out on Tuesdays, you might wonder?

Well, it's this. Last January – that's nine months ago now – Trevor and Sharon were going to a traditional music night in a local pub. They asked us to join them, and we did. I don't love the Irish music, if the truth be told, and I know it's sacrilege to say that – I'd be forgiven easier if I set fire to the flag and danced naked around it – but there you have it. But Sharon is my best friend, and she was a bit down in the dumps, so I went. Chloe Desmond, always known as Chloe from the chipper, who went off with Sharon's now ex, Danny Boylan, was pregnant again. She had the baby a few weeks ago. It bugs Sharon, even though she wouldn't touch Danny with a barge pole if he came crawling back to her on his knees; she's really happy with Trevor these days. Something about Danny Boylan can still get under her skin.

There was a fella there playing the uilleann pipes; in fact there were three pipers. And to my astonishment and dismay, my husband was transfixed. He'd heard the national instrument before, of course, but whatever it was about that night, something happened in his brain, and since then he's been learning them. I'm trying to be supportive. He works really hard – he's got his own roofing business that he built up from scratch since he came back from the States – and he's not a big drinker, and he doesn't bet on horses or look at other women. But really and truly, what a dose. They sound bad when played by professionals, but I can just about bear it, but if you've never shared a house with someone learning to play the Irish uilleann pipes, then don't tell me you know pain.

They're like a bagpipe, just as loud, but without the kilts – thank heaven for small mercies, I suppose. The Irish word for elbow is uilleann, so you kind of squeeze an air-filled bag with one arm and play a tune on a kind of flute affair called a chanter at the same time, but as well as that, there are other things called drones that emit – and yes, you've guessed it – this mournful droning sound under the tune, and it's a combination of noise that could be used to force confessions out of innocent people, it's so bad. You'd agree to anything, literally anything, to make it stop.

But he loves it, and that's where he goes on a Tuesday night, to his lesson with a woman called Gobnait, who has wild hair and mad eyes and lives out in Connemara right in the middle of the bog. She's hilarious, I have to say, and I love meeting her because she has absolutely no filter whatsoever. Whatever she thinks, she says, which is refreshing, and she's an amazing piper, even to one as averse as I. He goes to her house, a cottage where she spins wool – she has a flock of sheep – dyes it mad colours and sells it online.

'You're doing it again!' he called yesterday as he squeezed the bag and a sound like someone torturing tomcats came out of the thing.

'Doing what?' I yelled as I added the jar of sauce to the curry for dinner.

'Wincing when I'm playing,' he bellowed. The pipes are so loud, you need to shout over them. 'This is a hornpipe, by the way, in case you were wondering.'

I wasn't wondering. I was only praying it would stop soon. But I am a loving and patient wife, so I said nothing.

I tried not to outwardly wince, but I was inwardly not only wincing but screaming, and daydreaming of wrapping the bloody things around his neck.

The girls encourage him. They say they love it, which I know is a lie, but they'd take his side every time anyway. And as if this situation could get any worse, Rollo has taken to howling along in sympathy. Kate made a hilarious TikTok of it the other night, Kieran playing and the dog howling, and it's had loads of hits or likes or whatever they get on that thing.

So that's why the peace and quiet of my house on a Tuesday night is good but also bad, because unfortunately he comes home each week with a new tune.

This evening, Rollo is asleep in the kitchen – he's 'afraid' to come in the living room with me – Frankie Velcro is in her cage in Ellie's room, and Knickers is hopefully safe in his enclosure, a huge fancy thing full of vegetation and branches to cling to that takes up two thirds of the utility room and which was built by Goosey, who has appointed himself animal welfare officer for our family. I suspect this is an excuse to see Ellie, though she continues to ignore him in favour of Carrot, who it turns out *is* aptly named because he's a vegan, which is no doubt why he always looks like he needs a good feed.

Ellie insists we eat vegetarian, at least when he comes over. 'To what end?' I asked her. 'He'll discover we are carnivores at some point, why not early on?' But that was met with a horrified gasp – she's dramatic, my girl – and the puzzling remark, 'Mam, you *know* I hardly ever touch meat.'

Er, tell that to the poor Aberdeen Angus that was sacrificed for your rib eye last Friday, Ellie, I thought, but I wisely kept it to myself.

I have an hour or two before I need to collect the girls from Mam's. I've had a sandwich, made myself a nice big cuppa and settled down on the sofa. I'm in the middle of a great book, *Mrs Dalloway* by Virginia Woolf. It says in the blurb that it's a book that 'explores the fragmented but fluid nature of time and the interconnectedness of perception and reality across individuals and social spheres'. But honestly, I think that's a bit highfalutin and would put people off. I'm enjoying it because it's just about a woman who is getting ready for a party just after World War One, and as she prepares, she goes backwards and forwards in time, and for me, it's just like this for most women. Always thinking, always worrying, planning, reminiscing, all of that. I honestly think male minds are totally different to females. Kieran is a deep thinker, and he's not insulated from worry, but the endless monologue of things to be done, observations made, predictions for the future, more reminders of chores to do that are on constant loop in my mind are not in his, I don't think.

I'm in the middle of a chapter when my mobile rings. It's Ellie.

'Hi, love. All OK?' Though I'm sure it is. My mother texted only twenty minutes ago to say they'd had their dinner and were determined to make a dress for the races out of frisbees and clingfilm.

'Hi, Mam. Yeah, grand. I was just wanting to ask, can we bring the twins to the disco on Saturday night? It's in Dalton's Hotel, and their dad is working abroad for a couple of months or something, and their mam had an operation on her knee, so she can't drive for six weeks.'

'Sure, no problem. And tell them they can stay the night.'

'Great, I'll snap them. See you later.'

'Bye, love. Will I collect ye?'

'No, Joe is going to drop us back. He's going to play cards in the Samovar anyway.'

'Righto, pet. See you later.'

We end the call, and I text Cat and Trish O'Leary's mother so she knows what's happening. Teenage girls can't always be relied on to communicate with their parents. *Hi, Anne. Either me or Kieran will collect Cat and Trish for the disco on Saturday night, and they can stay here after. I'll run them home Sunday morning after breakfast. I hope the knee isn't too painful.*

Sent. Two ticks. And then Anne is typing, and a moment later, a message pops up. *That's so kind of you. I really appreciate it. The knee is not bad, but I'm on crutches for six weeks, so sorry.*

Really, it's no problem, I text back. Anne's always polite, but she doesn't need to thank me. All the kids around here are in and out of each other's houses all the time; it's no big deal, and we kind of raise them together. Besides, I'm delighted Ellie has become best friends with the O'Leary twins since the big falling out with her 'frenemy', Jess, who it turned out was only inviting her around all the time so Ellie could do her homework for her.

Ellie has handled her break-up with Jess really well, and it is a sign she is growing up. I asked her a few months ago if she ever spoke to Jess any more, and she seemed surprised I'd asked.

'I do, but I don't trust her. I'm friendly and say hi and all of that – I'm not going to bother my head with not talking to her, way too stressful. But as Taylor Swift says, Mam, the trash always takes itself out in the end.'

It's a great thing to see your kids making smart decisions and knowing their own worth.

I'm just settling into my book again when another text flashes up on the screen. Sharon. *Did you know Róisín is coming home for good????*

I wince. I knew Sharon would make a big deal of this, which is why I've put off mentioning it to her.

Róisín Duggan is Kieran's old girlfriend. They moved to New York together in their twenties and were due to set up their lives there, except he came home for a family funeral after a few years and met me in the pub. We'd known each other all our lives, but he was a few years ahead of me in school. Anyway, we hit it off and had such a laugh together that night, and the next night he took me out, and the following day, he rang Róisín and broke it off. She was devastated but decided to stay in New York, posted him back his stuff, and she's been there ever since, hugely successful as a litigator, which is what they call barristers over there.

Things were a bit frosty for a few years – she came home twice a year to see her parents – but time went on and everyone got over it. She met a Mexican American man called Joel Barrera. He is lovely, a great cook, handsome and charming and with an impressive job working as a political adviser to a New York senator. We started meeting up with them whenever they came home, and they always brought nice things for the girls. She even invited us to visit them two years ago, and that holiday in New York is one we still talk about. It was all very friendly.

I think Róisín enjoyed showing off her new life to Kieran. Fair enough. She wants him to know she did fine without him, and I don't blame her for that. She and Joel lived on the thirtieth floor of a really swanky apartment building off 7th Avenue in Manhattan, no children but a very yappy Pekingese dog called Princess. Joel took us on a tour around the New York Senate building where he worked, we went to the Top of the Rock, ate Chinese food in Chinatown and saw *Hamilton* on Broadway. It was a trip of a lifetime, and Róisín and Joel were wonderful hosts. He even helped Ellie with a school project last year on different political systems around the world.

Róisín's heart was broken by Kieran, I know it was, and at the time, we genuinely felt terrible about it. But we just fell in love, and as soon as he knew, he did the right thing and told her the truth. So it was a relief to see her and Joel so happy together and that was all water long gone under the bridge.

I did hear something about that, I text back. Might as well admit it now; Sharon will worm it out of me sooner or later.

I can't believe you didn't tell me!!!! A raging emoji.

CLOSER THAN YOU THINK

I send an apologetic face. *Sorry, must have forgot.*
She's going to be living in Ballycarrick!!!!!
We don't mind where she lives, Shar. It's fine.

This is true, though I was a bit taken aback when Kieran told me she was moving home for good, especially as she and Joel both have such great jobs in New York. But her parents are getting older, so I expect she wants to be near them. I'd hate to live in a different country from Mam; I'm going to miss her when she's away on her cruise of the Caribbean, they are spending some time in Miami too so she'll be gone for ages.

She and Joe Dillon are off next Thursday, and even though I'll miss her, and my peaceful Tuesdays, I'm delighted for them. Mam had a health scare earlier this year, her heart, so now they've both retired to spend more time together. Sharon bought Mam's shop, and it's going great for her, and Joe's shop is being run by a young lad he hired, Conal Keane. Conal has bought one of the new houses at the other end of the town, and he'll buy Joe's shop as soon as he can afford it on top of his massive mortgage.

Another text. *Did you know she's bought the Old Rectory?*
I did. Kieran went and looked at it for them before they sent the surveyors in.

The Old Rectory is a beautiful old Georgian house in the centre of Ballycarrick. I can't remember the last time anyone lived there, and it's been in a pretty poor state for years, but there has been work going on for the last few months; a big Galway company has been in doing all the renovations, upgrading of plumbing, wiring and all of that and installing Wi-Fi.

And you never said a word????? Me and Trevor are in the Samovar, and Foxy Clancy just told us.

I wish she wouldn't make a big thing of this, but she will. I've always loved that house. I suggested buying it to Kieran once – it wasn't priced at much more than our own house – but he pointed out it would cost five times what it was on the market for to renovate it.

Not my story to tell. That place is lovely, but it was getting very run-

down. I'm glad someone bought it, and the builders have done a great job of it, I text back. *I hope she and Joel are happy there.*

OH, STOP BEING SUCH A SAINT!!! You cannot be cool with this.

I laugh. I can just imagine Sharon rolling her eyes and huffing. I send her five angel emojis to wind her up even more, then go back to my book with a grin. After Danny betrayed Sharon with Chloe, it really ruined her belief in men, and she was blue in the face warning me not to let Kieran and Róisín see each other when Róisín came home for visits. I was always having to explain that Kieran wasn't like that, until gradually she came to accept he wasn't. Even so, she clearly thinks Róisín is not to be trusted.

CHAPTER 4

*D*elia and I are off for a quick coffee break after a hectic morning, leaving Zoë in charge; hopefully she will cope. I've had the talk with her about not taking selfies at work, and she's doing her best, though the habit is so engrained in her, it's clearly a huge effort. I keep seeing her hand twitch towards her phone and jerk away again. She is trying though, in all fairness, so I'm going to coax rather than berate.

I'm also doing my best to get her to talk normally to people who come into the station, just chat about the weather and that instead of compulsively oversharing.

She gave Tatiana a terrible fright last week when Tatiana popped in to get something certified for her Irish citizenship application. The Russian woman is definitely not one to get into personal conversations. We still don't know what really happened between her and her ex, Benny, just that he's alive somewhere in England, but Zoë started telling her that she was working on her own attachment issues because her relationship with her mother could be described as code-pendent, based on her mother's insecurity. She went on to explain to a horrified Tatiana how her mother's father was an alcoholic and so as a child of addiction, she needed to have her inner child nurtured.

I get it, and to a large extent, I actually agree with Zoë, but Tatiana's reaction was comical.

'Stop telling me this. I must go now,' she'd bluntly announced. Zoë, to be fair to her, took it in stride. I'll give the Gen Z kids that – they don't get insulted easily.

It's a bright, clear morning, about twelve degrees, not bad for October, and Delia and I walk instead of taking the car. It's not that far, and besides, I like my officers to patrol the streets on foot as much as they can; I'm old-fashioned that way. People talk to you, and you see the way things are going much better than from a car. I'm a big believer in creating and maintaining good relationships with the community you are trying to police. It makes life easier when you do need to deal with an issue.

It will also help with my step count. I did a miserable twenty-five hundred yesterday, but I had so much paperwork to do, I had no opportunity to go for a walk. So today is the day I'm going to hit ten thousand and burn a million calories. The only flaw in this plan is our destination: Teresa's Bakery aka the Pit of Despair for those of us trying to keep the waistlines in check.

As we turn out of the station towards the town centre, Brian Magee whizzes past in a flash of cerise Lycra. That man is obsessed; he's never off that racing bike. Delia leaps to avoid the plume of water his wheels spray. It's not his fault; this is flooding season, and the gutters have spilled across the road because the drains are blocked with leaves. When Brian's father, Otter Magee – don't ask me why he was called Otter, he just was – was alive, the drains were never blocked, but now everything is being administered from Galway; the local county council office was closed down after Covid. Now the leaves are gathering, and if we get a heavy rain, it will be a disaster. I make a mental note to contact the council and try to get it looked at.

We stroll on down Main Street, and the people of Ballycarrick are going about their business as usual. I love to see the hustle and bustle of the town, and the new people arriving have really added to the place, despite the concerns of over-populating. There's a Ukrainian shop now, selling all sorts of exotic things. Ellie is friends with several of the Ukrainian refugee kids and has developed a taste for *deruni*, a kind of Ukrainian pancake served with sour cream, and I have to admit they're delicious. I might pop in and get some for dinner later.

Outside Bertie's butcher shop, Howya Phelan, one of the butchers, is taking a break from cleaning the windows. He's chatting to Lavinia Moran and Elsie Flanagan, and I catch Minnie Melodie's name before Howya sees me and waves.

'Howya, Mags,' he says cheerfully in his Dublin accent.

'Hi, Howya,' I say, resisting as ever the urge to say 'Howya, Howya.' I presume he has a real first name, surely his mother loved him, but I've no idea what it is. I'm curious to see him talking with Lavinia and Elsie, though; they would definitely think they were a cut above the likes of Howya.

'Hello, Sergeant Munroe,' twitters Lavinia in her posh little voice.

'Hello, Lavinia, good to see you.' She's a pain, but she'll never know I think that. 'Hello, Elsie.'

'Me and the lovely ladies here, we were just talking about the witch and the warlock. You know, Minnie and Neil, that's after moving into the Lodge?' says Howya, as Lavinia and Elsie tinkle with amusement at being called lovely ladies.

'Oh, yes.' I smile. 'Those two are definitely causing a stir, all right.' Delia, beside me, emits a slight snort.

Howya glances at Delia, then leans closer to me. 'Well, I'll tell you what, Mags,' he says conspiratorially. 'And you can believe this if you like, but I lost the key of the shed – looked high up and low down and no sign of the blasted thing. And eventually in desperation, I went to Minnie, and on comes my nana on the auld magic short-wave, told her 'twas in the pocket of my donkey jacket, which I never wear out any more, only around the garden. And sure enough, there it was.' He sounds like he's just revealed the last secret of Fatima.

I don't know. It does strike me as an obvious place to look. I might have suggested it myself if he'd asked me, but I don't say so. And I'm not saying I don't believe in all of that. God knows I've poor St Anthony tormented with pleas when I lose my phone or that pygmy hamster of Ellie's gets mislaid, and I'm very grateful when they're found, so that's the same kind of idea, I suppose.

'And did you hear, Mags,' says Elsie, 'she told Julie Dullea from the chemist that her chap – remember the lad that died off the motor-bike? Well, she told Julie he said she should go on soulmates.com and that she'd find love. And she did, and now she's doing a line with a lovely fellow altogether, very high up in pharmaceuticals apparently.' Elsie is like Nora, always impressed by people who are 'very high up'.

'And when I went to see her,' trills Lavinia, 'my grandmother came through and said my Raymond was a credit to me and that he was a marvellous lad and destined for great things politically, she hinted, and Raymond has joined Young Fine Gael at Trinity – did I tell you he's gone to Trinity, Mags?'

'I think you mentioned it,' I say politely. She's told the entire parish around eighty times.

'Yes, well, Granny told Minnie that Raymond is destined for high office. Isn't that just amazing?'

'It is, Lavinia.'

It isn't. The dogs on the street know of the wonder that is Raymond Moran. He's like King Midas – everything he does goes fabulously for him. According to his mother anyway. Of course Lavinia wants to hear her son is a future Taoiseach, and it wouldn't take Minnie very long to figure that one out.

'Isn't that just amazing, Delia?' presses Lavinia, who likes everyone to ooh and aah over Raymond.

'Amazing,' says Delia, looking bored.

We head on to Teresa's, and as soon as we're out of earshot, I ask, 'Still not impressed by our witch and warlock?'

She shrugs. 'I'm a police officer, Sarge. I don't judge.'

I nod, pleased with her. 'Good woman.' It's what I've taught all my officers, that it takes all sorts and unless someone's actively breaking the law, it's not up to us to express an opinion on their behaviour one way or another, especially when we're out in public. As I'm fond of saying, each to their own.

I'm surprised at how dismissive she is, though. I've always thought

Travellers were into psychic readings and lucky charms and stuff like that. It's not like Delia isn't proud of her heritage and true to her roots, even though she's always lived her life a bit differently. Maybe that's it. Maybe she thinks settled people have no right to go in for that sort of thing?

* * *

IN TERESA'S, we take the table for two in the window. I wouldn't normally sit in full view of the street – I like a bit of privacy on my break – but it's the only space left. We go up to the counter separately. I choose a brown scone to have with my coffee, and to my surprise, Delia comes back with one as well.

'I don't know why you didn't get the custard slice. There isn't a pick on you,' I say enviously. The same could not be said for me; it's necessary for me to be good and avoid the deliciousness of Teresa's cakes. I was fifty-two last birthday, and despite some effort – not total abstinence but general trying to be healthier – the belt of my uniform pants is on another notch. I look with envy on the young metabolisms of the likes of Delia. I had it when I really needed it, I suppose, but honest to God, it's a battle.

'Ah no, I'm not a mad fan of the sweet stuff, to be honest,' she confesses, and I wish I could feel the same way, but then wouldn't I be missing out on one of the great pleasures of life? It's a conundrum.

'How are the carpets looking?' I ask. She and Darren have just bought a house, a three-bed semi-detached in the back of an estate, and they had the bedrooms carpeted yesterday.

Delia beams. 'Oh, Sarge, you should see them, so beautiful. And they make the upstairs look huge. I never had anywhere so luxurious. I swear, I just walk around the house gazing at everything. Darren thinks I'm half cracked.'

'I'm delighted. And what did your mam think of the kitchen?' Delia's mother is a great cook; she could give Teresa's Bakery or the Samovar restaurant a run for its money if she chose to.

'She thinks it's lovely,' says Delia, a bit quietly.

'Would she ever think of settling?' I always think life on a halting site must be hard, especially in the winter, though the Travellers do have huge modern caravans these days with running water and electricity, not like Dacie's time when they lived in wooden horse-drawn carts and often slept under the stars.

'No, Daddy couldn't live in a house, 'twould kill him, so they'll be in a caravan till they die.'

I take a sip of my coffee. It's nice but not as good as the Samovar. The whole town is addicted to Tatiana's coffee, but she is very tight-lipped on her supplier, as she is about most things. Teresa was supposed to have been caught rooting in the bins behind the pub trying to find evidence of where Tatiana gets it from, but to no avail.

'And do your parents mind you being settled?' I ask.

Delia's dark eyes flash at me, and she sticks out her chin like she used to do in the early days when she was always having to defend her Traveller heritage. 'I'm not "settling", Sarge.'

'Oh?' I set down my cup and look at her, waiting for her to explain.

'"Settled Traveller" is what actual settled people call Travellers who have houses,' she says. 'As if we've betrayed our heritage and somehow got more like them. But I'm a Traveller, not a "settled Traveller". The garden is big, and our children, if God blesses us, will have room and animals, and Daddy will help us grow our own food, and there will be a concrete stand for a little caravan, and we'll spend plenty of time with my family in the summer.'

'Well, that sounds lovely, like you're getting the best of both worlds,' I say. 'And I'm sorry I got it wrong.'

'Ah no, it's just the words, Sarge. I know you didn't mean any harm.' It's nice of her to be magnanimous; she's still a bit bristly, though. The Carneys, who are not Travellers, aren't any happier than Delia's parents about her and Darren's relationship. In fact it would have been hard to decide which family needed the defibrillator more when that romance came to light.

'Still, words are important,' I say.

Then she relaxes and grins. 'Now you sound like Zoë, Sarge,' she teases as she splits her scone in half and butters it liberally, adding a teaspoon of Teresa's home-made blackberry jam, which is as much tangy as sweet. 'Mm…gorgeous,' she pronounces happily.

I halve my own scone and debate about butter and jam. There are raised voices outside, and I glance through the window to see Caelan Cronin getting shooed by Tatiana out of the Samovar across the road. He was probably in there trying to cadge a drink, though he's only sixteen. A couple of the Carmodys are with him, Patrick and Kenneth, and that's not good; they're underage as well.

They're always in trouble, the Carmodys, in a pathetic, petty-thieving, dope-dealing way. They have a squalid site up the Tuam road, and Darren, who is our Juvenile Liaison Officer, is driven demented by them. He's always having to testify in the children's court and hates doing it, especially as most of the kids are Delia's cousins. Not all of the Carmodys are crooks. Martin Carmody is nice, but he is a weak patriarch, unlike Jerome McGovern. The McGovern teenagers know to keep on the right side of the law or else they face him, a much more daunting prospect than the courts, and Jerome also insists that they keep the site immaculate, despite all the chickens and dogs and horses and donkeys.

Caelan legs it across the road to get away from Tatiana, and he glares in the window of the bakery as he passes, as if I'm his enemy. He's such a sad case, Caelan Cronin. Ellie's a year behind him in school and says he has the teachers' hearts scalded. He used to be as cute as a button, and he still looks like butter wouldn't melt – he's as good-looking as his mother was – but he really needs to get away from those other young hooligans he knocks around with.

'He painted "murderer" on Mike Cantillon's van again last night,' says Delia quietly, watching Caelan storm away by himself up the street.

I sigh heavily taking a bite of my scone. 'Has Cantillon made a complaint yet?'

'Not yet. He's probably still sleeping off last night's session. No, I heard it from my cousin Olivia. She's quite friendly with Kenneth's younger sister Bridget, and Bridget told her, Caelan and Kenneth… How are the uilleann pipes coming along?' She instinctively changes the subject from police business because Annette and Martha have just come in the door, and they'll probably come over to say hello.

'Don't even ask,' I say darkly. The whole station knows of Kieran and his new hobby and finds it hilarious.

'Hi, Mags, hi, Delia.' Sure enough, the two women have headed straight for our table.

'Hi, you two. I saw Finbarr on the front page of the *Western People* last week with the city farms thing. Fair play to him – that's amazing.' I smile up at them.

'Oh, he's telling us we need to get it framed and he wants it on the wall when he comes home on Friday.' Annette grins, rolling her eyes in pretend exasperation.

Annette's son, Finbarr, has Down's syndrome and lives during the week at a residential centre in Galway, where he's making huge news with organic micro-farming and helping people set up allotments and all the rest. It's all supervised by a wonderful team, and Finbarr and his friends get huge satisfaction from helping people raise a few hens if they have a garden or grow a tub of new potatoes on a balcony if they don't.

'He's after teaching people that special way to lay chicken wire around the coop to keep the foxes out, like Olivia showed him,' Martha says to Delia. Finbarr and Olivia McGovern, Delia's cousin, are great pals, and so Finbarr spends a lot of time at the Drumlish halting site. Olivia learnt everything she knows about chickens from Delia's father, Jerome, and she's passing it on to Finbarr.

'Yes, he's as proud as punch that none of his clients have lost one chicken to the fox this year.' Annette is clearly very proud as well; she's beaming at her son's achievements. Thirty years ago she'd been told by a cruel social worker that he would never amount to anything. Finbarr's father disappeared the moment he knew his son was different, and Annette scraped by for years doing market gardening and supporting her boy. The arrival of Martha Turner a few years ago changed her life. She and Annette are a couple now; they got married last year. I like them both enormously.

'Oh, don't be talking about chickens,' Delia says, getting up to leave. 'Olivia talks of nothing else these days. My dad is letting her run the egg business, so we're all delighted Finbarr is as into the hens as she is – she'd wear the ears off you.'

'Well, he's lucky to have her. He hangs on every word she says. We have the gospel according to Olivia every weekend when he's home.' Martha laughs. 'She's the ultimate authority on everything, according to him.'

'Well, if you ask my Auntie Assumpta she'll tell you Miss Olivia is a great young one for getting her own way, so don't have her be leading Finbarr astray now.' Delia is joking. Her younger cousin is a sweet girl, but like all teenagers, she has her moments.

'He'd follow her through the gates of hell, so he would,' Annette agrees cheerfully as she glances around for a spare table. I'm finishing my coffee and the last bite of delicious scone.

'You can have our seats if you like. We're going back to work,' I say, getting to my feet.

'Would we be into your grave as quick?' Annette asks with a wink as the two of them slide into our places before anyone else can take them.

CHAPTER 5

*D*elia sets off back to the station – she's due to go out on car patrol with Michael later this afternoon as it's not possible to do the country lanes on foot – and I ask her to check how Zoë is coping on the public desk.

I should go back to the station myself, as I need to write to the council about the drains, but instead I take a detour down MacDiarmada Street, which contains a row of small, neat houses with well-maintained front gardens behind low white walls. I stop at a house where the garden is more overgrown than the rest and the fence broken and the gravel weedy. I let myself in the creaky gate and go to knock on the front door.

A grey-haired, grey-faced man opens it. It's Caelan's father, Liam Cronin, and his shoulders slump when he finds me on his doorstep. 'Is he in trouble again, Sergeant?' he asks, and my heart goes out to him and his children. They are a family grieving ever since Caelan's mother was knocked down and killed by Mike Cantillon.

I'll never forget that day, Trish taken away in the ambulance from where she lay, broken, in the middle of the road outside the primary school. Her body was catapulted up in the air, such was the force of Cantillon's van. She'd been dropping Caelan to school, so it happened in full view of him and of the whole town. She was rushed to hospital but died a week later of her catastrophic injuries. Cantillon got seven years for being three times over the legal limit, served four and a half, and it wasn't the first time he was caught drink-driving either. He's been out for a while, and at first he stayed away from the town. His wife, Sandra, had moved back to her parents' place in Mayo, taking their son, Kevin, with her, and he joined them for a couple of years. But it didn't work out, they got divorced, and recently he's moved back to his home place in Ballycarrick, which fell empty once his mother passed away.

And now as a result, Caelan is increasingly out of control and headed to a life of hardcore crime if he isn't stopped now. Liam is doing his best as a father to his two sons, and Fiachra is a grand young lad, to be fair, but Caelan, who is older than Fiachra and was there when it happened, can never forgive Cantillon, and he hates me too because I represent the system that to his mind let his mother's killer walk free.

'No, no one's in trouble, but I'd like a quick word with Caelan,' I say. 'Is he in?'

Liam nods towards the sitting room door, which is closed. I take that as giving me permission and open it gently.

'Caelan? It's Sergeant Munroe. You're not in trouble. Can I have a quick word?' I square my shoulders and walk purposefully into the room. Caelan jumps to his feet, his smartphone in his hand. He looks belligerent, terrified and heartbroken, all at the same time.

'Sit down, please,' I say, no trace of my normal friendliness.

He flops back down into the armchair, sullen, his head down, fiddling with the phone, his silky dark-brown hair falling over his face. Such a handsome boy; he'd pass for a young Johnny Depp.

I sit on the sofa opposite while his father hovers miserably in the doorway.

'Caelan,' I say, still speaking in my professional voice, 'you've been cautioned on seven occasions over the last eighteen months for harassing Mike Cantillon. The Garda Juvenile Liaison Officer has spoken to you repeatedly.'

Caelan mutters something under his breath that I don't quite catch, but it's safe to assume that it's very derogatory of Darren's efforts.

'You have vandalised Mike Cantillon's garden, spray-painted his wall, you've called him names on social media, and now I hear you and Kenneth Carmody painted graffiti on his van last night. I expect he'll be in to complain today, so I want to ask you, Caelan – what's the end game here? If Mike wants to press charges, I'm going to have to arrest you for the crimes of wilful damage to property under the Criminal Damage Act of 1991.' I spell it out to make sure he understands this is serious.

'That scumbag murders my mam, and *I'm* the one that's in the wrong? This is a joke.' A laugh, more like a bitter bark, erupts from him, the sound of a disillusioned adult, not a sixteen-year-old kid. This boy is so full of rage, it is palpable in the room.

Caelan is not a bad person; I've seen evil and he's not it. He's hurting and he's right to be angry. Four and a half years in jail for killing someone when you were drunk is not enough. But it's how it goes sometimes. In the eyes of the law, Cantillon has served his time, and he is entitled to live where he wants.

'Caelan, the law is very clear that you are in the wrong. And if I have to arrest you, the law will require you to be sent forward to the children's court, and you could end up with a custodial sentence in a juvenile correction unit.' I don't want to do this to him, or his father. I try to support Liam; the poor man has been through enough. But sometimes support and understanding have to come in the form of tough love.

'I don't care what the law says. It's the law's fault he's out. It's the law's fault Cantillon only got manslaughter and not murder, so you can piss off,' he spits at me.

'Caelan, please…' Liam begins, but the boy turns on him then.

'Shut up, you. I'm sick to death of listening to you bleating on.' The boy does a whiney impression, presumably of his father. '"You've got to move on, Caelan. We've got to look to the future, Caelan." *You* might be soft on that murderer, 'cos you don't care about Mam any more. Nobody cares – they let him out. But I care, and I won't forget her.' And he goes back to his phone, his eyes bright with unshed tears.

I stand and join Liam in the hall, closing the sitting room door behind me. 'Look, Liam, I'll say to Mike Cantillon what I always say, that pressing charges against Caelan will be a bad look for him and the paint will wash off, but this can't continue. I'm serious. I keep promising Cantillon I won't let it happen again, but then…'

'He's been talking to his mother,' says Liam unexpectedly.

'I'm sorry?' My brain scrambles to make sense of this. 'Do you mean Mike?' I thought Mike Cantillon's mother was dead.

'No, I mean Caelan. He's been down to that witch woman and had a séance, and apparently Trish came through for him.' He glances at me to see how I take this, and I give a noncommittal nod, so he carries on. 'He was so happy when he came home and told me about it. Well, it made me think it could do him good, if he believed Trish wasn't… well…gone…' Poor Liam, he has tears in his own eyes. 'He was on about how proud she was of him and everything he did, and I thought that would help. But it's all gone worse now, Mags, because he thinks she's proud of him for harassing Cantillon. And though I said to him his mother would never approve of that, she wouldn't want him in trouble, she would want him to be happy and get on with his life, he just screamed and yelled at me that I don't care…'

Liam looks so weary and battered by life, it's hard to watch.

* * *

I ALWAYS KEEP my office door slightly ajar, and my heart sinks when I hear the familiar tones of Detective Inspector Donal Cassidy, known behind his back as Duckie.

A while ago Duckie got a promotion I didn't even want, and he's been lording it over me ever since. He never has a reason to pop in, but he does with annoying regularity, always mentioning how he was having dinner with the Minister for Justice or how he played golf with this CEO or that dignitary. Kieran says he does it because he's desperate to show off to me, which means he's actually insecure about his position, but I really wish he'd leave us alone. He's sexist and racist and thinks he's hilarious, which he absolutely is not. He's shaved his head, which is a mercy – the purple dye and combover look was fooling nobody – but he's doubled down on the stinky aftershave to make up for the lack of hair. Poor Nicola got an asthma attack after his last visit to our station.

'Someone like you is wasted here in Ballygobackwards,' I can hear him saying through the gap in the door. The cheek of him. 'Maybe I can pull a few strings, get you a transfer to Galway…'

I can't see who he's talking to, but I can guess it's Zoë because he's in full flirt mode. Duckie has two modes. The first is nasty and rude; he reserves that for men he considers beneath him and all women over thirty-five or over seventy kilos. And the other is what he imagines is flirty and charming, to men he's sucking up to and beautiful young women. It's enough to make you want to gag, truly.

Nicola is his usual target here, but she's off today, thankfully, so he's turning it on full whack for Zoë. I wonder should I go out and rescue her, but at the same time, I'm interested in how she'll deal with him. I stop writing my email to the council about the drains and listen.

'Yeah, her indoors dragged me to see the witch woman.' That's what he calls his wife behind her back – her indoors. He wouldn't dare do it to her face, though. 'Everyone is on about her. I mean, I'm not into it myself, but to be fair, she did comment on how young I looked and how I was a very astute person – remarkably intelligent, I think was the phrase she used – and that there would be something big happening for me career-wise in the coming months. I've always lots of irons in the fire. Can't go into it, obviously, with you. Senior members only, I'm afraid. But it makes you think, doesn't it?'

'About what?' asks Zoë, and I realise to my amusement that she is totally impervious to Duckie's ham-fisted flirting. He makes Nicola's skin crawl, but it seems that for Zoë, he might as well be an actual duck quacking at her for all the impact he is having.

'Well, all of that, you know, magic or whatever… Or are you a more down-to-earth kind of girl? Likes to get down and dirty? You

CLOSER THAN YOU THINK

look like someone who'd be very easy to deal with, knows how to show a man a good time, not carping on about equality and women's lib and all the rest of that nonsense, like some people we could mention.'

The last bit is delivered sotto voce. Clearly he means me. I have certainly raised the issue of language in the workplace and objected to him calling women 'birds', and Travellers 'knackers'.

'Younger girls are better, I always find,' he drones on. 'Make a man feel good about himself. Young fillies like yourself could teach the auld harridans a thing or two, I bet. Maybe I could take you out sometime? I know everyone, and a pretty girl like you could really go places if you had the right connections – you know what I mean?'

'I think I do know what you mean, but I think you should talk to your therapist about it?' says Zoë kindly.

'Ha, ha, my... *What?*' He's suddenly heard what she said, and he's confused.

'Your therapist? You surely have one? Talk to them about your longing for female acceptance, you know? I think we can put a lot of deep-felt trauma down to primal wounding, where your mother deprived you of love, and you spend your life searching for the elusive maternal bond? Were you cuddled? Were you breast-fed?' She asks these questions as innocently as if she's asking the time.

I stifle a giggle and take a mouthful of my coffee. I wish I could see Duckie's face.

'Ah, no... Well... Breast?' Duckie splutters. This has caught him off-guard. He's used to rejection, I'd have to imagine, and he delights in making women feel awkward, but this will be a new one on him.

'Yeah, I thought not? I suspect Minnie might be appealing to your inner child, the longing for praise, for endorsement, the baby Duckie...'

I almost spurt the mouthful of coffee I'm drinking. Nobody calls him Duckie to his face.

'Maybe the toddler Duckie, or ten-year-old Duckie or teenage Duckie craved love and was rejected, and now you see that acceptance of yourself as you are on offer with Minnie, which is why you see what she said as flattering?'

Oh, I wish I could record this – it's hilarious. The best thing is, I think she is being quite serious. She reads a lot of self-help books and is forever quoting podcasts on wellness.

'Ah no, that's a load of auld crap, inner child...' He's got no answer for her, though, and she ploughs happily on.

'And skin-to-skin contact in the first moments after birth is so vital, but I know years and years ago they probably didn't know that. I think they only discovered that in the 1950s or maybe even the '40s, so probably they didn't know about it when you were born?'

'I'm forty-six,' he splutters, which is not true – he's closer to fifty-six – but Zoë talking to him like he's an old, misguided, unloved child of the war years is priceless.

She misunderstands. 'Born in '46? That explains it. Like, they were probably all suffering from PTSD after the war, that's post-traumatic stress disorder –'

'I bloody well know what it is. Where's Mags?' he snaps, furious now.

'One sec, I'll call her,' Zoë answers, totally unaware of his outrage. She rings me on the internal line. 'Sarge, Duckie is here to see you.'

'It's Detective Inspector Cassidy to you,' he barks. I can picture his face, probably a deep purple now.

'Oh, right, sorry.' I hear her still on the line. 'Detective Inspector Duckie Cassidy is here, Sarge.'

'Oh, never mind! I'll come back another day, when the lunatics aren't in charge of the asylum,' he roars, and I hear him storm off out of the front door.

'Sorry, Sarge, he's gone. He must have remembered he had a meeting or something,' says Zoë, before she hangs up.

I'm unable to speak. I'm hardly able to breathe. I think I love Zoë after all.

CHAPTER 6

On my way home, I call in to see Jerome, Delia's father. I want to ask his opinion about Rollo. Jerome's a bit of a dog whisperer, so maybe he can whisper to Rollo that I'm not trying to murder him.

There are about ten caravans in all on the Drumlish halting site, each housing another cousin or aunt and uncle of Delia's. The place is spotless. Dogs, ponies, hens, rabbits in hutches – they are everywhere, but they are well cared for. I park outside the entrance and take off my Garda jacket, pulling on the plain hoodie that I keep in the car for when I want to be off-duty. The McGoverns are law-abiding, but they're naturally wary of law enforcement and with good reason. Travellers and the guards have not always seen eye to eye over the years, and the kids can get scared if they see a Garda uniform.

Besides, this is a social call.

'Ah, Mags, 'tis yourself,' Jerome says as he opens the door of his van to me. Dacie used to live here, his mother who died a few years ago, and I get a pang of sadness for her; I was so fond of her. She was a real Traveller woman, lived a hard life on the road, but she'd always say she had it better than settled women like me who are expected to do it all. It was Dacie who asked me to get her granddaughter Delia a start in the guards. Jerome was dead set against it, there being an inherent mistrust of the gardaí in the Traveller community. As well as that, working women are not their way; girls in that culture marry young, and their husbands provide for them. But Dacie and Delia together brought him round.

'I was just passing, thought I'd drop in.' I smile up at him.

To my disappointment I see a shadow cross his big, handsome face. Jerome McGovern is the head of his Traveller family, and he has a body like a tank. His dark hair is always brushed back off his forehead, and his skin is like leather from a life spent outdoors. His hands are tattooed, and he was, I believe, the bare-knuckle boxing champion of Ireland when he was a lad. Travellers love bare-knuckle boxing. Such practice is illegal, of course, but as a guard, you pick your battles, and it's part of the Traveller way. I don't understand it or like it, but they are kind of self-regulating with regards to that, so I stay out of it and pretend I've no idea what it even is.

I feel a pang of disappointment that no matter how many years we are friends – and I was friends with his mother before him, and his daughter is a guard under my command, and we've been through some scrapes together – he's still capable of being suspicious of my motives.

'Nothing bad, don't worry,' I say. 'I just wanted to chat to you about my dog.'

He stands before me for a beat. Then, 'Tea?' he asks, and I nod.

'I'd love one,' I say, following him into his caravan.

Delia's mother, Dora, seems to be out, and he places the kettle on the gas hob and gestures that I should sit. The van isn't as big as some of the modern Traveller caravans, and his bulk makes it feel even smaller, but it is neat as a new pin. I sit on the U-shaped sofa at one end; the bedrooms and bathroom are at the other, with the little kitchen in between. He makes the tea in silence while I tell him about Rollo, then hands me a steaming mug and places a packet of biscuits on the table. If Dora was here, she'd be horrified; she always serves tea in cups with saucers and biscuits on a plate.

'So you've come to me for help,' he says.

I sense an edge to his tone, and I wonder if something has upset him.

'Well, I just thought, since you are so good with animals...' I raise an eyebrow. 'Jerome, are you all right? You seem a bit...'

'I hear you're offerin' all sorts of protection to the pair in the Lodge.' He glowers.

'What? The witch and warlock?' I'm confused.

Jerome snorts, much like his daughter did at the briefing meeting. 'Witch, my eye. She's no more a witch than I'm the king of England. She might be well and good at the cold reading, but that's where it ends.'

Again, I'm puzzled, like I was with Delia. Yes, maybe Minnie and Neil aren't the real deal – and I make a mental note to look up what 'cold reading' means – but still. 'Ah sure, they're just doing their thing, Jerome, hurting nobody. What harm are they doing?'

'Harm? What harm?' He is astonished. 'Tell me, is there not a law to stop criminals and liars takin' people's hard-earned money off them and makin' them believe things that are not true?'

'Well, there's a lot of legislation now to prevent fraud, online scams, that sort of thing...'

'Ye know that's not what I mean. I mean the like of that pair takin' money off innocent people, makin' out like they have the sight when they've no such thing.'

He's not wrong about me knowing what he means, but I'm not sure what to say to him. Getting money from someone by selling them a fake product, that's clearly illegal. But faith healing and predicting the future and stuff like that – who's to say if it's fake? Especially if the customers are happy?

'Well, whether this pair can or they can't cleanse auras and things, if people want to consult them, sure it's their own time and money they're spending?'

'Mags,' he says fiercely, 'if anyone around these parts wants to talk to the dead or know what is comin' down the tracks for them, where do they go?'

I'm even more bewildered now, and I know my face shows it.

'Dora's sister Kathleen, she has the sight,' he says in exasperation, like I'm being deliberately obtuse.

'Oh, is she married to Boxer Carmody?' I vaguely remember Dora's sister now, a haggard-looking woman with a pockmarked face and dyed purple hair, who lives with her husband on the Tuam road site.

'That's her, and she's out of business nearly from that pair. And we're gettin' it day and night from the other families since we're so friendly with ye, and Delia is one of ye, for God's sake. That pair of chancers over here from England, gettin' all kinds of help from ye, with Kieran fixing their roof for them and ye putting the run on a good devout Catholic like Oscar when he went to ye about it, and 'tis making life very hard for us, Mags.'

I've never seen him so upset; Jerome is normally stoic if anything.

'Her son's wife had a child, and we weren't even asked to the christening. Dora's very vexed, and they're all sayin' we're after gettin' like country people and forgettin' our own. And we were tryin' to keep it quiet like, about Delia livin' outside of marriage and even buying a house with that feen Darren, but it got out, of course, so we're disgraced. I knew 'twas a bad thing to have Delia join ye, and now I'm proved right.'

'Delia never said you were still upset –'

'Sure, what would she understand! She's as bad as ye now, learnin' your ways instead of her own, and herself and her mother are after an awful fallout. Dora thinkin' Delia was boastin' about her new kitchen, not a word spoken between them these last three weeks. So I suggest ye make it up with your own dog, Mags, maybe just treat him with a bit of respect ye can't seem to give us.'

I've never seen Jerome like this, and I feel terrible that he believes it is his good relationship with me that is at the heart of his troubles. I had no idea that Kathleen Carmody was Dora's sister, but then there are so many of them, it's hard to keep track. Dacie had sixteen children, and Dora was one of thirteen, all of whom are married to Traveller men, and they too have lots of children. Still, I don't know what to do to make this better.

'Ah, Jerome, look, I'm sorry. The last thing I wanted was to cause problems for you, but there's nothing much I can do about Minnie and Neil – they're doing nothing illegal. And as for Delia, look, she's a young, independent woman. She's proud of her family, but she wants to just live her –'

'Don't, Mags.' He speaks through gritted teeth. ''Tis different for ye. We're not the same, and Delia needs to remember she's one of us, much and all as she'll deny us. I said 'twould end badly, and nobody listened to me, and now here we are.'

I'm reminded of something Mam always says, that it's never about what people say it's about, that there's always more behind it. Jerome is still upset about Delia becoming a guard, and everything else for him stems from that. To her father's way of thinking, instead of forging her own career with us, she should have married a Traveller boy approved of by the family, and on top of that, it should have been done years ago. Delia is in her twenties now, and Traveller girls usually marry in their late teens. But instead, she's living in sin with a man from the settled community.

I think Delia understands on one level how hurtful and embarrassing this is for her parents, because she has promised them she and Darren will get married someday, but not yet.

But I doubt she really gets how painful even this is for her parents. A huge extravagant-to-the-point-of-bankruptcy church wedding is an important part of Traveller culture, but Delia doesn't seem to realise how much her parents want to do this for her. I heard her telling Nicola that a wedding like that is a massive expense and that she is saving her parents from having to pay for it. I can't interfere; it's for her and them to work out.

I stand. 'I'm sorry if you think I brought trouble to your door, Jerome. It was never my intention, and I'm very sorry that your friendship with me and Delia's career have put you at odds with the rest of your family. If I can help, I'll be happy to.'

The look he gives me speaks volumes. *Stay away from me, that's the best thing you can do.*

* * *

I'M RATTLED AND UPSET, so instead of going straight home, I drive out the road and turn down a side boreen to the stony beach. The autumn nights are drawing in, so the sky is gunmetal grey and the sea a shade or two darker. Angry-looking waves crash relentlessly on the shore, which suits my mood. There are some picnic benches there, but it's too cold to get out, so I stay in the car, facing the sea.

A short way from the car park, on the beach, there's a lone fisherman casting out, dressed from head to foot in green oilskins. The things people put themselves through, I think bad-temperedly. I wonder if he knows he can buy fish in the supermarket and save himself all the misery.

Then I wonder where the fisherman's car is; it seems odd to be there without a vehicle of some kind. I look around and see it, a large black one parked at the other end of the car park near the dunes. Weird that someone would park all the way over there and drag the gear across the big car park and down onto the shore.

I don't know why, but I get out and walk over to have a look at the vehicle. An Audi, but I don't recognise the plates.

I glance back. The fisherman is looking in my direction, so I carry on walking straight past the car to the ramp on the right-hand side of the car park, glad I'm still wearing the anonymous hoodie and so appear like a middle-aged woman out for her health rather than a nosey-parker guard.

Maybe I should do some steps while I'm here anyway; my Fitbit is showing a pathetic two thousand despite my vowing to do ten thousand today. I've hardly even walked off Teresa's scone, especially as I gave in to the butter and jam.

I carry on down the ramp and up the beach, heading away from the lone fisherman, the pounding waves on my left. A short distance in front of me, a couple of people, a man and a woman, are picking up driftwood and piling it together, probably to make a fire. Strictly, they shouldn't be doing that – we're not supposed to burn anything these days because of carbon – but I decide to leave them at it. I know we need to save the planet, and I do my bit with organic veg and recycling, and Kieran's new work van is all electric, but right now I'm in my hoodie, I'm off-duty, and I'm not going to spoil someone's innocent fun.

I'm heading past them when the woman calls my name. 'Sergeant Munroe!'

I turn, and speak of the devil – metaphorically, of course – it's Minnie, with her partner, Neil.

She comes straight towards me, her hands stretched out in greeting. She's a stocky woman, with very straight waist-length silver hair, and she's dressed in hiking boots, green leggings and an oversized black tunic type thing that goes down to her knees, with a long pointed hood. It's embroidered with silver stars. She looks very theatrical, as if she's dressed up as a witch for Halloween. On her delicate hands are several big silver rings set with mood stones. She has remarkably smooth skin for a woman I imagine is in her sixties; she must have magicked her wrinkles away.

Neil, her partner, who has followed her over, looks much more ordinary – lanky and thin, with grey curls and a long straggly beard that covers most of his face, wearing a hand-knitted striped jumper and jeans.

'Sergeant Munroe, we've been waiting for you!' cries Minnie, in a big, strong voice. 'What took you so long?'

'Waiting for…?' People seem determined to confuse me these days. Maybe I just keep missing something obvious, or maybe I'm going senile.

'We wanted to see you, so we manifested you, and here you are!'

It gives me a bit of a chill – there's something very unpleasant about the idea of being supernaturally summoned – but I remind myself I have no reason to believe Minnie just jerked my psychic chain. They were here, and I turned up, and I've only this woman's word for it that there's any sort of connection.

'Well, you're always welcome to pop into the station if you need to talk to me about anything.' I smile rather stiffly.

'Oh, no, no, no. The spirits arranged it this way for a purpose.'

53

Minnie comes closer, blocking the direction of my walk. 'Do you know a man called Desmond Dunne, Sergeant?'

My heart sinks. I can guess what's coming next. 'I do.'

'Well, he is running a smear campaign against us, Sergeant Munroe. He keeps taking down our sign, saying it's evil, even though we've explained I'm a white witch and Neil here is a white warlock.'

Damn it. I'd meant to talk to Desmond about the sign, but it went right out of my head when I heard about Caelan.

'We've tried to reason with him, Sergeant, we really have...' Neil's soft voice is soothing; he seems like a gentle soul. 'I even offered him a free aura cleanse because I sense something is wrong with his health.'

I'm sure Neil's right about that, and I'm sure Dr Harrison senses it too; one look at all the broken veins and the big red nose would tell you Desmond Dunne is heading for an early grave. And the bash over the head with the flowerpot hasn't made things any better. I did tell him to get himself checked out before I left that day, but I suspect he didn't, and now he's acting stranger than ever, hanging out with Oscar and being all holy.

'We've done nothing to provoke him. He's just a menace.' Minnie is really cross, and I don't blame her. 'So we've decided we want to make an official complaint.'

'Well, before you do that, how about this?' I suggest soothingly. 'I'll have a word with Mr Dunne, explain that he needs to stay away from your property, and if he does that, we'll say no more about it?'

Here I go again, trying to smooth things over, turning the heat down, not escalating things.

'We've told you, we've tried that,' Minnie complains. She's clearly beginning to wonder whether it was worth manifesting me at all.

I smile and nod. 'I appreciate that, but I would be doing it in an official legal capacity, with the implication being I will have no option but to proceed with a formal caution if he refuses to comply with the instruction.'

Neil turns to her then. 'We can just try this way first, love. It's worth a shot.'

I wonder what alternative course of action they were considering. Eye of toad and toe of newt? A spell of some kind? But I say nothing.

'Fine, but this is his last chance,' Minnie says back to him. She's not speaking in a particularly threatening way, but my senses tingle nonetheless.

'I have to caution you and Neil against doing anything to take matters into your own hands, Minnie,' I say warningly.

'Oh, don't worry, Sergeant, we won't do anything illegal,' she says, and holds my gaze with hers. Her eyes are incredibly dark, I notice then, dark, dark brown, almost black in the evening light. And then she laughs, like she's just having fun with me. The tension breaks, and I smile too. And I have an idea.

'Can I ask you a favour, Minnie?'

'Of course, Sergeant.'

'A boy called Caelan Cronin came to see you recently, and his father told me…well, that Caelan thought he was speaking to his deceased mother through you. And she was telling him how great he was and she was proud of him, which is nice.'

'I was very glad to help him make contact,' she says, with a gracious tip of her head.

'The thing is…' And I explain the circumstances, how Caelan took his mother's approval as carte blanche to vandalise Mike Cantillon's property and how the poor, stricken boy is in danger of getting into terrible trouble with the law, and that if Caelan came to her again, could she possibly make sure Caelan's mother said something about looking ahead to the future and…

'I beg your pardon?' Minnie bristles, like she can't believe her ears. 'Are you asking me to lie? You want me to *pretend* to channel that poor boy's mother, and put false words into her mouth? You want me to *fake* it?' She's either genuinely offended or an excellent actor, hard to tell which.

'I didn't mean to offend you, Minnie,' I say. 'I just meant, perhaps there is a way you could let Trish Cronin – that's Caelan's mother –'

'I know Patricia,' snaps Minnie, her dark eyes flashing.

'Oh, yes, well, if you could let her know what was happening with Caelan, so next time she speaks to him –'

'Those that have passed on know everything,' she sighs wearily as if everyone should know at least that. 'It is not my duty to tell them what to say when they choose to speak – through me – to their loved ones.'

'Of course...' This is hopeless. I should never have got into an argument with a witch.

'Mike Cantillon is his name? The man who killed Caelan's mother?' asks Neil, coming to my rescue in his gentle, soothing way. 'That's terrible. And only four and a half years in prison? No wonder Caelan is hurt and upset. He must feel that justice has not been done.'

'Well, that's the law,' I say noncommittally. 'And I know it seems unfair to Caelan, but Mike Cantillon did his time and he's out now, and the law requires he's left to live his life in peace.' I'm hungry now and I check my watch. It's getting to dinner time, so I should be getting home.

'I'll remember this conversation,' says Minnie suddenly, in a much kinder tone.

'Thank you.' I hope this means she'll take my request on board, even if she can't admit to being in control of what is said in a reading. I say goodnight to the two of them and walk back to the car park.

As I get into my car and slot the keys into the ignition, I see that the fisherman is still there, a black figure against the setting sun, which is bleeding red across the waves. Out on the horizon is a boat, silhouetted against the fading glow.

* * *

BACK HOME, the girls and Kieran are watching television.

None of us have eaten, so I peel potatoes to boil for mash and throw on some sausages and onions. Kieran comes in behind me as I'm turning the sausages in the pan, puts his arms around my waist and kisses my neck. The girls produce vomit sounds from the table, which makes us both laugh. Then Kieran screams, not a manly yell now, but a full-on girlie scream.

Knickers has just leapt out of the cupboard above the cooker, over Kieran's head, and thundered down his back, much to the hilarity of our daughters.

'Ah, Knickers. Did my dad scare you with his squeaky voice?' Kate dives under the counter, where Knickers has taken palpitating refuge, and soothes the thing by gently caressing his side.

'What in the name of all that's holy was that thing doing in the cupboard?' Kieran splutters.

'He loves the heat of the cooker, I think. I found him draped across the grill the other day – lucky he wasn't served with the fish fingers,' I say cheerfully. Secretly I'm delighted it wasn't me screaming this time. I must be getting used to Knickers suddenly popping up everywhere.

'Did you know he was in there?' Kieran is flabbergasted.

'Oh yeah, I store him there, Rollo in the bed, Frankie Velcro up my sleeve. You know me, Kieran, the Dr Dolittle of Ballycarrick.' I take the sausages from the pan to the plate and bring the plate to the table. 'Of course I didn't, you daft eejit. That thing loves hiding and jumping out at me – it's his favourite pastime.'

'I didn't know you could make that sound, Dad.' Ellie chuckles. 'Very macho.'

'Yeah, well, that thing should stay in his enclosure,' he grumbles as he throws a heart-stopping amount of butter into the potatoes before mashing them.

'He's very intelligent, Dad,' Kate explains, 'and he can escape from everything. Besides, he likes having the run of the house.'

'And what if Rollo eats him?' Kieran asks, and the girls laugh.

'Knickers is the same size as Rollo, and anyway, Rollo is the biggest baby on earth. He's more scared of Knickers than he is of Mam.' Kate giggles. 'And he's absolutely terrified of Mam.'

CHAPTER 7

J'm applying some cream the kids got me for my birthday on my eyes, which are looking very saggy these days. I have to remember to open them wide in pictures now or else I look like Droopy dog, super sleuth. It's a choice now between that or appearing permanently startled. The joys of gravity, eh?

'Do you want to come to the tionól with me on Saturday night?' asks Kieran, from the bed. He says 'tionól' like of course everyone knows what that is. But I've no idea. I turn to look at him questioningly. He's sitting up reading a music magazine with an Irish fiddle on the cover.

'It's a gathering of pipers,' he says, clearly amused by my ignorance. 'Loads of pipers from all over the country are coming. It's going to be brilliant.'

I can't help but smile at his enthusiasm. 'No, it's OK. Ellie and the twins have a disco on Saturday, and the twins are staying over here, so they all need picking up, and I can't leave Kate by herself all evening. So you go and enjoy, and I'll sort the girls out.'

'That's a shame you can't come. Donál Óg O Sé is coming and everything,' he says earnestly, and I haven't the heart to say I never heard of Donál Óg O Sé any more than I knew what a tionól was before he told me, so I just nod sagely.

'He's absolutely amazing. I could listen to him for hours.'

I smile. I've never seen my husband star-struck before. He's always liked music. We went to see Bruce Springsteen a few times and U2 of course, and he took the girls to Ed Sheeran last summer, which he was allergic to the idea of but actually enjoyed. But this is a whole other thing.

I know I complain about the noise of Kieran practising the pipes, and I swear that's all you could call what he currently produces, noise, but I assume he'll get better and it's lovely to see him enthusiastic and happy. It's been a rough few years between one thing and another, but life is getting easier, and I'm so glad he has time for a hobby. Kieran is a big strong Irishman, a hard worker and a great dad, but his mental health took a knock when I got shot and nearly killed while thwarting the efforts of a gang of people smugglers.

I know you might think that being shot at sort of goes with the territory of being a police officer, but that's not the case in Ireland. Some branches of the serious crime and detective squads have access to firearms, but the rank and file of us gardaí are not armed, and neither are most of the ODCs (ordinary decent criminals, as we call them). And so while getting shot in the line of duty is not impossible, neither is it very likely.

So when it happened, Kieran took it badly. Up to that point, he'd thought being a sergeant in Ballycarrick was just dog licences, drunk drivers and domestics, and that's still true, but after the shooting, he was seeing danger around every corner. He got so worried and over-whelmed by it all, he wanted me to quit the job, which I refused to do, which meant some tension between us, and he was living on his nerves for a while.

Being reared by the overbearing Nora and the taciturn Kevin didn't help; not much room for open and honest conversation in that house. So bottling things up is Kieran's MO, but gradually with medication and a good therapist, he's feeling much better.

59

He told the girls at my suggestion what was going on with him – we're determined to do things differently to his parents – and they've been brilliant. He's an adoring dad, so in the light of everything, we're all happy to let him perforate our eardrums with the uilleann pipes. Kate even says she's loving it more and more, which I very much doubt, but she's a kind little soul. Are there days that we wish he'd found stamp collecting or watercolour painting? Well, maybe, but we love him, so we grin and bear it.

'Oh, and Mam wants us over for lunch on Sunday,' he adds apologetically.

'Can't wait,' I say with a rueful smile, screwing the top back on the cream. Nora and I have reached what they call in international conflict an 'entente cordiale', which is a tacit agreement to avoid all-out war but with an understanding that there is not now, nor will there ever be, anything approximating warmth.

My monster-in-law is an incurable snob, and despite all that the family have been through, it seems to not have resulted in any great personal growth for her, as they are fond of saying on *Oprah* and the like.

She nearly had a breakdown when Kieran's dad, the monosyllabic Kevin, discovered she'd had a baby before she got married and that he was the father. She refused to look for the child at first, terrified the neighbours would find out she wasn't 'respectable'. After a very dramatic time of slammed doors and long silences and Kevin showing uncharacteristic gumption, the whole thing was resolved and everyone was reunited.

Of course it helped a lot when Nora discovered her long-lost first born was 'very high up in television'. Oilibhéar, which is Irish for Oliver, but everyone just calls him Ol, works for the national broadcaster, RTÉ, and this is a source of great delight and bragging rights. Am I horrible for secretly wishing he'd turned out to be a binman or a van driver? Anyway, these days she's over the moon with her well-got son. And we all like him; Ol's a dote. He lives in Dublin but visits often with his charming wife, Muireann.

Nora does love her children to be 'very high up' in things. She is proud that her daughter Orla is married to Fergus 'very high up in the bank', and Aoife's husband, Leonard, is 'very high up in education' – he's the principal of a posh secondary school. And Catriona is married to Seamus, who is 'very high up in medicine', a cardiologist no less. Gearoid, the baby, runs the Irish language theatre in Galway and is always pictured in the society magazines, so as you can imagine, he's 'very high up in the arts'.

So you can see how devastating Kieran's choice of wife has been for her. We live in a very ordinary and sometimes very messy house, and I'm a rank-and-file member of the police, on a civil service wage, and nobody could say I'm high up anywhere.

There was a promotion opportunity there a while ago, and Ronan Brady, a friend and senior colleague, recommended I go for it, which is Garda speak for I'm a shoo-in. I talked to Kieran and was tempted, but in the end, I decided against it. I like my current job; I love knowing everyone and helping where I can. But Kate in her innocence told her Nana Nora that I turned down a big promotion; she was only defending me from another snide remark probably. But once Nora got wind that I turned down the chance to be 'very high up in the guards', she was furious. It was hilarious. She rang Kieran, telling him to more or less order me to take the job. Luckily for me, Kieran takes not a tack of notice of her.

I sound a bit like I'm feeling sorry for myself, but I'm not a bit. I think my monster-in-law is ridiculous for finding me disappointing, but there you have it. The strange thing is, it was to me she came when she couldn't bring herself to talk to anyone about the baby she'd had before she married Kevin, not even her own husband. So we have kind of a bond now we never had before, but it doesn't mean she has to like me, nor me her.

'Ah, it will be grand,' Kieran says as I climb in beside him. 'Everyone's coming, Ol as well, and apparently even Seamus is gracing us with his presence.'

'I'll believe that when I see it.' Seamus the cardiologist almost never turns up to anything. Catriona goes to every family event on her own. I've actually only met the man a handful of times, and that's the truth.

'I know, but Catriona says he'll be there, and she usually makes an excuse, so we'll see. It was meant to be last weekend, but Seamus was on call and Gearoid said he wanted everyone.'

'Really? Gearoid wants everyone there? So is it to do with him and Enrico finally setting a date?'

'No idea. He wouldn't tell me either way.'

I snuggle into him. 'I hope they *are* getting married. I love Enrico – he's hilarious.'

Enrico is fiery and passionate, and prone to great outpourings of love for Gearoid, often at Nora's dinner table, which makes all the Munroes squirm and me laugh. Gearoid didn't tell his family he was gay until he was approaching thirty; he said he couldn't be bothered to draw that drama into his life, and I don't blame him. The Munroes are not OK with emotions of any kind.

His siblings and father are fine about it, and even Nora has come round, though she was horrified at first. It's *de rigueur* now to have a gay child apparently; everyone who is famous has one. She watched some programme – don't ask me what it's called – about gay men in America and the love they have for their mothers, and now she's styled herself as the Ruth Bader Ginsburg of the west of Ireland, the epitome of acceptance and love. Any day now she's going to refer to Gearoid as being 'very high up in the gays', and woe betide anyone who recalls how she refused to accept it at first.

Kieran sets his magazine aside. He wears glasses to read now, a new development, and he takes them off and throws them glass side down on the locker. We're not the kind of people who put them in cases or use that little cloth they give you when you get new glasses; he wipes his on his t-shirt mostly. Then he opens his arms as he always does, and I rest my head on his chest. I feel the familiar but so welcome strength of his arms around me.

'Enrico loves you too. He told me just how much at great length after that horrible play you dragged me to.' He laughs, a deep rolling sound in his chest that reverberates against my ear.

'It was art, you philistine.' I slap his side playfully.

'A play about a fella stuck in a box, from the point of view of the box, *in Irish*. I swear if you ever drag me to something like that again, I'll file for divorce. We should tell the prison service about it – they could put it on instead of solitary as a punishment. The bold boys would behave if they thought that desperate drivel was their fate, let me tell you.'

'Well, I thought it was brilliant, a caustic condemnation of the bourgeois. The box was metaphorical for the trappings of a consumerist society.'

'Ha! You did in your eye! I saw you asleep at one point.'

He's not wrong; it was absolutely dreadful. But Gearoid knew it was terrible and begged us to come to fill out the numbers.

I laugh. 'Well, at least I didn't snore.'

'You owe me a few piping concerts now after all the rubbish you made me sit through over the years. Remember the poetry reading you dragged me to, of your one from Tuam that *moved* to Tibet, she said, and when I asked her how long she lived there, she said four weeks. And the Ukrainian opera in the Protestant church in November, where we nearly froze to death on the hard seats for *three hours*.'

'Hey, that was to support art in the community as a local guard. But please, I'd rather have bowel surgery in the back garden than go to a piping concert. Please don't make me,' I plead jokingly.

'You might like it. Give it a chance...'

'I wouldn't. I can say few things categorically, but I definitely one hundred percent wouldn't. And don't forget there's the disco. You go, though, have a brilliant time.'

'Róisín's home, landed back on Friday,' he says then, out of the blue.

'Is she?' There's nothing surprising about this because I knew she was coming soon, but something about the way he said it feels weird, and I pull back a bit from our cuddle.

'She's been through a bit of a bad time recently. That's part of the reason she's back.'

'Really? When did she tell you that?'

'She rang me, and I met her for lunch today.'

'Oh. You didn't say?' I don't want to sound jealous, and I'm not; I trust Kieran completely. And Róisín ringing him and meeting him for lunch and telling him all her woes is fair enough; they go back a long way. But I'm still a bit surprised.

'I would have, but I wanted to wait to talk to you without the girls, because what she told me is a bit sad and private.'

I lean up on an elbow. 'What was it?'

'She lost a baby, Mags. More than one.'

I'm so sad to hear that news. Róisín's lovely, and she doesn't deserve more heartbreak. 'Oh, poor her, that's terrible. But she and Joel both decided not to have children, I thought?' When I met Róisín in New York, she'd had that well-polished look of women with no kids and loads of time, money and inclination for gyms and facials. I wouldn't swap my girls for any of that, but I thought she was happy with her decision.

He shrugs and sighs. 'That's what she thought too, but then Joel changed his mind and said it was all he wanted, and, well, she was in her early forties by then, so they spent a load of money on IVF, three cycles, and none of them worked out.'

'That's so awful.' I'm raging at Joel, typical man thinking there's all the time in the world to make a choice about whether he wants children or not, fooling around during his partner's most fertile years and then making the woman feel old for not being able to pop out a baby at the drop of a hat when he finally feels 'ready'.

'And then Joel had an affair...'

'*What?*' Oh my God, this got worse.

'Classic case, his secretary from work, half his age, the whole thing.'

This is so unfair. Why does it always seem to be the men? Sharon's ex, the slimy Danny Boylan, did the same thing, though to be fair, Danny would get up on a gust of wind and everyone knew it; the whole parish is full of little versions of him, as he's wheedled his way into the beds of so many women, the mind boggles. He is utterly gross, with all the charm of a bedpan, but maybe I know too much. But Joel is nothing like Danny. I thought they were happy.

'It's a big part of the move back to Ireland. It's about her parents getting older, of course, but it's also about a new start for her and Joel.'

'And Joel was prepared to give up his job in the New York Senate in order to make a go of his marriage?' My opinion of Joel goes up slightly. Very, very slightly.

'Well, the senator he worked for lost their seat in the last election, so he was at a loose end anyway.'

'Ah...' That makes more sense. His market value had clearly plummeted with the loss of his job, and I'm willing to bet it was the secretary who sent him packing, back to Róisín.

'And she wanted to get away from New York, put all the sadness behind them, and her law partner agreed to buy her out, leapt at the chance actually, so she and Joel have a good pot of money to start afresh over here. She's going to set up a one-woman law firm in Ballycarrick for starters, and Joel already has an interview for a job as the public relations officer for Shannon Airport.'

'So everything is good between them now and she's happy?' I ask. I trust Kieran implicitly. He wouldn't ever think of going back to Róisín, I know that, but I'm not sure I like the idea of her crying on his shoulder. He's such a sucker for tears. Even the girls know that if they start crying, they can get whatever they want out of him. I'm not much of a one for tears – I'm more likely to roar at someone. I do cry – like I'm not totally frozen – but it's not something that happens often.

'Yeah, well,' he says, stretching to turn off the bedside light, 'like I said, they're working it out.' In the darkness he adds, 'Oh, by the way, she's coming along to the tionól tomorrow night. Joel doesn't fancy it, but she loves the traditional music. That's all right, isn't it?'

I don't say what I really think. That it's OK with me but that it will have every tongue in the parish wagging that Kieran Munroe's glamorous ex-girlfriend from years ago is back and they're going on dates together behind their partners' backs.

'Of course it is. Go and enjoy it, love, and hopefully it will cheer Róisín up a bit.'

I go to sleep feeling very virtuous and magnanimous, and honestly, I do feel sorry for Róisín. And I'm not Nora – I don't care what the neighbours say, just so long as I know it's not true.

CHAPTER 8

*I*t's Sunday morning and I'm the only one up. It's lashing rain outside, and I don't bother to get dressed. I'm wearing the pyjamas the kids got me for my birthday that have the official harp emblem of the Irish government on it with the title 'Minister for Cop-On' in official font.

Apparently I'm always urging my daughters to have a bit of cop-on, Irish speak for be a bit wise as to what's really going on. And I regularly diagnose most people's problems as being because they lack basic cop-on. I am, of course, right. But they thought these pjs were hilarious.

Ellie and the twins were awake all night giggling and God knows what else. The table is littered with the remains of pizza and fizzy-drink cans, so I clear it all away and put the kettle on. The girls were in great form after the disco and on the way home were telling me all about this one and that one and this boy and all the rest. I must admit I'm relieved that from what Ellie was saying, Carrot seems to be off the menu. Call me Nora, but while I'm never going to go and demand a full Dermot the dentist or Alistair the quantity surveyor as a match for my eldest, I am hopeful she can do better than the emaciated

Carrot, who says he's giving up school when he's sixteen to become a hip-hop artist.

I make myself a cup of tea and take it into the conservatory we built last year. Kieran has banned the girls from it, saying he wants one tiny part of his own house where he isn't tripping over shoes and schoolbags, and where he and I can relax. We have no sockets out there, or screens, so that's enough to deter them. He got the triple-glazed glass for it and built it himself, and it's lovely, warm in winter and cool in summer. We spent a fortune on furniture for it. Most of our furniture in the house is hand-me-downs or got second-hand from DoneDeal – we don't care about stuff like that – but we treated ourselves to this, and it's so comfortable and looks lovely too. There was a dodgy moment when Goosey wanted to co-opt it for Knickers' enclosure, saying it would be perfect and just the right size, temperature, etc., but I vetoed that idea immediately. It ended in me giving up half the utility room, which means I have to do a lot more tumble drying because there's hardly anywhere to hang anything any more, but it's worth it to keep the conservatory for ourselves, and Knickers adores the humid heat of the dryer.

I've finished *Mrs Dalloway* and have moved on to a great book I got from the library, *A Man Called Ove* by Fredrik Backman. Very funny. So I curl up on our fancy leather recliner sofa with my cuppa and book, and I'm the happiest woman alive.

Kate will get up around ten, but the other girls won't surface till noon at the earliest. And Kieran must have been very late at the tionól – I was fast asleep by the time he came home – so he'll probably have a rare lie-in too. Bliss.

I'm absorbed in the life of Ove in Sweden when I hear tyres on the gravel outside. Who could it be at this hour? It's only half nine. If it's Nora, I'll scream. Mam and Joe are gone on their cruise, so it's not them. Sharon? Unlikely at this hour.

There's a very gentle knock on the front door, like whoever it is will go away again if nobody comes. I'm curious, so I drag myself up and go to answer it, remembering as I open the door that I've no bra on. I think women in the world can be divided in two, those who sleep in a bra and those who don't, and neither will ever understand the other. I'm a no-bra woman, and I cannot for the life of me think how someone could bear to be trussed up all night. But my friend Sharon has always slept in hers and even puts it back on after sex before going to sleep. Inconceivable, but there you have it.

A tall, slender woman with a long blond bob and wide blue eyes is standing on my doorstep in the rain, which has briefly eased off. She's dressed in a smart cream waterproof coat with the hood up, she's carrying a plate covered in tinfoil, and over her other arm is a red anorak.

'Hi, Mags!' she says, a bit uncertainly. She has a slightly husky voice, and her accent is transatlantic, a musical mix of Galway and the States. 'I know it's mad to call so early, but I was thinking I could leave these on your porch and creep off again.'

'Except we don't have a porch.' I smile, holding the door open for her. 'Hi, Róisín.'

'I'm so sorry if I woke you.' She's making no effort to intrude, just holding out the coat and the covered plate. 'I was going to leave these cakes as well to say thanks. Kieran was so good to lend me his coat when we were leaving the tionól. My car was at the other end of the car park, and I'd forgotten it rains all the time in Ireland.'

That's when I realise the red anorak is Kieran's. But I'm a magnanimous woman. 'Come in out of the rain and have a cup of coffee,' I say. 'Everyone else is still fast asleep, so I'm on my own.'

'I really don't want to inconvenience you...'

'It's no trouble at all. I was up anyway.' I lead her into the tidy kitchen, offering a prayer of thanks once again for Klara.

Klara Shevchenko, one of the Ukrainian refugees staying in Ballycarrick, has set up a house-cleaning agency. I gave her a start cleaning the Garda station, and knowing that we trusted her meant she was inundated with enquiries from other people, and now she has five or six of the Ukrainian women on her books. She tried to insist on doing my house for free each week to say thank you. I had to explain that it was impossible for me to accept that as a gift, as it would look very bad to my superiors, but that I was happy for her to come and I'd pay her. So now each week she leaves a large box of washing powder or a tray of home-made cakes or something. I've given up telling her not to.

It's so great to have the house tidy at least once a week. Nora dropped the girls home from camogie and Irish dancing last Tuesday evening – I was late at work and Kieran had his piping lessons, but luckily Klara comes on Tuesdays – and when Nora met me on the doorstep, her coat already on, she said she was 'pleasantly astonished' at how tidy the place was. Ellie, standing in the hall behind her, cast me a glance of solidarity. She knows her nana is a trial.

'Tea or coffee, Róisín?'

'If you're sure, a coffee would be lovely.' She smiles as she hands me the plate. 'I'm a terribly early riser these days, after working in New York. I've been up since six thirty and thought I'd do some baking.'

'That's so kind of you. There was no need, but' – I lift the tinfoil, and a delicious aroma of buttery pastry wafts up – 'let's have one with our coffee before the barbarians above land and devour them all. How do you take it?'

'Just black please, no sugar.' She takes off her damp coat and hangs it over the back of one of the kitchen chairs; she's dressed in a cream woollen dress, burgundy tights and brown boots. She looks like a full-page ad in one of those airline magazines. I bring over our coffees and sit opposite her at the table, and I take one of the tiny pastries and bite into it; the filling is of sour cherry, and the combination of sweet pastry and fruit is delicious.

'Oh my God, you'll be giving Teresa a run for her money with baking like this. They're amazing.'

She laughs, a deep chuckle. 'I did a pastry course in New York. I have a limited repertoire, I'm afraid, but what I can do is good.'

'I can't bake if my life depended on it, but probably just as well. I'd be high on my own supply.'

'I know,' she agrees, taking one too. 'I have a terrible sweet tooth.'

I laugh then. 'That's not the problem. The trouble starts when your pants won't button, and that's not an issue you have, so no sympathy, I'm afraid.'

She grins. 'Except I get pimples like I'm fifteen again if I take too much sugar, so you're not the only one with problems.'

I like her for sharing that, as Zoë would say, and I am predisposed to be sympathetic to her anyway, because of her struggle with IVF and then Joel having an affair. I think about hinting that I know about her troubles but decide not. If we end up as real friends, which we might or might not, she'll tell me in her own good time. Meanwhile, I have to have another of her little cakes. I bite and close my eyes at the bliss of it all.

She smiles at my reaction. 'I hope these make up for me showing up at such an ungodly hour on a Sunday morning. I'm still learning how to be Irish again, instead of a New Yorker.'

'Ah, most normal houses are probably up by now. Kieran's an early riser usually, but he was at some mad gathering of pipers...' I catch myself. 'Of course you know that. How did it go?'

'Oh, it was wonderful – I love the pipes!' she exclaims. 'I heard Liam O'Flynn play *The Brendan Voyage* in New York a few years ago, and I just fell in love. They're such an evocative instrument, aren't they? Like how in a world that moves so fast and changes all the time, the pipes are the constant, and the same sound we hear was what people heard hundreds of years ago.' She catches a glimpse of my expression and laughs. 'You're not a fan?'

'Well, I had no opinion on them at all until recently, but now that Kieran is learning, and he's in the early stages, I'd have to say no...not so much.' I smile ruefully.

'Well, I'd love if Joel played an instrument. It might be good for his soul.'

There's a long pause, and I wait to see if she's going to open up about Joel and their recent history. I wonder if she realises Kieran would have told me. Maybe not. I suppose not all husbands and wives have a relationship where they tell each other everything.

Instead of saying anything more about Joel, she looks around her.

'Your home is so lovely, Mags, and your garden is so peaceful. You must love it.'

'Well, we're not really gardeners, so we just planted trees that kind of take care of themselves, but yes, it's nice.'

'And how's your mam? I see the boutique is called Sharon's Boutique now, not Marie's?'

'Yes, Mam's in her seventies but fit as a trout. She married again recently, would you believe, to Joe Dillon from the menswear shop, and they're off on a Caribbean cruise right now – you'd envy them in this weather. I miss her, though. How are your parents?'

'OK. Sort of. The doctors say Dad has a bit of dementia.'

'Oh, I'm sorry to hear that. That's awful.'

She exhales, and the sadness is palpable. 'Yeah, we hoped it was just normal forgetfulness at first, like a "where are my keys" sort of thing, but it's more than that. Sometimes he has the keys in his hand but isn't even sure what they're for. My mother refuses to see it, though – she says he's fine. And you know what? That just makes the whole thing harder.'

My heart goes out to her. Such a weight of sadness this woman is carrying.

'I can imagine. It's hard to accept, I suppose, for your mam as much as your dad.'

She nods, and I try to think of a bright spot. 'How are you settling into the Old Rectory? It's great to see it lived in after so long. The builders seem to have done a great job.'

'Oh, it's lovely. We love it. Apart from there's a leak in the back bathroom,' she says mournfully.

Poor woman, she can't seem to get a break. 'Oh no. I'm sure they'll fix it for you. Is it the shower?'

'No, the roof. And the builders say they can't get back to us for four weeks at least, and then they're saying we might have to have major roof surgery, replace all the flashing and the slates around it.'

'Seriously?' I'm horrified. 'How did they not know at the time it was going to need so much more work?'

'I have no idea. Maybe they're chancers despite the big fancy

Galway website. I told Joel we should use Kieran for the roof, but he is a big believer in keeping friendship and business separate. He's not Irish and doesn't really get it… They've cost us a fortune already. I just wish…' She sees my expression and says quickly, 'But don't worry. I know we can't ask Kieran to come along and mop up someone else's mistakes when we didn't give him the work in the first place.'

She's right, it would be bad form, and I'm glad she understands that. But then my heart goes out to her… I find myself saying, 'Well, I don't know how busy Kieran is this week, but I'm sure he can take a look if you like?'

'Ah, I don't like to ask him…'

'He won't mind, Róisín, and he'd hate to think the lovely renovation was being water damaged.'

She is so thrilled and grateful. 'I would love it. I'm scared to death the whole bloody thing is going to come down on our heads at this stage.'

I grin. 'Sure, I'll ask him.'

'Ask him what?' Kieran says as he comes through the kitchen door in his holey green jumper and jeans. He loves that jumper, and it's been darned by my mother – not by me, I hasten to add – around twenty times. He's unshaven and his hair is standing on end, but I see it, the admiring glance from Róisín.

It's not just her, though. Women love my husband. Not in a pin-up kind of way – he's too unpolished for that – but he's big and muscly and handsome. And I don't feel jealous at all; I'm used to it. If anything, I'm proud he's mine. To add to that, he's a genuinely nice guy, sound, kind, a laugh, you know exactly. Not that I'm not fit to kill him sometimes, of course I am, but he's a good man.

'Morning, Kieran,' says Róisín. 'I brought back your coat. And some cakes to say thank you for saving me from a soaking last night.'

'Hmm, I wondered what was smelling so good…'

'No fear it would be me baking up a storm, is there?' I grin again at Róisín as I stand up to make Kieran a coffee. 'I tried to make an apple tart a few months ago, but it had a soggy bottom, as they say on the cooking shows, and was only fit for the bin. I follow the recipes and everything, weigh all the things, but each time I try it, it's an unequiv-ocal disaster.'

'My wife is a multiskilled woman, but we'd all have to admit at this stage that baking isn't her strong point. Thanks, love.' Kieran takes the steaming cup from me and joins us at the table. Róisín pushes the plate of cakes towards him, and he bites into one of them and has the same reaction I did. 'Oh my God, they are amazing.'

My poor husband is deprived of nice treats at home. I don't buy cakes and biscuits because I'll be the one eating them, so a low-sugar granola bar or a cracker is usually the best we can do. Nora is a wonderful baker, so he grew up with all sorts of lovely things; the lack thereof in our house is yet another reason for Nora to be disap-pointed in me.

'Thanks. It's nice to bake for someone who appreciates it.' Róisín smiles. 'Joel is always watching his figure – I guess it's a midlife-crisis thing.'

'I could do with that kind of crisis myself.' I sigh.

'Oh, stop it, love, you're perfect the way you are. Now what were you going to ask me?' Kieran smiles at me.

So I tell him all about the builders and the leak, and Róisín apolo-gises and says of course she's not expecting him to do anything about it.

'I don't mind taking a look,' he says to her. 'It'll be the flashing most likely. Those hipped roofs are notorious for leaks, and with a preser-vation order on it like the Old Rectory has, you have to work with what you have. To be fair to your Galway builders, they couldn't have known it was going to leak. You need a long wet spell to check it.'

I love this about Kieran. He's not the tyre-kicking type of trades-man, saying the last fella must have been a right eejit altogether to have done such shoddy work.

'That would be so kind of you. I'm worried if we leave it much longer, we'll sail out in the tub,' Róisín jokes in her husky transatlantic accent. She really has spent a long time in New York. Everyone here calls it a bath; only Americans call it a tub. Mind you, there is so much American influence here nowadays, a lot of people have picked up

Americanisms, like my kids seem wont to do. Only yesterday Ellie told me that I sound like a right eejit saying I'll ring people when you should say call them.

This resulted in a lecture from me – she was in the car, so a captive audience – on the beauty of cultures and diversity and how we shouldn't all strive to be the same, look the same, sound the same. And that the Irish ring people when they want to make a telephone call and that's the way it should stay.

She thinks I'm daft, of course, but it had to be said.

'Hi, everyone…' It's Ellie, up earlier than I thought she'd be. The twins drift in behind her, pyjama-clad and bleary-eyed, and I think how the three of them have absolutely no idea of their innocence and beauty. Last night, all dolled up, trying to look older with false eyelashes and fake tans, they thought they were only gorgeous, walking like newborn deer unsteady on their vertiginous heels, but their real beauty is now. No make-up, hair around their faces, in their pjs. If only they could see it. The sheer beauty of youth. It is wasted on the young, it's true.

Kate trails in behind them, yawning, rubbing her eyes, beautiful in a different way, still no more than a child but delighted to be hanging out with the cool sixteen-year-olds.

'Hi, girls. You two have grown since I saw you last.'

'Hi, Róisín.' Ellie greets her warmly. 'These are my friends Cat and Trish.' The twins smile hello and eye the plate of pastries.

'Róisín brought home-made cakes, but maybe have some cereal first?' I suggest as Kate plunges her teeth into a pastry, grinning guiltily.

'Ah, 'tis Sunday…' Kieran winks and puts his arms around Kate, drawing her onto his knee.

'You've grown into such beautiful girls,' murmurs Róisín, admiring Ellie and Kate.

I remember her troubles with IVF and feel almost guilty for my luck. My phone pings.

It's Sharon. *Fancy a coffee?*

Can't, I'm afraid – house full of teens, I respond quickly.

Róisín gets up to go. 'I'll get out of your way now. Mags, thanks so much for the coffee, and Kieran, thanks for offering to look at the roof. I'm around all week.'

'Look, you don't want to leave it. We're passing on the way to Mam's for lunch – why don't I drop in and have a quick look on the way,' Kieran offers.

'Oh, I couldn't ask you to do that – you're going to a family occasion. Please, next week is fine.' She looks embarrassed now.

'It's no bother, and sure, it won't take ten minutes,' Kieran insists.

'But it's pouring. You'll get soaked,' she protests.

'The thing about leaks, Róisín, is it needs to be raining to find the bloody things. So a roofer afraid of the rain is a bit like an ashtray on a motorbike!'

'If you're sure? That's a really big favour. You'd never get this in New York!'

Trish pipes up, through a mouthful of cake; the girls are busy devouring every morsel. 'Oh, I nearly forgot, Mags. Mam said can she borrow that high-sided pan of yours? She's steaming the puddings this evening.'

'See?' I smile. 'We all do each other favours here. Welcome home to Ballycarrick, Róisín.'

* * *

'WHAT ARE YOU WEARING, MAM?' Kate asks gently, and I know she wants me to make an effort, not for me or for her but so Nana Nora won't cast one of her head-to-toe glances.

'My black jeans and my pink jumper?'

'The pink jumper that has the hole under the arm from when you caught it climbing into Boomerang Butler's field?'

'Ah, yeah, I forgot that,' I admit. I had to drag Rollo back again only yesterday, and this time it was my best cashmere jumper I tore.

'What about the rust-coloured dress, the one Sharon gave you for your birthday?' Kate suggests.

'I don't think I've any shoes for that, though, and isn't it a bit overdressed?' I ask doubtfully. I actually trust her in fashion matters – she has my mam's eye for what works – but I don't want Nora thinking I've tried too hard.

Kate peals with laughter. 'Mam, you could be accused of lots of things, but being overdressed is not one.'

I smile. She's probably right. I'm too old to fit my wide feet into crippling shoes; years of Garda-issue boots has turned my feet to puddles. And I can't be bothered waxing my legs in the winter, so I wear trousers all the time. And while I'm not a total slob of course, I'm not one for cosmetic stuff really.

'I suppose you won't wear these?' She pulls out a pair of gold sling-backs Sharon insisted I buy last year even though they feel like you're wearing cheese graters on your feet.

'Y'know, Kit Kat, if you ever wonder if something is sexist or not, just ask yourself, would men do that?'

'What?' she asks, her head in the bottom of our wardrobe, rooting for other shoes. I realise I'm braced for Knickers to come bursting out, but thankfully he doesn't.

'Well, men don't squeeze their feet into shoes that hurt them, or shave all the hair off their body, or tweeze their eyebrows, or wear underwear that cuts off their circulation… The list goes on and on.'

'Well, we're not going to solve that today, so for now let's just get you fixed up for Nana Nora's lunch, and we'll close the gender gap tomorrow.'

It's my turn to laugh then; she's a funny one.

Once we are all ready – I've settled on a nice pair of jeans with a pair of pastel-blue flats with a wide-fit toe and a navy silk blouse Mam gave me about two years ago but I rarely wear – we pile into the car. Kieran is still wearing the dark-green Aran jumper with the holes. His mother despises that garment with a venom normally reserved for worst enemies, but he loves wearing it to wind her up. And to be fair, it detracts from me. I think he kind of does it to protect me.

CHAPTER 9

*T*he rain is coming down heavily again – it's relentless, this weather – and sure enough Main Street is running like a river. As we drive we leave a wake that laps over the pavements. I've written three emails to the council this week, and still no sign of anyone clearing the leaves. The shopkeepers are doing their best, but there's just too much water in the system. It needs a root and branch go at the drains, or the next thing it will be up to the doors of the shops.

I think of the Carmodys in their halting site that floods every year. I hope they are prepared. The McGoverns at Drumlish fare better, being up a hill, but life for the Travelling people in this weather, it can't be pleasant.

On the far side of the town, we pull up outside the Old Rectory, and Kieran jumps out, flipping up the hood on the red anorak that Róisín brought back to him. 'I'll only be fifteen minutes,' he says. 'Stay here in the dry.' He takes a box of tools out of the boot and runs up the front steps and rings the bell; someone lets him in.

A few minutes later, carrying an umbrella, Róisín appears and knocks on the window. 'Will you come in to see the place? Kieran's looking at the roof – he insisted on going up the fire escape.'

I'm actually dying to see what she and Joel have done with the house, so I get out.

'Ellie and Kate? Do you want to come too?' She smiles at them.

'Ah no, we're grand, thanks,' murmurs Ellie, and they stay in the car on their phones.

There are leather slippers inside the door, for people to take off their shoes, and so I slip on a pair, and then Róisín walks me around. It's so beautiful. The front of the house has to be preserved exactly, but the kitchen is at the back and they've been allowed to put in a huge glass wall, so even on a day like this, it's full of light, with navy blue units and copper handles. Off it is a snug, with two squashy leather couches and a big TV mounted on the wall over the original fireplace. At the front of the house is another large sitting room, beautifully furnished, but this in a more 1930s Art Deco style, with a fabulous old gramophone with a copper horn. The white marble fireplace is definitely not original – the old one was taken out years ago, Róisín tells me – but the original oak floorboards are polished to a golden sheen, two large silk rugs in pinks and creams cover some of the floor, and there's a three-piece suite upholstered in a turquoise fabric with peacocks and gold flowers. Standing on a side table is a ceramic vase the size of Kate, holding a large fan of bamboo fronds.

The whole thing is quirky and mismatched but perfectly harmonious.

'Please tell me an interior designer did this and not you,' I exclaim.

She laughs. 'Mostly me, I have to admit. I'm a total control freak about interior design, so I sent all the instructions. The designer here hated me, but I was paying good money so...' She shrugs. *Everything has its price* says the shrug. 'Anyway, I wanted it to be ready when we got here so we could hit the ground running. We left all our New York furniture behind, and that made life easier. We had so little to bring with us, and we... Well, I wanted everything to look different from day one.'

I wait a moment to see if she wants to say more, but she doesn't, so I walk over to marvel at a collection of small oil paintings in gilt frames hung seemingly haphazardly on the chimney breast, but of course, like everything here, it is in perfect symmetry. 'Well, all I can say is I'm glad you were in our house before I came here. If I'd have seen this place first, I could never have let you in the door.'

'Will you stop?' She dismisses my remark. 'Your house is gorgeous. Nobody could be uptight or stressed in that house. I love it – it's a real family home. I'm not surprised your daughters' friends love being there. That's what I'd want if I had daughters like yours, for them to have their friends over, to veg out on the sofas, to watch movies and eat pizza and not be terrified they'll mess it all up.'

Again, I feel a bit guilty for my happy family life. 'I do like having it like that,' I admit. 'My mother had to work so hard to raise us as a widow. You remember how she was always in the shop. We were kind of half reared in there. We lived upstairs, so it wasn't cold or very tidy, but it lacked a mother's touch, I suppose.'

I find myself telling her something I don't often vocalise. I know Mam worked her fingers to the bone in the shop for us – she had no choice – but I missed her. I wished she'd not had to stand behind the counter from nine till seven, six days a week. In the evenings then, she used to do alterations, so she was always busy. I try to be different, to be around for my kids, and that was a big part of why I turned down the recent promotion.

'You're lucky you have such a good relationship with your mother now,' says Róisín. 'I know you lost your dad, but you can't psych your way out of a terrible mother, they say, and I know, I've tried.' She laughs, self-deprecating. 'I grew up in a cold house. Not a hair astray, everything perfect, but no love or laughter or life.'

I'm surprised to hear this; I never realised Róisín had an unhappy childhood. I suppose I've internalised from Nora how perfect Róisín Duggan was, with her gynaecologist father who was president of the local golf club and her respectable GP mother. I've listened for twenty years to the life Kieran could have had if only he'd stayed with this woman. That's not Róisín's fault, though, I remind myself.

The master bedroom is beautiful, a huge sleigh bed with a rose-coloured throw over it, and Sliderobes. I know without opening them that everything is neat and tidy; there is no chance an avalanche of clothes and shoes will engulf you if you open the door, which is likely in our wardrobes from IKEA, not to mention the distinct possibility of a huge frilly lizard bursting out, giving everyone a heart attack.

The lead windows with their Tudor diamond pattern have been supplemented with VELUX skylights, facing away from the road. The landing, the bathrooms, even the leaky one – everything is gorgeous. Quirky, quaint and expensive. Whatever she sold her New York law firm for, it generated plenty of money, that's for sure.

There's one last door off the landing, and Róisín says, 'We need to clear this room out,' before she opens it.

It is a small, cluttered space lit only by a high VELUX window, and it's clearly being used as a storeroom for what little they had to bring with them from America. And to my surprise – I'd almost forgotten he was around – Joel is in there, crouched with his back to us. He's just taken a phone that looks like it belongs to a child out of a cardboard box – it's got a Daffy Duck cover – and he's staring at it with a shocked expression.

'Oh, there you are, Joel. Do you remember Mags?'

He obviously hadn't heard us come in, because he gives a slight cry of alarm as he jumps to his feet. 'Hi, Mags, nice to meet you again,' he says, with a forced smile. He is as handsome as ever, tall with beautiful brown eyes and curly black hair, expertly cut. Like the house, everything about Joel Barrera is understated but expensive. He wears a cream shirt that was definitely tailored for him and Versace jeans. I know those jeans cost six or seven hundred euros because Sharon bought a pair in Dubai about ten years ago and is still going on about the price. I recall his cologne from when we visited. Something woody, with hints of chocolate.

'Hi, Joel,' I say. 'Róisín is just showing me around the house while Kieran investigates your leak.'

'That's great.' He seems not to know what to do with the phone in his hand but then pops it up onto a high shelf, just under the VELUX window, like he wants it out of sight.

'I hope you're settling in to Ballycarrick OK?' I ask.

81

'Yeah, it's a great little place. We love it.' He's waiting for us to leave.

As we descend the stairs, a loud banging comes from the roof. 'I hope Kieran is all right up there.' Róisín looks up to the ceiling, worried.

'He's fine, honestly,' I reassure her. 'He's rarely on the ground, don't worry.'

As we enter the kitchen, Kieran is on his way in, shaking the rain off his red coat, his toolbox in his hand.

'Well?' Róisín asks in trepidation. She doesn't seem to mind he's wearing his boots in the house, despite the slipper thing.

He shrugs. 'Well, it's hard to tell without a proper survey of the roof, but there are lots of places where the lead flashing, that part that covers the seams and transitions between slates, can go wrong. I've just put some sealant where I think the worst parts might be, and I've also sealed the counter flashing around the chimney – that's definitely one of the main offenders – but that's only a stopgap. Some if not all of the flashing needs replacing.'

She pulls a face. 'Is that a huge job?'

He shakes his head and smiles reassuringly. 'You have two options really. One, go with your current builders, replace all the flashing and the slates around it. But honestly, if I was you, I'd see what can be done with roof sealant first. If it's applied well, it can work. Some of the flashing nails are exposed too, and they should be sealed. It's the cheaper and faster option, and it's not guaranteed to work, but worth a shot in my opinion, though.'

'I don't suppose...' She winces, knowing she's being cheeky to ask.

'I can pop over on Wednesday if it's dry, but as I say, it's not guaranteed to work. It will cost you around six hundred euros for labour and materials...'

'What would we be looking at cost-wise to do it the way my builders want to do it? Roughly.'

Kieran thinks for a moment. 'Off the top of my head, and this is just a ballpark, that's expensive and is major roof surgery – I did something like it for the Lodge recently. Maybe something in the region of 20K, if they don't overcharge you?'

Róisín exhales. 'Right, well, that's it. Let's try the six-hundred-euro option, with the full and certain knowledge that it may not work, but it's worth a shot. What would you give me odds-wise? If I was a betting woman?' She winks at him.

'Fifty-fifty, truthfully.' Kieran is not like the many cowboy operators. He doesn't take on more work than he can handle, he turns up when he says he will, he charges people a fair price, and he's always honest about what to expect.

'I'll risk it.' She sticks her hand out and he shakes it. 'This place has almost bled us dry as it is.'

'Right. I'll be here at eight on Wednesday if it's dry. I'll text you anyway, but if it's raining, don't expect me.'

'Wonderful. Thanks, Kieran, I really appreciate it. See you soon, I hope, Mags? We should all go to the Samovar for dinner or something.'

'That would be lovely,' I say, and I think maybe we will end up as friends.

CHAPTER 10

e're all groaning after eating so much. Nora has outdone herself – again. I'll give her that. She might be an absolute pothole, as in best avoided, but she makes a great roast dinner. Today was a leg of lamb with all the trimmings, followed by rhubarb crumble that must have had cocaine in it or something – it was impossible to stop at one helping.

Now we're sprawled like beached whales on sofas and armchairs around the living room, the shrine to the wonder that is the Munroe children.

I tease Kieran all the time about all the photos, medals and certificates Nora has on every available bit of wall. There's one certificate that's in the hall that Kieran won when he was in primary school, a grade-two 'Printer Use Proficiency' certificate; we all take the absolute mickey out of him about it. But he's not alone; every one of the Munroes is much celebrated for even the tiniest achievement.

The grandchildren are in the kitchen – they prefer it to the stuffy living room – and raucous laughing and messing can be heard between all the cousins. So it's just us adults, the Munroes and the outlaws, Nora and Kevin and ourselves, Orla and Fergus, Catriona and Seamus, Aoife and Leonard, Gearoid and his partner Enrico, Oilibhéar and Muireann.

Nora is deep in conversation with Seamus, and by conversation I mean she is talking at him and he's just 'listening'. I like him, though we rarely see him; he just works incredibly hard, and also I suspect he uses it as an excuse to avoid Nora. And who can blame him? He's from a very normal family, and she's such a snob; she's always trying to put him on a pedestal. It was him that Mam went to last year when she had a heart attack, and he diagnosed her, arranged the surgery and took excellent care of her, keeping me and Kieran informed every step of the way.

Leonard and Aoife are telling Muireann how they each got a green flag for their schools, a sign of their commitment to ecology and the environment. They're all right, a nice couple if a bit sanctimonious. They'd be horrified if they knew I'd let Minnie and Neil build a bonfire on the beach. Which reminds me, I must check in with our local witch and warlock. I had a talk with Desmond Dunne about leaving their sign alone, and I hope he's kept away from the Lodge since.

The room is very warm between the open fire crackling and all the people. Full of food, it's hard to stay awake.

Ol is dozing on the smaller of the two sofas with his eyes closed and head tilted back – he and Muireann were up early to get here from Dublin. I find myself studying his face. I often find myself staring at Ol, because he looks so like Kieran. It's almost disturbing, as if I've accidentally married an identical twin. It's really strange, because Gearoid looks nothing like either of them.

Nora is talking to Orla now. 'I must go to see the white witch in the Lodge. I didn't think much of it at first, but Lavinia Moran and Elsie Flanagan swear by her, and they're very respectable women...'

At the other end of the same sofa, Orla's husband, Fergus, is definitely asleep. Or maybe just pretending to be. He's still a bit traumatised from the time he happened to mention that some very distant cousin of his in America was running for political office and Nora got it into her head that someone in her family was going to be the next

JFK and started flying a huge Stars and Stripes on her front lawn. It all ended when the man decided to 'spend more time with his family' (was caught with his hand in the till, in other words) and dropped out of the campaign, much to Fergus's relief.

'Isn't it wonderful Róisín is home?'

I am nearly asleep, but the sound of Róisín's name jerks me awake again. Nora is telling Orla how pleased she is Róisín is setting up a law firm in Ballycarrick. 'As good as the one in New York! Frances was only saying to me the other day what an asset it will be to have someone in the town who knows something about the law,' she twitters.

I doubt Frances said anything that daft to Nora, or even spoke to her at all. Nora would love nothing better than to be on a best-friends basis with Frances and Martin Duggan, Róisín's parents, but she's not.

'I think Mags knows something about the law,' says Orla, with an amused glance in my direction. She's the most good-natured of the Munroe daughters, though she's still scarily perfect, never a hair nor a cup out of place in her house. Her daughter, Evie, is Kate's best friend, so we see each other a fair bit, at least in passing.

'Oh, but, well, you know...' Nora is caught. She can't exactly say a police officer has nothing to do with the law, but of course in her mind, a local sergeant is on about the same level as a lollipop lady in the great pecking order of things. 'Well, anyway,' she recovers, 'I met Róisín in the hairdresser's on Saturday, and she's looking absolutely gorgeous, not a day older than when you and she first left for New York, Kieran...'

If I wasn't so overstuffed by food, I might say something pointed yet witty, but my brain is so pleasantly sedated, I can't come up with anything clever. Kieran hasn't even heard her; he is half-asleep himself, weirdly in the exact same position as Oilibhéar.

'So can we tell them?' Enrico asks Gearoid, talking straight across Nora, who is now informing everyone in the room about the lovely, elegant outfit Róisín was wearing in the hairdresser's.

'You're going to anyway.' Gearoid sighs theatrically but nods. Enrico is a pet. We all love him, and after a bumpy start, he and

Gearoid seem really solid, despite the occasional fireworks. They announced they were engaged a few weeks ago, but that was after a big bust-up that had Enrico rushing off to Sitges in Spain and Gearoid running after him to make it up, followed by lots of lovely photos of them on Instagram. They've been on and off for years we think, but Gearoid always kept his romances out of the family chat.

'We've set a date for the wedding.' Enrico claps his hands, so delighted with himself, it's touching. He's handsome in a slim, Spanish way. He can't weigh more than sixty kilos, but he's so stylish and glamorous, and his Spanish-accented English and naked enthusiasm charm everyone he meets. Gearoid adores him. Today he's wearing a midnight-blue lace tunic, I kid you not, complete with frilled cuffs and collar, and tight black leather leggings. His long dark curls are tied back in a ribbon, and his fingernails are painted baby blue. He wouldn't look out of place at Versailles when the *sans-culottes* were chopping heads off.

There's a round of applause from those of us still awake, then a fresh round from those who were woken by the first lot of applause, and Nora's silent husband, Kevin, gets up to shake Gearoid's hand, then Enrico's, bless him.

'Ah, wonderful!' Nora is also thrilled, a far cry from her initial reaction to having a gay son, but to be fair to her, she's embraced it with gusto now. 'Well, where will it be?'

She's longing for somewhere posh, I know. The girls all got married in castles or really swanky places – Orla went to Dubrovnik – but as usual Kieran and I were a source of pained disappointment. Our wedding was in the local hotel, the Carrick Arms, and was low-key and low budget.

We loved it, just our families and close friends, a nice dinner and a great band. We all danced all night, and the party went on in the residents' bar till the dawn allegedly; we were well gone by then. But it wasn't upmarket enough for Nora at all, and she spent the entire day sitting in an enormous white picture hat that would have been better employed at a royal wedding. She wore white, by the way, a long white ankle-length dress and that giant hat. She looked ridiculous. I've rarely seen my mam absolutely furious, but she was that day.

'Well, it was Mags gave us the idea actually.' Enrico grins at me, and Nora's face falls in horror.

'No, no, not the Carrick Arms,' she begs.

'What?' Enrico bursts out laughing. 'No! Castle Dysert. So we went there, and we met Conor and Ana, and oh my goodness, it is so beautiful, so atmospheric, the castle and the big fires and everything. We fell in love right away...'

'Conor charmed him, as you can see,' Gearoid adds, with a wry smile.

'Well, he did, and he said we can do it whatever way we want. So we have some ideas, but it will be a secret, so you can all be surprised on the day.' He claps again, and his excitement is infectious.

'Oh, that will be lovely, so exclusive. They won't allow any riffraff there, I'm sure.' Nora preens. (Subtext: Unlike the Carrick Arms, where they even serve the McGoverns and the Carmodys.) 'So when is it to be?'

'Don't go mental now, but we booked it for the end of January.' Gearoid drops this in casually.

'The end of *January*?' Nora gasps. 'But we can't possibly be ready in that time, Gearoid! For goodness' sake, that's only three months away. There's too much to be done... We'll never –'

'Mam, seriously, there's nothing to be done. I'll get dressed up, this peacock here will no doubt look like something from a pantomime, and we'll tie the knot and have an old shindig in the castle. Conor will take care of everything. All you need to do is get your dancing shoes on, and away we go.'

Nicely done, Gearoid, I think. The longer she has, the more she'll stick her beak in and drive him cracked.

'Well, even getting everyone else dressed, Gearoid...' She isn't letting go. 'All the grandchildren have to have something suitable to wear, sort of matching. I can go shopping for them in Galway.' She's desperate to have something to do.

Orla, Catriona and Aoife all look slightly uncomfortable. All three

CLOSER THAN YOU THINK

of them are well and truly under her thumb, but they don't want a mutiny in the house either; all their children are teenagers and might refuse to be dressed up like lampshades.

Catriona, who is the most like Nora and so can get around her more easily, says, 'Of course, Mam. We'll all talk to each other.'

Nora says a bit huffily, 'Well, I know you girls like to shop for your own children, and you have great taste of course...and Muireann... but... Oh, *I* know!' She turns to me, like she's just had the best idea ever. 'Mags, you're very busy – I know you never have time to buy suitable clothes for Ellie and Kate. I mean, they can look a bit...well, a bit scruffy from time to time...'

I grit my teeth. The cheek of her, singling my girls out as ones likely to turn up in ripped jeans or a dirty t-shirt, but I will not rise to it, I just won't.

'They wouldn't think of themselves as looking scruffy, Nora,' I say calmly. 'But I can see how the fashion of your era is different to what they wear nowadays.'

She laughs a little, fluttering her fingers. 'No, but really and truly, that dress Ellie has on today, she's grown out of it – it barely covers her backside, poor child. And Kate's jeans have an actual hole in them, Mags.' She sounds so reasonable, you'd swear I was on the roof of a building with a Kalashnikov and she a chief negotiator.

'Don't worry, Nora,' I say, equally reasonably. 'Ellie's dress is actually designed that way, to be worn with the thick tights she has on under it, and Kate's jeans are brand new. She bought them with the rips – it's the style.'

'Well, I don't know about that, but surely it's not right that Ellie is having to wear Kieran's work boots.' Nora persists with another light laugh and a smirk at Catriona, while Orla decides to find something interesting on her phone and Aoife studies her hands. Muireann is also staying out of it, but not out of fear; she's just not sure of the family dynamics yet.

'Honestly, it's fine, Nora. They're Ellie's boots.' I smile sweetly. 'You can tell, because she is size four and Kieran is a size twelve, and his are DeWalt safety boots and hers are Doc Martens. She saved up for them, and they're very comfortable and good for her feet.' I have no idea if this last bit is true or not, but I throw it in anyway.

'Look, here's what we'll do, Mags,' says Nora patiently. 'I know you're on a budget, and I think it's wonderful the way the girls help out, with Kate buying her own jeans, like you said, and Ellie saving up for some footwear. So for the wedding, I'll take care of them, and I'll make sure they're dressed, well' – she pauses – 'appropriately.'

Kieran is wide awake and getting restless. He's raging, I can tell. He has his own issues with the shortness of Ellie's dresses and the fake rips in Kate's jeans, but he won't have his mother denigrating his daughters and trying to make out we can't afford to buy them decent clothes. Kieran works hard so the girls can have everything they need, and he knows I do too. I can tell he's about to say something – he's very protective of us, especially when it comes to his mother – but I squeeze his hand warningly.

'Thanks so much, Nora,' I say calmly, 'but it's fine. I'll take the girls to Sharon and get them something. Don't worry about them. You just look after yourself.'

'Oh, Sharon's Boutique is lovely,' says Muireann helpfully, obviously thinking this a noncontroversial thing to say.

And Orla says, 'It's nice, yes. Evie spends her own pocket money in there sometimes.'

'My darling nieces and nephews will *all* look wonderful, I'm sure, and Sharon has a wonderful eye, no more than Mags's mother before her.' Gearoid also backs me.

'Ah, no, no, no.' Nora screws up her face. 'You're being very nice, all of you, and of course I support buying locally if possible. And Sharon's little place is fine for cheap things to wear for fun, I know that, but for a *family* wedding, in *Castle Dysert*, we'd need to go more upmarket than a little shop in Ballycarrick – surely you can all see that?'

'Sharon's will do fine for my girls, and that's where we'll go,' I say firmly, and she and I lock stares. The expression on her face, her lips pursed like a cat's bum, would make me laugh if I wasn't so cross. Kieran is still fuming beside me, but I was right to restrain him. If he lets fly at his mother now, the tension will last for weeks, and we don't want that coming up to the wedding. 'So who are you having as the celebrant?' I ask Gearoid, changing the subject.

'Our friend Sapphire Storm,' he says. 'She's so experienced – she does lots of weddings.'

'Is that the drag queen you and Enrico took me to in Dublin?' Now it's Catriona's turn to look horrified.

'Yes!' Enrico bursts in, delighted she remembers and oblivious to the look of sheer panic on his future sister-in-law's face. 'Oh my God, she's hilarious. We were lucky to get her, but she'll do an amazing job.' And he gushes on about the wonders of Sapphire Storm, totally blind to the varying degrees of despair – and amusement – on the faces of all those present.

'I know you can't be married in the Church, Gearoid,' says Nora, cutting across Enrico in the same way he did to her earlier. 'But I wonder if someone a little more' – she searches for the word – 'more *formal* would be better, to lend it a bit of gravitas?' My monster-in-law looks like she's swallowed a wasp, but she knows she must tread lightly. She can't bully her youngest son in the same way she can the girls.

'Oh, but we don't want formal, Nora,' Enrico says, glad to be able to clarify. 'That is not the vibe we are going for at all. We want it to be fun and beautiful and full of love.'

And Gearoid shrugs and smiles as if it is entirely out of his hands.

Oilibhéar starts reminiscing about when Sapphire Storm was on *The Late Late* and how the audience loved it. Catriona says no more, and Nora knows better than to push it.

'Why don't you and I make us all some tea and coffee?' I suggest to Kieran.

Enrico follows us to the kitchen, where he lines up all the kids – they adore him, each and every one – and teaches them a hip-hop dance that they are all going to perform at the wedding apparently.

'I don't know how you don't head-butt her,' Kieran murmurs to me as we load up two big trays with cups and cafetières and teapots and jugs of milk and bowls of sugar.

91

'Tempting, but the last thing we need now is another family feud,' I murmur back. 'Leave her to me.'

Back in the living room, we relax over tea and coffee and the conversation flows on without further incident, until Ol and Muireann have to hit the road before it gets too dark, and Seamus needs to cut someone's heart out or something, and Orla and Fergus suddenly remember Evie has a dance recital.

Evie and Kate are in the same dance school, and I've heard nothing about a recital, but I don't say. Orla spoke up for Sharon's shop earlier, which was nice of her, so of course I'm not going to blow her and Fergus's cover.

CHAPTER 11

A few days later, I have a half an hour before I need to be at the neighbourhood watch meeting, so I pop into Sharon's Boutique to see if I can get something for the wedding. Not for the girls – they'd need to be here for that – but for myself.

Sharon is helping Mrs Harris, who used to clean the Garda station before she retired, to select a new cardigan from a choice of five almost identical beige cardigans. All of which are also almost identical to the one she's wearing.

Eventually Mrs Harris says she'll need to think about it and leaves.

'That's the third time she's had me drag out all the cardigans.' Sharon shakes her head.

'Maybe I should consider a beige cardigan for Gearoid's wedding?' I joke, but something about her face makes me pause. She is perfectly made-up as always, but her brow is furrowed, which is unusual, as she has regular Botox injections. I don't think she needs them, but she thinks she does, and each to their own. She always looks gorgeous to me. Sharon is blond, tall and slim and wears edgy-but-cool clothes. How we're best friends is a mystery really. We not only look nothing alike, we *are* nothing alike. She hates reading and I love it; I'd go out in a bin bag and she's always on trend.

'What's up?' I ask.

I can see she's wavering, weighing something up, debating whether to say it. She makes her decision. 'Nothing.'

'Shar?' I nudge.

'Really, it's nothing.'

'Come on, spit it out.'

She inhales and exhales quickly, then says, 'Is Kieran doing some work for Róisín?'

My hackles rise. But I smile and keep my voice even. 'Róisín's roof has a leak, and Kieran happens to be a roofer, so it makes perfect sense for her to ask him to fix it.'

'Oh, I see,' she says. 'I thought that must be the case. I was just confused to see him going in there, because didn't she have some posh builders from Dublin doing all the work?'

'She did, but they left behind a leak that only showed up when it started raining for days at a time.'

'Oh, I see…' But she still has that doubting tone in her voice.

'What?' I say, and it sounds sharp to my ears.

'Look, Mags, I just think you should be careful, you know? People are talking, and there's no smoke without fire.'

I'm hurt now, but I keep on smiling, trying to keep it light. Sharon is on my side, I know she is. It's just her take on men is still coloured by that Danny Boylan. 'Come on, would you have a hair of sense? Kieran is not having a thing with Róisín Duggan, as well you know.'

'If you say so.'

'I do say so,' I say firmly.

She makes an effort to smile and get things back to normal. 'So Gearoid and Enrico are finally getting married, are they? You'll need something a bit original then, without being too mad. You don't want to upstage the…um, groom…' She giggles a bit at her own joke, but I can't laugh with her. There are tears stinging my eyes, but I don't want to let her see them.

'Sorry, Sharon, I've just remembered I have a neighbourhood watch meeting…' I hurry out the door before I can burst into tears. Luckily it was raining, so I came in the patrol car, and I slip in behind the wheel, drive around the corner into a one-way street between two sets of back gardens and sit there crying in private without being seen.

Why am I crying? Why am I so upset? This is nothing new. Sharon is always telling me to watch my back with Kieran because he's such a good-looking man and women are lining up to get their claws into him.

I wipe my eyes and blow my nose on a scrunched-up tissue. I miss Mam so much. I want to go and see her for a cup of tea and a bun and tell her all about everything and have her roll her eyes and say, 'Well, that's Sharon for you,' and reassure me I have nothing to fear from Róisín because I'm so much more wonderful than any other woman on the planet. Not that I think I am, but sometimes it's nice to get a mother's perspective on things. It's no good, though; I can't, because Mam is off sunning herself somewhere in the Caribbean, having a wonderful time with Joe.

I'm delighted for Mam. But I wish she was here in Ballycarrick with me.

CHAPTER 12

I'm writing yet another email to the council about the drains when I hear roaring and bawling from the public office, where Nicola is holding the fort. I hurry out of my office to find Darren leading Mike Cantillon into the station. Mike's clearly plastered – the stink of booze would knock a donkey – even though it's barely four in the afternoon.

Zoë brings up the rear, looking terrified. This is the coalface of the job, and I'd say whatever just happened has been a rude awakening for her.

'Get him into a cell, you two,' I say brusquely.

Darren manoeuvres him into the corridor that leads to the cells – we have two of them – but as he does, Cantillon lashes out, and drunk as he is, he's powerful. Darren is punched and winded, and Nicola rushes to help him. Zoë gathers up her courage and manhandles Cantillon, fairly expertly, to be fair, but she then makes a rookie mistake.

You may not know this, but you lead a prisoner into a cell as if they were a horse, straight in, turning with the prisoner on your side all of the time; you never want a situation where the prisoner is between you and the door, so you ensure you have a clear line of exit at all times.

Zoë fails to do this and gets ahead of him, and Cantillon kicks the door of the cell closed, locking both himself and Zoë in. Zoë screams, and I rush to open the cell. Cantillon is using his considerable body weight to pin poor Zoë against the wall. I shove him to his knees and cuff him behind his back – he should have been cuffed up to this, but we try to use the minimum constraint if we can – then force him on the floor, my knee ensuring he remains there. Nicola helps Zoë out, and then I retreat, locking Cantillon in.

I close the public office and lock the front door, leading them all into my office. 'Everyone all right?' I ask.

Darren nods, touching his stomach tenderly. 'Fine, Sarge.'

'Let's have you checked over all the same. Zoë, are you all right?'

She also nods and says, 'Fine, Sarge,' but she still looks panic-stricken, and I remember that first time for me too. Everyone knows notionally what the job is, but the first time you are really faced with someone the rest of the community will cross the street to avoid and it's your job to tackle them, it's a steep learning curve.

'Did he hurt you?' I ask gently.

'No, I'm fine.' For once she's not oversharing, or sharing at all.

I decide it's best not to make too big a thing of it now, but I mentally take note to check in with her later.

'OK, what's the situation?'

Darren debriefs. A brawl in the Samovar, someone making some remark about how well it is for Cantillon to be able to sit at the bar and poor Trish Cronin above in the churchyard and her children without their mother. A few slaps thrown, Tatiana expertly removes everyone involved – you do not mess with her – and the brawling continues on the street. Someone calls us, Darren and Chloe attend, Cantillon is arrested, charged, shoved into the back of the squad car and brought here.

'Nicola, get Cantillon's solicitor on the phone. Let him sleep off the drink, and we'll interview him once he's coherent. He's clearly in breach of the terms of his bond, so he'll be up before the judge tomorrow.'

Cantillon is on an early release programme, bound by a good-behaviour bond, so brawling in the pub combined with an assault on a member of An Garda Síochána will mean instant return to custody, so at least Caelan Cronin has got his wish. I wonder briefly if Caelan's mother is indeed looking after him. Maybe Minnie Melodie did have a word with her spirit after all.

I call Kieran to tell him I'll be late, and he tells me he'll ask Nora to pick the girls up from camogie and Irish dancing and drop them home, because it's Tuesday and he goes straight from work to his pipe-playing session and Mam is still off cruising the Mediterranean with Joe.

* * *

As I pull into our driveway, I see Nora's car parked outside the house. My heart sinks a little; it's nearly seven, and I'd hoped she'd be gone by now. The girls are perfectly fine at home on their own.

I back out onto the road again and park alongside the wall, so as not to block her exit. Nora meets me at my door with her coat already on.

'The girls have a lovely surprise for you, Mags,' she announces as she jumps into her car, putting on her seatbelt. 'I'd love to wait around to see your face, but Kevin needs his dinner. I'd never let him do for himself. I don't know how my poor Kieran manages to cook his own dinner when he works so hard all day.' And with this parting shot at my domestic failures, she starts her engine and whizzes off.

'Bye, Nora, lovely to see you too,' I say under my breath as I enter the house.

I am greeted by a furious scream from Ellie. 'Mam, no. Just absolutely no way. And it's not just me – Kate hates hers too...like *hates* it...'

I turn from hanging up my jacket by the door and stifle a guffaw. Ellie is standing in the living room doorway dressed in a garment that makes her look like a floral couch. Kate behind her is in a matching horror. Pink peonies on a white background, full skirts gathered from below the bust, puff sleeves with lace trim and a velvet collar. You know, the kinds of dresses you see on those creepy china dolls? Well, that's exactly what is on my daughters right now.

'Nana Nora bought them,' wails Kate, 'and she says she wants us to wear them for Gearoid's wedding.'

Nora has always been this way, sending really frilly, flouncy dresses each Christmas, and for diplomatic reasons when they were little, I put them in them, the poor misfortunes, each Christmas day, even though one time the lace irritated Kate's neck so much she came out in a rash. But those days are gone. I don't try to placate Nora any more, and to be fair, she doesn't usually push it, until now.

'Mam, seriously, I'm telling you now, I'm not going across the road in this. No way…absolutely no way. You have to do something.' Ellie is close to tears.

'Why didn't you just tell her I had your dresses bought already?' I ask, still trying to suppress my mirth as I head into the kitchen to make myself a sandwich. My furious daughters come stomping after me like two scary dolls.

'But you hadn't, had you?' Ellie rants, pink in the face. 'I picked out a lovely dress in Sharon's – she said for you to ring her – and I was going to wear that, but you just kept saying you were too busy to even go and look at it!'

It's true. Sharon has left me several messages since I left her shop in a hurry to hide my tears. The truth is, I haven't wanted to see her. I'm too conscious of the fact that Kieran is still doing the occasional bit of work on Róisín and Joel's roof, as other leaks make themselves known, and there was another tionól last week, which they were both at. In a small town like this, these things don't go unnoticed, and even though I trust Kieran completely, I don't want to have Sharon warning me again about how handsome Kieran is and how Róisín is a scheming whatever she is.

'Well, you could have said they were already picked out…'

Ellie jerks her thumb furiously at Kate. 'I would have done, if this muppet hadn't said you hadn't even been into Sharon's to look!'

'I didn't know she had these in her car, did I?' Kate cries, stung that this fiasco is somehow her fault. 'She asked me what we were wearing, and I said you hadn't been to Sharon's yet, which you hadn't, and then she said she knew that would be the case and it was just as well someone cared what we looked like. And then she came out with these.'

'Well, just say you don't want to wear them,' I suggest as I get the ham out of the fridge.

'Refuse Nana Nora? Are you on drugs?' Ellie exclaims.

'You'll have to do it, Mam,' says Kate. 'She's a bit scared of you. You're the only one not terrified of her.'

I laugh then. 'Indeed, and I will not do anything of the kind. This is between you and your grandmother. Leave me out of it.' I get the bread out of the bread bin and start slicing. 'Call her up now and tell her you don't like them.'

'Maaam!' they both wail. 'We can't say that to her, she'll –'

'What?' I ask, not unreasonably, giving up on my sandwich and turning to face them. 'Seriously, she'll what? Combust? Come at you with the breadknife? Walk into the sea?'

'No, but...' Kate looks on the brink of tears. 'They cost a fortune, she said. She had to get them sent specially from Germany...'

'Girls, Nana knows you wouldn't like those kinds of dresses. Sure, doesn't she see the way you dress all the time? So it was kind of aggressive on her part to buy these dresses without asking you. But we teach people how to treat us, you know, so if you let her do this, and you go along with wearing them, then she wins.'

'But we can't say no, Mam. And then I know she'll put it on Facebook – you know she's obsessed since she found out how to use it – and my life will be over,' Ellie says miserably. 'You have to help us, please.'

'I thought Facebook was only for the aged and infirm?' I ask, quoting my daughter back at her.

'It is, but someone will share it, and then it will be on the Gram and Snap and everywhere, and Kate and I will have to emigrate.'

I relent with a sigh. 'Fine. She must be home by now. Hand me my phone. "Once more unto the breach."'

'*Henry V*,' Ellie says gratefully. She's still a member of the Galway Youth Theatre, and over the summer holidays, they were doing lots of scenes from Shakespeare.

'I'd rather be facing the French Dauphin at Agincourt than your nana, though...' I pull a face, and they both smile a bit, though their eyes are full of trepidation as I scroll for Nora's number – it's not among my favourites. Before I reach it, I get a message from Sharon, which I open.

Fancy lunch and a glass of wine Friday? X

Can't, I'm in Galway at a meeting. X, I reply quickly, and return to finding Nora's number.

Nora's phone rings and she answers. 'Ah, Mags, it's you.' She is delighted with herself. 'I suppose you're ringing about the dresses I got for the girls...'

'That's right, Nora, I do want to talk to you about the dresses.'

'There's no need for thanks. They were very dear, I know, but sure they'll look lovely in them, and I just –'

'They won't be wearing them, Nora, so I hope you can get a refund.'

'I beg your pardon? Don't they fit? Kate said they fitted perfectly?' She sounds very vexed, and poor Kate, who can hear as I have Nora on speaker, pales and looks nervously at Ellie, who narrows her eyes at her.

'They fit fine, and it was very generous of you, but they don't like them, and to be honest, neither do I.' Honesty is the best policy with Nora. I know it might sound harsh, but every move that woman makes is calculated, and you have to fight fire with fire where she's concerned. She will refuse to pick up on subtle because it's not what she wants to hear, so blunt as a bag of hammers is the only way. 'The style isn't really the kind of thing they're into, so I'll repackage them, and we can return them, and hopefully you'll get a refund.'

For once she's silent. The girls look like rabbits in the headlights, rooted to the spot in terror and the horrible dresses.

'Well, I must say, I'm very hurt. Yes, hurt and offended and… Well, to have my generosity thrown back in my face like this, when all I wanted was to make sure the girls looked nice for Gearoid's big day.'

Ignoring the hurt and offended business, as that's her standard response to anything she doesn't like, I reply gently, 'I know it's disappointing, but you wouldn't wear something someone picked out for you that you didn't feel comfortable in, so the girls shouldn't have to either.'

'But Mags, with all due respect…' None. That would be the amount of respect I'm due apparently. 'I'm just making sure for their sake they look as nice as their cousins.'

Ellie's eyes open wide, and Kate is in tears now.

I'm boiling, but I keep my voice even and light. 'They'd look beautiful whatever they were wearing, Nora. But you're right, I do want them to look nice, and that's the reason they won't be wearing those dresses.' I stick my tongue out at the phone, which makes my girls giggle a little. 'So if you want to give me the address, I'll ship them back, or else I can get Kieran to drop them to you?'

'I really think children have too much say in everything nowadays. When I was a girl –' she begins again, but I cut across her.

'When you were a girl, children were seen and not heard and their opinions were irrelevant,' I say, and she knows not to go there with me. She was drummed out of her home when she was found to be pregnant, and her parents never spoke to her again, so she can't pull the good-old-days card with me. I know too much.

'Will I send them to you or to the shop, Nora?'

A long pause. 'To me,' she spits sourly.

'Righto, and thanks for thinking of them, but maybe next time a bit of consultation might save us all this hassle. Bye now, Nora,' I coo, before hanging up.

'We're dead,' Kate says darkly.

'She's going to kill us,' Ellie agrees.

'Ah, girls, stop. She's an eighty-two-year-old wannabe dictator. She only has the power we give her, and we're giving her absolutely none. Now take those awful things off. I'm getting a headache looking at them.'

Then they both launch at me and hug me tightly.

'You're a legend, Mam, an absolute legend.'

I watch them as they run up the stairs to their bedrooms, and my heart swells with love for them.

CHAPTER 13

'*R*ight, I'm going to Galway to a meeting this afternoon, so I'll be out of contact from' – I check my watch – 'around 2 p.m. till four thirty. Either side of that, get me on the mobile.'

I dismiss my team from the day's briefing meeting and make myself a coffee in my office. I honestly have no idea why I've been called to a meeting in Galway, and not in the Garda Headquarters either but in a hotel on the north side of the city.

Apparently it's just a small meeting, but Assistant Garda Commissioner Ronan Brady wants me to attend. He didn't elaborate further except to say he really would like me to be there, and could we grab a cup of coffee afterwards if I have time.

I ponder the invitation to coffee. Is there a discussion he wants to have without Duckie's ears flapping? Because Duckie Cassidy will probably be there at the meeting; he's not going to countenance being left out if I'm invited. Or is it just for a personal catch-up because we haven't seen each other in a year?

There was always a certain frisson between me and Ronan, and if things were different, who knows, though I never considered it obviously. I won't be telling Sharon about meeting him for coffee; she'd be very nudge-nudge. She always thought it was such strong willpower on my part not to allow things to go further than friendship with him, back in the days when he was Detective Inspector Brady. But I don't need willpower. I would never, ever do that to Kieran. And he would never do it to me. No matter what Sharon has to say about it, with her suspicious mind. I trust my husband and love him, and he feels the same about me.

I do like Ronan, though, and he likes me. He respects me as a police officer, which is more than can be said for Duckie.

I text him back agreeing to the coffee – we are colleagues, after all – then text Kieran to tell him I'll be late and that there's a fish pie in the freezer for their dinner. If he's working late, he'll always tell me, but he never texts me about dinner except to ask what we're having. The weight of motherhood, being a wife, responsible for a house, as well as having a full-time job, sometimes feels overwhelming. Kieran is a good man, but he has never once stripped a bed or bleached a toilet. He can make dinner, and he kind of tidies up, but his version of tidy is everything shoved someplace else, not actually put where it belongs. He has used the washing machine twice. And he's one of the better ones. It's a man's world, no doubt about it.

I pull out of the station and head for the Dublin road, passing the Lodge on the way. It looks great. The stone house is made of cut limestone, and our mysterious couple have had it all sandblasted so it's back to its original glory. The garden is almost bare now as autumn is turning to winter, but a few hardy plants are still blooming in pots outside. You'd wonder how they make so much money, but then the roadside is lined with cars; clearly the business of predicting the future is brisk. I'm not sure why people want to know what's going to happen to them. Best let the future unfold as it will, I think.

The broomstick sign is up, advertising aura cleansing, tarot card reading and crystal ball readings, so it seems Desmond is still keeping away, which is good. Mind you, he's definitely gone a bit strange since Maeve knocked him cold with the flowerpot and has been seen on the street with his new best pal Oscar, warning people how dancing with demonic forces is dangerous for their current and eternal existences and that it would be safer not to dally with witches and warlocks.

Minnie arrived into the Garda station a few days ago, wanting to know why Desmond and Oscar were continuing to defame her and her husband, and I had to explain that since nobody is committing any public order offences like trespassing or behaving in a threatening manner or being abusive, the gardaí can do nothing. 'I thought you'd show a bit more gratitude after I granted you the favour you asked me for!' she barked at me, before storming off, her eyes glittering with fury, not very white witch at all despite all the peace symbols and mood stones.

It unnerved me a bit, her talking about granting me a favour. I only ever asked her for one favour, and that was to do with Caelan Cronin, asking her to somehow get him to stop harassing Mike Cantillon. But surely she had nothing to do with Cantillon ending back up in jail... No, I decided firmly, she's just decided to claim credit for it, or even really imagines she had something to do with it, the same as she claimed to have 'manifested' me when I appeared on the beach.

I remember now I have a podcast about cold reading on my phone. I downloaded it because of what Jerome said about Minnie being a fake witch, but I haven't got around to listening to it yet. I pull over to the side of the road and Bluetooth it to my radio speakers before I drive on, listening.

It's interesting. Apparently a good cold reader can elicit information from their subject by making scattergun statements like *There's a relative of yours trying to come through... They're smiling at you... They're wearing an item of clothing they love, and it's blue? Maybe more green, or turquoise... I'm getting M... M...* And the chances are the person who has come to them, who wants this to work anyway, will then tell them all about their father Michael or Uncle Martin or their mam, and add another piece of information, such as 'yes, he had an old blue jumper he was never out of around the farm' or 'Mam must be wearing that lovely green dress she wore for my wedding.' It doesn't sound to me a million miles from how I question people myself. I always try to give the impression I know more than I do, like 'Let's talk about what you were doing last night, Richie,' and then Richie assumes I know already, because of course I have eyes everywhere, I'm a guard, and he gives me the information for free without realising it.

Then there's some stuff about being able to help people find things by saying, 'Auntie Margaret says it's somewhere you've already looked a few times, but under something, like a book or a cloth, or slipped down behind something else...' And then the person searches much more thoroughly and think it's a miracle when they find it. I wonder if Howya's grandmother told him not so much to look in his old donkey jacket for his shed keys but to look in an item of clothing he doesn't often wear.

Then I imagine Minnie getting indignant with me for being such a doubting Thomas, and I feel like a bit of a killjoy. I do like to believe there's more in heaven and earth. I switch off the podcast, and the radio blares in its place, Mariah Carey's 'All I Want for Christmas Is You'. Ah, lads, it's only October. Too soon. I switch that off as well, and in the silence, my mind drifts away to other matters. Ellie has a rehearsal on Saturday, and I might take her into town and have a wander around the shops to find something for the wedding. Something is stopping me going into the boutique.

Ellie is still set on being an actress, but I wonder if she'll change her mind as she goes into leaving cert, so many do...

My hands-free phone rings, and it's Róisín.

'Hi,' I say brightly.

After Sharon upset me in the boutique, I'd decided to invite Róisín out to Teresa's for a custard slice (I know, bad) to prove to myself how wrong Sharon is and that I have nothing to fear from Kieran's ex. We got ourselves a quiet corner, and after a lot of beating around the bush, she finally confided in me, as I already knew from Kieran, that her marriage had gone through a very rocky patch, with three failed rounds of IVF and then Joel having his affair, though after she found out, he'd begged her for another chance. She'd agreed, and the house in Ballycarrick, near her parents, was their fresh start.

'Hi, Mags, am I disturbing you? I probably shouldn't ring in the middle of the day.'

'No, no, you're grand,' I say. 'I'm driving but you're on speaker.'

'I was only ringing to let off steam. I'll go if you're busy.'

'Not busy. Just bored driving, so work away.'

'Well...' I can hear her settling down for a confidential chat. 'I'm fit to strangle Joel since he got this new job in Shannon Airport.'

'How so?'

'He's working from home this week, so I thought I'd see more of him, but he just won't come out of his office.' I can hear the edge of frustration in her voice. 'If he wants to work on our relationship, he isn't showing much sign of it.'

'I suppose moving country and job and everything is taking a lot of his energy?' I'm sure this is true, and he seemed very on edge when I met him that day.

'I know, I know, I'm being unfair, and I do love him.' She sighs. 'I wish he'd take an evening off, though. You're so lucky how close you and Kieran are.' There is something genuine about her; she isn't afraid to be vulnerable.

'And how's the new office?' I ask.

'It's great, and Gerry is as good as my old stylist in New York.' She's taken the empty rooms above Gerry's Hairdressers for her one-woman law firm and is delighted with the bargain. Not only is it cheap rent, but she gets a free cut and blow-dry every month, which in Ballycarrick is like winning a Golden Ticket for Willy Wonka's chocolate factory. Appointments are very hard got at Gerry's.

'Any customers yet?' I ask.

'Oh, yes, there's this gentleman who keeps coming in, wanting me to do something to stop Satan taking over Ballycarrick. He's offering to pay me by the hour, but I've explained I can't in all honesty take his money, that it's more of a job for the Church. Though he says he's tried that, but your priest here is a bit soft in the head apparently, and as for the guards... Well, I won't tell you what he said about the guards.'

We're both laughing now.

'Mags, he was on about this aura cleanse the warlock does, said it was obviously a way of stealing people's souls. But I don't know – it sounds pretty good to me. I might get myself one and put it down as expenses doing research for a client.' She chuckles, a throaty sound.

'Let me know if it transforms your life. Maybe I'll get one too,' I say, still grinning.

* * *

To my surprise, there's an armed detective standing outside the door of the meeting room, on the landing of this unremarkable Galway hotel. I don't recognise him. He is young, with a shaved head and a muscular frame busting out of his suit jacket, which I suspect he wears slightly too small on purpose. He hands me a ziplock bag with an electronic tag on it. 'You can keep your phone,' he says officiously. 'The bag just blocks the signal.'

He waits until I put my phone in the bag and zip it closed before opening the door for me, which leads into a long room with white walls and a central table.

Ronan Brady stands from the table as I enter. He looks strange in his commissioner's uniform. I only ever knew him out of uniform; he was a plain-clothes detective when I met him and detective inspector before this latest huge promotion. He is after ageing, I notice, crow's feet around his eyes and his hair has a lot more grey than it used to have. Still drop-dead gorgeous, though.

'Mags, so glad you can make it. Thank you for coming,' he says. 'This is John Greene, Assistant Director of the Garda National Crime and Security Intelligence Service. John, this is Sergeant Mags Munroe from Ballycarrick.'

'Ah yes, I've heard all about you,' says the only other person present, also bobbing up from the table with a friendly smile. He is a short, jolly-looking man, so unassuming that if you told me he sold shoes, I'd believe it. He has a fleshy baby face and a halo of brownish curls. His suit is well cut; it can't quite disguise his soft, pudgy body, though. His accent is unplaceable.

'Thanks for coming, and thank you, Ronan, for arranging this meeting. It is a little unorthodox, you might say' – he grins impishly at me, as if this is all some big lark – 'but we have a potential situation, and Assistant Garda Commissioner Brady has suggested it might be handy to have you on board. He has fully vouched for you, Sergeant, as someone with a good head on her shoulders, and who can be trusted to say nothing to anyone, but I will emphasise the need for absolute discretion, for reasons that will become clear in due course, and matters discussed here today must remain within this room.' His warm brown eyes rest on me. 'Am I clear?'

'Very clear, sir.' I take a seat at the end of the table, resting the ziplock bag down by the leg of my chair. I look towards the door to see who else is joining us. But no one else comes in. No Duckie. No anyone. What is going on here? I catch Ronan's eye – he's sitting opposite John Greene – but his face is impassive.

'So I'll get straight to it,' says Greene, still addressing me directly. 'As I've already explained to Ronan, we in the security service believe we are facing an existential threat to Irish and European security.'

'I see.' I do my best to sound calmly interested, as if this sort of thing happens to me every day. Inside, I've decided this is probably a dream and I'm going to wake up any moment. Still, it's an intriguing dream, so I stay with it rather than pinching myself.

'We have several recent sightings of military ships or ones somehow connected to the Russian government in our coastal waters, which is, of course, a cause for concern. Given the war in Ukraine, and the West supplying weapons to Kyiv, any disruption of the NATO alliance and the Western economies would be ideal for Russia. We have information that Putin intends to attack our essential infrastructure, and we need to ensure he fails. In Ireland we are setting up a joint task force, bringing together all the security services, and it will be called Operation Greengage. And this is where you come in.'

Yep, definitely a dream, and any minute now, James Bond is going to walk through that door and I'm going to be sent off with him to save the world. I pray my alarm doesn't go off too soon, or if it does, I hope I sleep through it.

'I know you must be wondering why you're here, Sergeant

Munroe,' the shoe salesman continues, and I nod and smile as I wait for him to explain my mission.

'Ronan has told us you are a very good officer, extremely observant, very hands-on and involved in your community. He says nothing that happens in Ballycarrick gets past you and your only flaw is being a little too heroic. Though of course those sex traffickers would have got clean away if you hadn't acted so promptly.'

This is great. I love this dream. 'I just did what anyone else would have done,' I murmur modestly.

'You did what I didn't do,' says Ronan sagely. 'And that's why you're here today.'

'So you see,' says Greene, 'we need someone on the ground who can carry out unobtrusive surveillance of the area around Ballycarrick, in particular Ballyloughane Strand, where one of the four transatlantic digital cables connecting America to Europe through Ireland comes ashore.'

This time I sit in stunned silence. An alarming sense of reality is creeping into this dream. There's a welded cover in the corner of the car park at Ballyloughane Strand, where I was only the other day. Kieran and I took the girls down to watch when the cable was being brought ashore. There was a weird-looking cable-laying ship lying off the coast and a pavilion in the car park, and lots of sailors and engineers milling around, and even a marine ecologist making sure there was minimal damage being done to the environment. The whole circus was quite the local attraction while it was going on.

'We've never really had a suitable level of security around these cables,' Greene goes on, 'but the sabotage of the Nord Stream pipelines has brought them into sharp focus. Three quarters of all cables in the northern hemisphere pass through or near Irish waters, as well as the vital four that actually come ashore. A lot of people think most global communications go through satellites, but that's not the case. These cables carry ninety-seven percent of financial transactions, business operations and everyday internet access, and any damage to them would be extremely destructive to the economies and defence systems not just of Ireland but of the entire Western world.'

Dear God. I'm beginning to realise this is for real. This makes it a lot harder to maintain my calm, smiling demeanour, but I do my best to stop my jaw from hitting my knees. 'And so what exactly...' I say, my voice a bit squeaky now.

'What do we want you to do? Well, not take the Russians on single-handedly, of course!' He laughs gaily.

I laugh along nervously. 'Well, I hope not.' The only Russian I know is Tatiana, and I wouldn't take even her on single-handedly – she'd crucify me. Luckily I'm not going to have to. She's not a fan of Vladimir Putin, which is why she left Russia in the first place, and she's furious about the war; she makes a point of employing Ukrainian refugees in her pub and restaurant and snarling at anyone who complains about them being in Ballycarrick.

John Greene is still laughing. We are having such fun. 'No, no heroics required, and in fact we don't want you to approach anyone you suspect – that would endanger the whole mission. We will be placing a naval vessel in the bay, ostensibly to monitor illegal fishing but crewed by intelligence experts, and we will be gathering intelligence as to the activities of possible Russian vessels. All we need from you is to keep your ear to the ground locally, pay attention to anything around Ballycarrick that changes or seems strange. And if anything strikes you, however minor, bring it to Ronan's attention. Now' – he checks his watch again and bounces up – 'I really have to fly. Another meeting about this in Dublin but wanted to meet you first. Ronan will fill you in on the details. Ronan, a quick word?'

Ronan is already on his feet. 'Mags, could you wait here, and I'll be back?'

'Of course,' I say. I was getting up myself, expecting to follow them out, but now I sit back down, feeling like a spare wheel. Ronan knocks to let the guard outside know they're coming out, and when they've left, the officious young man closes the door on me again.

In the dead silence, I sit thinking about what I've been asked to do. John Greene, from the highest echelons of Garda intelligence, wants me to look out for something strange in Ballycarrick? Well, that's a simple assignment. Clearly he has never been to Ballycarrick; there's nothing but strange behaviour there on a normal day. There are the lunatics in Tidy Towns who think the world owes them paint. And Elsie Flanagan, who daubs the exact same scene of Carrick Lough in her art class in the community school over and over again; there are a hundred of them hanging framed on the walls of her house. And Lydia the Turkish Barber who is neither Turkish nor a barber. Bertie the butcher, who is the proud owner of the pope's medal for services to the Church but simultaneously organised a group sex evening in cars for strangers that I had the great misfortune to happen upon. I could go on. And on. And on.

Ages have passed. My foot has gone to sleep, and I stand up and walk around. Where is Ronan? I can't distract myself with the phone because it's still in the ziplock bag. I try to see the screen to tell the time, but it's upside down and I feel afraid to take it out. I sit down again and stare at the wall.

At last, after what feels like an hour, Ronan finally arrives, carrying two cappuccinos in takeaway cardboard cups. He hands me one.

'I'm so sorry. John wanted to arrange a time for our next meeting that suited a few more people,' he says, drawing up a chair beside mine. 'I would say let's go down to the bar, but we've had this place swept for bugs and so on, so it's safer here.'

'Ronan, what on earth is going on?' I ask, turning my chair to face him.

He exhales and runs a hand through his greying hair. He's aged a bit, not as boyish-looking as he was when I first met him, but I suppose we all have, and being Assistant Garda Commissioner must be a stressful job.

'There are spies operating somewhere on the island of Ireland, we think,' he says. 'They seem to know a lot of what we're doing to try to intercept Russian traffic, and we are under serious pressure from everywhere to rout them out.'

'But aren't they on the ships?' I ask, realising I sound thick as a ditch.

'Yes, undoubtedly they are, but possibly on land too – we don't know. But we need to make sure.' He sighs. 'We're the weakest link between America and Europe, honestly, being an island with two thousand miles of coastline, almost all of it unprotected. We are not resourced or equipped to deal with a threat like this, but we'll have to work with what we have.'

'So seriously, what do you expect me to do?' I feel stupid even asking. 'Because, Ronan, I'm way out of my league here.'

He lifts his cappuccino and smiles at me over the rim. 'That's not true. I know you can do this, Mags. You're wasted down there really, though I know you love it. And I know I can't convince you to move up to Dublin, but if you ever take a notion, just say the word. But will you do this for me? I kind of promised the top brass... This is Interpol, MI6, CIA, German Federal Intelligence Service, you name it, the highest possible level.'

'Of course. I just wish I knew what I was looking for.'

'Just like he said, anything that strikes you about a new person in town, anything out of the ordinary, come directly to me, personally, in private. There will be other meetings soon that will be less restricted, several other officers, so not just you, but I wanted John to meet you personally because you're the best person we have on the ground.'

'And about those other officers, dare I ask...' I give him that look.

He returns it with a rueful smile and drops his voice, though nobody is in the room except us. 'Yes, I'm afraid DI Cassidy is already part of this operation as well, operating out of Galway...'

My heart sinks. I don't hate anyone, truly. But Duckie Cassidy really is an absolute dose.

'But look, Mags,' Ronan carries on. 'You're the main person here, no matter what that plonker thinks. Just ignore him, if you have to deal with him at all. He's looking to go up a grade, trying to secure a fatter pension for himself, so he's all over this like a rash. But he's not here today and you are – remember that.'

'Sure. Thanks, Ronan.' I suppose if the Free World is under threat, Duckie Cassidy should be the least of my problems.

'Meanwhile,' says Ronan, pulling his chair slightly closer, 'I want to chat to you a bit more about what you might be looking for.'

'A man with an eye patch, stroking a white cat and sounding like

Alan Rickman?' I'm not a big James Bond fan, so I don't know if I've got the stereotype right, but that's the best I can come up with. 'I'm afraid that wouldn't exactly stand out in Ballycarrick.'

Ronan splutters with companionable laughter. 'Yeah, I realise that.' But then he's serious again. 'We have it on fairly good authority that there are Russian operatives in the region, and with the beach at Ballyloughane Strand being the main target, we think they'll be some-where close by. But apparently they're not at all like you'd expect. I was in The Hague last week, at a meeting about this exact thing, and the Interpol officer who gave the talk was really interesting. A foreign agent might be one half of a married couple or a family or whatever, and they're most likely to be bland. Possibly living in one of those new houses getting built. They deliberately blend in. They are usually Mr or Mrs Average, occasionally both if they're operating as a pair, which they do sometimes, normal car, normal looking, everything run of the mill, nothing memorable at all.'

'Really?' I'm fascinated.

'Yeah. He told us a story of this couple they recently arrested, for example. The husband worked in IT, she in retail banking, two kids, very normal looking, living in Brussels. Kids going to school, the whole lot. She said she was French, and he said he was from South America someplace, but in fact they were both Russians. Even their own kids had no idea. The couple were deep undercover and had done nothing basically for fifteen years, but then she worked her way up in banking, in Brussels of course, met loads of EU people and got information that way. Then she befriended, even went so far as to make really good friends with, another couple with kids the same age.' He sipped his coffee. 'Loads of playdates, spent all the holidays together. The friends even minded their kids for them when they went skiing to Austria for a long weekend. Looks like the Russian woman had planned it all so that if and when she and her husband were picked up, the innocent couple would feel obliged to take their kids in and look after them. Which they did.'

'And what happened to the children in the end?' I'm shocked at the callousness of it all.

'Ended up back in Russia with the parents, who were part of a spy swap or something – he was a bit vague on the details. Poor kids had never been there before, didn't know what was going on. Even the skiing trip had been a complete scam. The pair of spies had gone to Moscow to be debriefed. They sent photos of them having a great time in the snow and the whole shebang, but the snow was in Russia, not Austria.'

'And how were they caught?'

'Well, this is the fascinating bit. These undercover agents seem to get caught in one of two ways. Rarely are they actually caught in the act – they're so clever and cautious and excellently trained. Like this pair had a web of invisible thread over all their clothes in the wardrobes, done in a specific pattern, so they'd know if they'd been disturbed, that sort of thing. But anyway, they seem to either give themselves away by something silly, like a gesture or a movement that's so inherent, it's hard to stop. This woman had both her children with no pain relief whatsoever because she didn't want to risk being out of it and saying something incriminating. Not a peep out of her apparently.'

I think back to having Ellie and Kate, and that would not have been possible for me. I have to admire that strength. 'And the second way?'

'The need for human connection, the need to be honest. With spies, no matter how deeply buried their true identity, it seems the urge to connect with someone, presumably someone other than a coconspirator, is strong. This guy ended up having an affair with a woman he was given as a contact. They should never have met in person, but they did, and they were able to open up about who they really were, I suppose. She was another agent living in Paris, I think, and they had a relationship, and that's how they got caught. Interpol had their eye on her but no idea about him or his missus. The affair led the police to the couple.'

'Wow, the poor kids, though… Imagine being ripped from everything and everyone you know and flown to Russia, no language, no idea what's going on…'

He nods, but not being a parent himself, I think he doesn't feel how horrible it would be. I can't imagine that happening to Ellie and Kate.

'So the thing is, we're looking for someone who doesn't stand out, you know. So what with the beach being close to Ballycarrick and lots of new people coming to the area...and it being off-season, the beaches aren't busy.'

'I'll be on the lookout. Though you've just described the vast majority of the new residents there. They're generally young couples, working in Galway, so it's not going to be easy.'

'That's their general idea.' He sighs. 'It will be massive for us if we can get them, Mags. They pose a real threat to international security and commerce, and I know our lot are keen to reassure all the foreign direct investment companies here that our security, cyber and regular, is up to scratch.'

'Well, I'll keep an extra-close eye. I think that's all I can do, right?'

He nods again. 'Thanks, Mags.' He stands. 'Fancy one more cup of coffee somewhere decent before you head away?'

'No, I'd better get back.' I want to be home before dark. I'm not going to be able to tell Kieran what I've been doing – he knows police work is confidential – but it can make him twitchy if I'm late home without an explanation. Shades of the time I got shot. As we wait for the lift, leaving the young guy with the gun to do a sweep of the room or whatever floats his boat, I ask, 'How's the new gig suiting you?'

He smiles and nods. 'Good, I like it. I had to move to Dublin, though. The commute was killing me.'

'I suppose you had no choice,' I say pityingly. It's widely accepted among people outside of the capital that to live there is the worst option on the island, and equally bewildering to Dublin natives that we don't want to live there.

'Yeah, I got an apartment in Castleknock, so it's fine.' He shrugs. 'You know the kind, glass and chrome, no soul.' He gives a small laugh.

'Did you sell your house?'

He shakes his head. 'I should do probably, but I don't know. I can't bring myself to do it.'

His wife, Evelyn, died of breast cancer in her thirties and he never really got over it. His house in Galway, a lovely period terraced home overlooking the bay, is one they bought together.

'You'll do it in your own time, if it's right for you,' I say quietly.

'My niece and her boyfriend are renting it from me at the moment. He's finishing his PhD in University College Galway and she's working at the hospital, so it suits them. How are the girls?'

'Great. Teenagers, you know yourself.' I roll my eyes with a grin.

'I don't know, Mags. I wish I did,' he answers sadly. He and Evelyn had no children. They'd been planning to, but then she was diagnosed with cancer the first time, and his pain is still there, though he doesn't wear it on the surface. The poor woman battled it twice, so it was a long road for them. I know he doesn't let his guard down like this with many people.

'It's not too late, you know,' I say. 'You're a fine catch, and you could meet someone, have a family.'

He smiles then. 'I could, if I had ten seconds to myself and I wasn't well known for being a cop. What am I supposed to do, Mags, go on Tinder? And have every criminal in the country taking the mick? I don't think so.'

Even though he's shaking his head, this is an advance. It's the first time he's even agreed in principle to meeting someone new.

'There are other ways,' I suggest. 'Meeting people through friends, for instance.'

'Well, keep your eyes open so. I trust your judgement, so if you see some woman that you think might like a workaholic, emotionally constipated Irish cop who hates foreign food, then by all means, give her my number.'

'I will.' And I find myself racking my mind for such a one. Ronan does work hard. His career is in the stratosphere and only going up; he'll definitely make Commissioner, which is the highest rank we have, but he probably won't even stop there. Interpol, the EU – the world is his oyster, but there is something deeply sad about him too. I would love him to meet someone; it's been too long.

* * *

ON MY WAY back from Galway, I'm called on the radio by Zoë, her voice coming through over the crackly system. 'Sarge, are you anywhere near Ballyloughane Strand?'

Instantly I'm on full alert. Heart racing. *The Russians have invaded... They've blown up the car park...* 'Copy that, Zoë, I'm about four miles from there. What's going on?'

'I have Mr Oscar O'Leary here claiming he has seen some satanic rituals and heard screaming coming from the beach and has asked us to investigate?' She says it like this is a perfectly normal request.

'Right.' On the one hand, I'm extremely relieved, but at the same time, I'm amused to note I'm a wee bit disappointed. So I do have some James Bond tendencies after all. I might as well check. The screaming is probably foxes or something. It's dark, but I pull over and turn back to go down the coast road. What was Oscar doing anywhere near here anyway? 'I'm on my way, Zoë.'

'Thanks, Sarge, over.'

The road down to the beach is narrow and dark and it's windy out, so I drive slowly. I'm starving. I've asked Kieran to drop into Bertie's on his way home and get one of their home-made shepherd's pies, which are delicious, and so all he has to do is defrost some peas. Neither of us are wonderful cooks, but we manage. I'm looking forward to a quick shower, dressing in my cosy pjs with no bra on and having a nice dinner. We're in the middle of a great series on Netflix, and I know Kieran will have the fire lit – he's great like that. Wandering around a windswept beach in the dark is about as far from my ideal night as it's possible to be, but hopefully it will be nothing and the evening can continue as planned.

I don't go as far as the beach but park in a lay-by that looks down on it from above. There's a vehicle in the car park below, a beat-up old VW camper van with faded stickers on the side. I know it's Minnie and Neil's van. So this is what Oscar's been up to. I've told him to keep away from them, but he's been following them around on the quiet, probably him and Desmond both. It's one thing badgering people about Satan on the street, but stalking is a whole different ball game. If that pair doesn't back off, I'll have to have words, I really will. I can't hold off an official complaint forever.

There's a fire going, but from up here, I can't see what's going on around it, though the chances that it's a ritual sacrifice or whatever Oscar thinks it is are minimal. But I remember I've been asked to keep an eye on the coastline now, so as I'm here…

Reluctantly I make my way down the steep sandy path, the wind howling around my head. Then I see them, and for a moment I don't believe it. All alone, on a dark, wet, cold October night, in a gale, beside a fire, Minnie and Neil are naked and writhing around on each other's wrinkly old bodies, deep in the throes of passion.

Beating a hasty retreat – they are too busy to notice me mercifully – I make my way back up. And I wonder how long it will be before I can unsee that particular sight.

CHAPTER 14

The removal for Desmond Dunne has a queue out the door of Caffrey's funeral home and down the street. I sigh. If you don't know, funerals in Ireland take between three and five days, and this bit, the removal of the body from the funeral home to the church, can take ages, as everyone connected to the family, even tenuously, will come to offer their condolences. I had hoped to duck in and out, meet Maeve, say how sorry I am – though considering she nearly did away with him herself a few weeks ago, those words sound hollow – and get home. But now I'll have to get in the line and accept the fact that I'll have to wait. A heart attack apparently. At least it's not murder. I've been worried it might come to that, though I think Maeve got a salutary lesson after she knocked him cold with the flowerpot.

Not that it stopped them fighting. They were like the Twits; you know, that Roald Dahl book about Mr and Mrs Twit who are always doing desperate things to each other? My girls loved that story when they were little. Only last week Desmond changed the locks while Maeve was visiting her sister in Mayo, and she called us expecting us to break the door down. Despite their terrible relationship, the wailing and gnashing of teeth now that he's dead will be next-level. It is always the way.

I get out of my car and join the queue. It is drizzling rain and very cold and the evenings are getting dark earlier now, so there isn't the chat there would normally be. Hoods up, umbrellas, heads bowed, but rain, hail or snow, tradition is important, and the people of Ballycarrick have come to say goodbye to Desmond and support Maeve and their daughters.

The thing about Irish funerals being for everyone is nice. I remember when my dad died, it was actually very comforting to have all the people troop through the house and shop in those days after, the rosary around the open coffin the first night, followed by tea and cakes supplied by all the neighbours, which then turned into whiskey for the men and sherry for the ladies and a huge sing-song that went on till the small hours. We celebrate the person's life really well here. My dad was so unwell for so long, it was a happy release for him, and honestly for Mam too; she'd been caring for him diligently and gently for so long.

The removal is hard. The closing of the coffin is something I'll never forget. Dad lying there, the white satin of the coffin only slightly whiter than him – and he was so thin by the time the disease finally killed him – his hands with the rosary beads intertwined, looking peaceful. But when Ernie Caffrey and his son Thomas, the undertakers, put the lid on and the brass screws were turned, there was something cruel about it. Mam and me, Delores and Jenny, my sisters – just standing there watching. I'll never forget it.

My mam always says that part, just like the coffin going into the ground, is necessary for the ones left behind; it helps you to believe your person is truly gone from this life. It helps the grieving. I don't know. I can't imagine how. If it was Kieran, God forbid, and me and Kate and Ellie had to watch that... It wouldn't do you any good to think about it.

I think my dad would be really happy that Mam married Joe. He and Joe liked each other a lot, and he wouldn't have wanted Mam to be alone for as long as she was. I think of him often these days, and I wonder if he's around, his spirit or soul or whatever you want to call it. Sometimes I'm sure he is, other times not.

The crowd shuffles on, and the rain settles on my shoulders. I don't have my Garda jacket on, though I wish I had because it is so weatherproof, it's incredible. But I'm here as a neighbour, not as a guard, so I'm just wearing my black wool coat over my uniform. I've no umbrella, so I'm really getting soaked.

Bertie the butcher and his wife, Maura, pass me on their way out. They've done their sympathising and are on the way home to their fire. I'm jealous. She smiles hello; he looks away, still mortified. I'd love to say to him, Bertie, just forget it. It was a moment of madness; we all have them. Though to be truthful, meeting a load of middle-aged random people for bodily antics in cars isn't something I'd ever consider, but each to their own.

Luigi is two people ahead of me, carrying a lovely wreath. I'd say he made it himself. He used to be a florist from Offaly and was called Leonard before upping sticks and opening a pizzeria in Ballycarrick and reinventing himself as Luigi.

Then I see Sharon and Trevor getting out of their car and coming to join the queue. Some young women, I'm assuming friends of the Dunne girls, are between me and them, but I smile and give a little wave while at the same time being quite glad there's people between us. Which is awful of me, because Sharon is my best friend. I really should stop avoiding her... Just then Róisín arrives and comes to stand beside me, holding a big umbrella over both our heads.

'Hi, Mags, thought you'd appreciate a bit of shelter.'

'Hi, Róisín. Thanks.'

Though I'd rather she hadn't joined me like this. I can hear a slight murmur among the young women behind me about queue jumping, and I'm sure I can feel Sharon's eyes burning into the back of my neck.

Funerals here are a highly evolved social dance, and without anyone ever saying a word, everyone knows where they fit in the order of things. For example, if it's the parent of a work colleague, you're not expected at the rosary but you would be expected at the removal. You could go to the funeral also but not the grave and certainly not the lunch afterwards. But if it's any blood relative, even a distant aunt, rosary and grave are essential. You could skip the removal if it's a distant relative, but for aunts, uncles, cousins, you'd be expected at the whole thing. Friends is a whole other thing. I can't really explain how people know where they fit, but they do.

Róisín coming to sympathise with the Dunnes is a bit wide of the mark, and her skipping the queue is a cardinal sin; she's obviously been in New York for far too long and forgotten her Irish funeral manners. But she means well and is obviously anxious to fit back into society here, so I'm hardly going to tell her she needs to go to the end of the queue where Sharon is standing. For one thing, I'm happy not to be rained on any more, and for another thing, Sharon will either flat-out ignore Róisín or spend the whole time shooting daggers at her.

The crowd shuffles on another bit. Oscar O'Leary comes out of the funeral home and stalls for a moment when he sees me. I know he wants to tell me how Desmond was a devout Catholic and so has definitely gone straight to heaven or whatever. But the rain is bucketing down, and he stays under the wide porch. Thank heavens for small mercies. It's not that I'm against religion, and at a time like this, it can be very helpful. But sometimes when we come across particularly horrific cases of what people can do to each other, it's hard to believe there's a God at all. Little children suffering, addicted parents, violence, abuse... If there is a God, he's got some serious explaining to do, as far as I'm concerned.

Eventually we get inside. There are easily thirty people ahead of us, but at least we're out of the rain. There's a low murmur of conversation in the foyer of the funeral home, distant family members who are not close enough to the dead to be in the line of the bereaved but who will be sticking around for the whole thing.

Maeve and her daughters come into sight, seated on a row of chairs near the coffin, dressed in black.

I go to a lot of funerals – it's expected of me as the local police sergeant – and so I've had a lot of opportunity to observe people in this, the lowest ebb of their lives. Some people cry; others don't. Some look as if it's just another day and another job to be done; others look lost and scared and sad. Mam at Dad's funeral was stoic, frozen. Numb really, I suppose.

As the queue edges past the row of chairs, the Dunne girls shake people's hands, accepting people's 'I'm sorry for your troubles' – the standard remark for sympathising – and they look exactly as you'd expect two young women to be when burying their dad. But Maeve is going all out. She is theatrically bereft, up for the Oscar clearly. Black lace dress, Morticia Addams style, her hair in a dark chignon, red lipstick and pale make-up. And – and this is frankly bizarre – a black mantilla partially covering her face. I've not seen someone with one of those on their head since I was a kid.

When I go to shake her hand, she jumps up and flings herself into my arms – literally flings herself – and clings to me, howling like a wounded animal.

'Sergeant Munroe, what am I going to do without my Des? How will I go on? How will I live? He was my life, you know it better than anyone…my whole life…'

I try to disentangle myself, but she's hanging on and everyone is watching. 'I'm very sorry for your loss, Maeve. He was a lovely man,' I say. Desmond Dunne was not a lovely man. He was a man trapped in a web of his own making, where he and this prima donna tore lumps out of each other for decades.

'He was, and oh, how he adored me… Treated me like a queen, he did, nothing was too much. I'll never know love like that again… never…' She stops just short of placing the back of her hand to her brow, Greta Garbo style, and some of the locals in the queue are hiding a smirk. The Dunnes' tumultuous marriage wasn't a secret. Only a few months ago, she came into the Samovar and dumped a full pint of Guinness over Desmond's head, destroying Tatiana's upholstery in the process. Needless to say, Maeve had to pay for the damage. People don't generally refuse Tatiana.

Maeve's daughters look mortified by the histrionics – they don't know where to put themselves – and I manage to release Maeve's grip on me and offer them my condolences too. Róisín does the same, and we leave together.

Róisín suggests a quick coffee in the Samovar, but I say I just want to get home. She comes with me as far as the car, holding her umbrella over my head. Sharon and Trevor pass us as I open the driver's door, and Róisín says cheerfully, 'I must drop back Kieran's damp gauge thing – he left it at our house. Maybe we'll go for a meal in the Samovar on Friday evening?'

I see Sharon's shoulders twitch. I know she's heard – she couldn't not have – and I wish she hadn't. Not that I'm doing anything wrong, but it feels horrible. Almost like she thinks I'm choosing Róisín over her. Choosing an enemy over a friend.

It's not Róisín's fault, though.

'Sure, I'll text you,' I say.

'Great, see you Friday hopefully.' Róisín walks on, and I get into my car and close the door.

Before I can drive off, Oscar pops out of nowhere, rapping on the driver's window. I think for a moment of ignoring him, but how can I, so I roll it down with a sigh. 'Everything OK, Oscar?'

'It is not, Mags,' he says through chattering teeth. He has no umbrella, and the rain is running off his thin silver hair. 'What if it's me that's next? What about that? What are you going to do about it?' I don't know what he's on about, but he's clearly very agitated, even frightened, and the departing mourners look at him in puzzlement as they hurry past.

I think sadly of the shepherd's pie awaiting me at home, which 'poor Kieran', as Nora would say, has been obliged to heat up himself. 'Get into the car, Oscar.'

He rushes around the car to the passenger side, soaking himself further because the gutter has flooded again – the council assured me it would be solved, but clearly it hasn't – and scrambles in, shedding water everywhere.

'I told you that man was a murderer, Mags. I told you about what happened in England, and I said what were you going to do if they take a set against a person here? And now they've done it. They've murdered Desmond for preaching against their master, Satan...'

'He had a heart attack, Oscar,' I say, realising what he's on about. 'There was a postmortem. Nobody murdered anyone except possibly the manufacturers of Benson and Hedges – he must have smoked forty a day. But you'd also have to blame the pints and the curry and cheese chips from the chipper.'

'He was giving all that up, Mags. He'd found salvation...'

'But he hadn't given them up, Oscar.'

'Mags, you have to believe me! Of course they made it look like a heart attack, but didn't I tell you they were at a satanic ritual on the beach? They had a bonfire lit, and I don't like to tell you what else. They must have been summoning an evil spirit to murder poor Desmond, and it will be me next if they find out...' His voice trails off.

'Find out what, Oscar?' I ask. 'That you've been following them around, spying on them and reporting on them to the guards?'

'Ah, don't go telling on me, Mags,' he whimpers, and his expression reminds me of Rollo, showing the whites of his eyes and quivering in needless terror.

I sigh inwardly. Or not that inwardly, truth be told. Bring on the Russian spies – they'd be easier. 'Well, Oscar, I don't know about witchcraft, but I do know about stress, and we don't want you getting a heart attack either, do we? So why don't you just relax and back off on the spying, huh?'

'If you think that would be the safer thing to do, Mags,' he quavers.

And I say I think it definitely would, and hopefully that's an end to it, especially now that Desmond Dunne is out of the picture.

CHAPTER 15

$\mathcal{T}$atiana has a new boyfriend, Victor. We've had a chat, and he's a distinct improvement on 'leery Benny', her husband who used to own the pub, and who found Tatiana on RussianBrides.com. Tatiana arrived, married Benny and then dispatched him with indecent haste to England, where he's lived now for years without sight nor sound of him.

Victor is not her first post-Benny relationship. A while ago she went out with the builder who did the massive extension to her restaurant. Her new man is a chef, mad into fishing, if in fact it was he who was fishing that time I went down to the beach. Kieran jokes she probably only dates what she needs at any given time. Like us all, though, he'd only say such things behind her back; we're all a bit scared of Tatiana. The seafood offerings in the Samovar, though, have really improved since Victor's arrival.

Kieran and I are meeting Róisín and Joel for dinner, and we cross the dark polished floor of the Samovar towards the restaurant. The bar is truly beautiful now, all gleaming brass and dark wood, with seating all around it, and the bottles on the mirrored shelves behind the bar glitter and shine. Klara Shevchenko, one of the Ukrainian refugees, welcomes us at the door of the restaurant and leads us to our table, where Róisín and Joel are already seated. Tatiana comes straight over to see if we want anything to drink.

'Ah, Mags, Kieran, welcome.' She is smiling, I think, though her smile is only slightly less threatening than her grimace.

'Hi, Tatiana,' I say. 'This is Róisín and her husband, Joel. They own the Old Rectory now.'

'Nice to meet you. I'm pleased to welcome you both to our lovely town of Ballycarrick,' she says in her heavily accented English.

It is a long way from Vladivostok, but Tatiana feels she owns the town now; she's a local through and through. She loves the place, to be fair to her. Last summer she, Luigi, Teresa from the bakery and Sharon's nemesis Chloe Desmond, now Chloe Boylan, who'd bought the chipper when the owners decided to retire to Spain, got together under Tatiana's direction to hold a food festival in the main square. Everyone was sceptical. A Russian publican, a greasy chip shop, a bakery and a pizza place in rural Ireland were not exactly on Michelin's must-visit list, but they all outdid themselves, and it was a great day. Tatiana is a force for good, despite her less-than-friendly demeanour.

'Thank you, Tatiana.' Róisín's smile in return is warm and friendly. She's looking beautiful in a cobalt-blue dress and baby-blue leather jacket. 'I used to live here a long time ago, but then I moved to New York...' Her eyes drift to Kieran, but that's natural. After all, it was him she moved there with. 'But I'm so happy to be home. And Joel's a New Yorker through and through, but he's loving it here, aren't you, darling?'

'Of course.' Joel is as handsome as ever, with his jet-black hair and huge brown eyes. He's in Prada chinos and a wine cashmere jumper, very elegant. I still think he looks a bit tense and diminished, though; he's not quite the same smooth, cultured guy I met in New York. 'It takes a bit of getting used to, but –'

'Ballycarrick offer everything New York offer,' says Tatiana firmly. 'We have extensive range of wine and wonderful food.'

'I'm sure you have –'

She speaks across him again. 'So for specials this evening, we have steak, ribeye, very nice, with garlic butter and roast potatoes and salad. Also we have trout, organic from the sea caught by my boyfriend, who is chef, and that with chips and salad or potatoes and vegetables from the garden. We have polytunnels, so very long season. And finally we have a shepherd's pie. That is specials, but all the usuals too, fish and chips, lasagne, crab cakes, roast chicken...'

'I'll have the trout please, Tatiana,' I say.

Róisín chimes in. 'Make that two. It sounds lovely. I'm sure it's better than New York.'

'It is and also not too fat making,' Tatiana replies bluntly, looking at me. Róisín casts me a startled glance, but I just smile and study the wine menu. Tatiana's not brimful of tact, it must be said.

'Well, I was going to order the steak, but maybe I should have a salad instead?' Kieran jokes, patting his belly.

Tatiana shrugs and doesn't laugh along. 'It's bad for business for me to tell people don't eat, so I say eat everything, but...' She makes that face of 'on your own head be it'.

'Yerra, I'll have the steak, and I'll go on the rabbit food all week.' Kieran beams and hands her back the menu. Tatiana raises her eyebrows but doesn't snarl about her salad not being rabbit food, showing she really likes him.

'Yes. Medium rare.' A statement, not a question. Tatiana decides how you would like your steak.

Joel is last to order. 'Remind me again?' He counts the options off on his hand. 'Steak, trout, some kind of pie, fish and chips...'

Tatiana seems to have taken a bit of a set against him, looking at him askance, but that's not unusual – she's very intolerant. 'Is all on menu and specials on board. You want I come back?' Her tone is one of ill-concealed impatience.

'No...' He scans the page again, almost apologetically. 'I'll have the pie please.' He hands her back the menu with a weak smile.

'Drinks?' she demands.

'I'll have a pint of Guinness please,' Kieran says, 'and a glass of the New Zealand Sauvignon Blanc for Mags.'

'A bottle of Malbec please,' Róisín says.

'Róisín…' Joel gives her a sharp glance.

'What? We're not driving. Mags, how are the girls?'

Róisín chats about what wonderful girls Kate and Ellie are, and they like her too. Róisín invited Ellie in for one of her amazing cakes the other day when Ellie was out shopping in town.

'I know you were there already, but it's so nice, Mam,' Ellie told me. 'It must have cost a fortune. Like art on the walls and really fancy furniture and everything, and they have this gorgeous Pekingese dog. She's just come out of quarantine from America – she's called Princess. And you have to take your shoes off going in the house, and Róisín has these lovely slippers for everyone, all different sizes. I think we should do that.'

I'd laughed. 'Well, if we could get you to stop leaving your shoes all over the sitting room floor, it would be a start.'

'Ellie seems to be very artistic,' says Róisín. 'She was admiring my paintings when she called the other day.'

So I tell her about Ellie wanting to be an actress and then about how Kate is entering the provincial athletics competition – she's quite a good sprinter. A look of sadness crosses Róisín's face, and I know she longs for a child of her own. And so I ask her about Princess, and that's clearly the right thing to do. She gushes over the dog as if she's a child, how sweet she is and the clever thing she did the other day…

'Joel thinks I spoil her, though, don't you, Joel?' she says, with a sudden glance in his direction.

'Well, you do,' he says. And though an exchange like that between me and Kieran would just be a bit of harmless banter, between these two it feels barbed.

The drinks arrive. Róisín offers the Malbec to Joel, but he takes only half a glass. I'd forgotten he wasn't much of a drinker; New York professionals can be surprisingly abstemious. But Róisín seems to be back in Irish mode and fills her own glass right up. 'You'll have to help me with this.' She grins at me.

I smile back at her. 'Well, I might.' We've left my car at the station and will be getting Marius, one of the older Ukrainian men, to take us home; he has just got a Public Service Vehicle licence to drive a taxi and is doing great business. I can allow myself more than one glass, I think. The food arrives, and the trout is so fresh and cooked to perfection. As I eat, I tell Róisín how my father loved to fish off the beach, just like Victor. She remembers her own father doing the same, and we discuss her ageing parents and how her father has started to forget her name, which is so very sad.

Out of the corner of my eye, I can see Kieran is struggling to make conversation with Joel. He is trying to get something going about Joel's new job, but Joel, though polite, is slow to let any conversation flow. Then Kieran tells him a funny story about his own work, how one of the builders he was working with last week discovered that his racing pigeon was in the North of England instead of in Dublin where it should be and the panic that ensued... Joel doesn't seem to know what a racing pigeon is, so that falls flat.

I would help Kieran out, but Róisín is monopolising me. She tells me how she had a tarot card reading with Minnie and thought she was really impressive. 'I mean, I know I'm not supposed to believe in these sorts of things – I'm a hard-faced New York lawyer. And I didn't exactly go to her. I met her in the street, and she gave me a card for a free reading, told me I had an unusual aura, so I thought, just for fun...'

I'm interested. 'So what happened?'

'It was amazing, Mags. She knew so many things about my life. She told me I'd had my heart broken in New York...' She glances at Kieran. He's eating and doesn't notice, but Joel does and frowns slightly. 'And then she told me about Joel, described him down to a T, even the sort of job he did. And then it was amazing. She said Joel keeps looking for something he's lost, and then she said it was a phone, a black and white phone...'

I remember then, the phone with the Daffy Duck cover that Joel was holding in his hand when we came on him in the Old Rectory, in the small room full of storage boxes. I remember noticing how alarmed he looked as he put it quickly away.

'So I asked her if she could find it, because Joel was really worried about it for some reason, and she offered to come to the house, and Neil came with her...'

'And to cut a very, very long story short, they didn't find it because it's all BS,' Joel says, still with that strained smile.

'They didn't find it because it's not in the house – it's outside near a body of water,' corrects Róisín, a bit irritably. 'So obviously you took it out with you and dropped it somewhere, probably walking on Ballyloughane Strand or something like you do.'

'Well, Minnie's on safe ground there,' says Kieran, trying to lighten the mood, which is getting a bit tense between Joel and Róisín. 'There's nowhere in Ireland that isn't near a body of water. The place is surrounded by sea and full of lakes and rivers.'

Róisín turns the full beam of her smile on him, as if he's just said the cleverest thing ever. 'Oh, I know, that's so true. I wish Joel wouldn't just dismiss everything that's a bit different. He's so closed-minded.'

Joel cuts into his pie, looking sulky. 'Look, stop going on about me losing that bloody phone, Róisín,' he says as he piles meat and gravy onto his fork. 'I don't care about it, and I'd rather not talk about it again.'

'I was only trying to *help*, Joel...'

'Well, don't.'

I need the loo, so I push back my chair and stand up. My husband gives me that look. The one that says *Don't you dare abandon me.* But I have to go.

'I won't be a minute,' I say apologetically.

When I come out of the ladies, he is waiting outside; apparently he needed to go as well. It's obvious he's just hiding, though.

'God, he's a bit of a dose, isn't he?' he says. 'I'm trying, Mags, but it's torture. Will we just bail out early?'

'He does seem a bit on edge,' I agree, though secretly I think there's two of them in it; I have a feeling Róisín is winding Joel up, especially the way she's cooing over Kieran. I don't say it, though. I don't want to come over like I'm jealous, and I know Kieran hasn't noticed.

As we make our way back to the table, Róisín and Joel seem to be having words; she's speaking intently to him, and he's staring at his plate. When we sit back down, Róisín turns her attention to Kieran, and soon they're chatting happily about the uilleann pipes. Róisín seems more interested in piping than ever and is thinking of taking lessons with Gobnait as well.

While they chat, I ask Joel some general questions about how he's settling in, which he answers with vague platitudes about how friendly the Irish are. He's still on edge, though. I wonder if I should say about seeing him put the Daffy Duck phone on a shelf. I'm sure he's looked there, but maybe something got put on top of it. Still, he seems sick of the subject. And I don't like people to think I'm always watching them and what they're up to. People get wary when a guard asks them the most perfunctory of questions, as if they're being inter-rogated all of a sudden. I asked Chloe Desmond how she, Danny and the kids got on in Lanzarote last week, and she nearly bit the head off me, saying a person is entitled to go on a holiday without having to answer fifty questions about it. It's very wearing.

Joel keeps glancing irritably at Róisín, who is gushing over Kieran, and I find myself being twitchy as well. I'm not sure what she's playing at. I know she'd be horrified if I accused her of flirting. Maybe she doesn't even realise, or maybe she does and she's getting back at Joel for his affair. Which doesn't feel very respectful, especially after I've been so welcoming to her. Then I think maybe I'm being ridiculously oversensitive because I'm picking up on Joel's narky vibes. Kieran, of course, is totally oblivious, as he always is to female attention.

Tatiana arrives with the dessert menus, but Joel announces he's too full for dessert, then says it's too late for him to drink coffee or he won't sleep. Róisín grumbles about him being a killjoy and rolls her eyes, but to be honest, I'm quite happy for the evening to finish early.

It's a clear night and I'm wearing flat boots, so when I suggest to Kieran that we walk home the two miles, he agrees. 'Do me good after the steak.'

We walk to the station to get the hi-vis vests from the boot of my car. I've only had one glass of wine and feel fine to drive, but I don't. I don't drink at all if I'm driving.

We walk hand in hand home and admire the clear starlit night. Kieran talks about a set of rare pipes that were donated to Na Píobairí Uilleann, the governing body of the uilleann pipes, totally oblivious to Róisín's flirting, and I realise she can do as she pleases; he won't even notice.

CHAPTER 16

'Mam! Quick! Help! Help!' screams Kate.

I assume she's let Rollo escape again, but when I come running down the stairs, Rollo is in the kitchen, butting the small furry Frankie gently across the tiles with his nose.

Kate is trying to drag him back by his collar. 'Rollo, stop...' she wails, but he ignores her.

'Rollo! Stop!' I snap, and this time Rollo backs off with a pathetic whimper and slinks into his basket, looking balefully up at me.

Kate also backs away from the scene of the crime, tears in her eyes and her hands to her mouth. 'Is she all right, Mam? Check if she's all right.'

I bend over the tiny body, which is splayed on its back, paws in the air. The hamster is a goner, methinks. 'Well, it was obviously her time, Kit Kat. They don't live very long, you know.'

'Maaam...she can't be. Ellie's going to murder me when she gets home.'

'It's not your fault, Kit Kat.'

'It is! It is my fault!' she sobs.

It turns out she was wearing Frankie Velcro as a brooch again but forgot and bent over a sleeping Rollo to pat him. Rollo woke up with a startled bark, and the tiny hamster suddenly came unstuck and peeled off and dropped like a stone to the floor.

Just as well Ellie went off early with Kieran again. It's her transition year, so they're always going on school trips to look at interesting things, and the bus always has to leave at eight because Ballycarrick is so far from anything worth looking at apparently.

'Ellie's going to mangle me when she gets home...' Kate is terrified of Ellie; we all are a bit, to be honest. And Kate, for once, isn't exaggerating. Ellie will indeed mangle her, and me with her, if she thinks we're to blame for this.

I think quickly, looking at the clock. I need to be at work in thirteen minutes. 'Here's what we'll do.' I pick Frankie up using the dustpan, with a wink at my youngest daughter. 'If there's one thing I know about, it's disposing of bodies and hiding evidence. So into the cage Frankie goes. When we both left for school and work, she was running around her little wheel there, happy as Larry.'

'We're going to lie?' Kate sounds shocked.

'Well, in a word, yes. But if it makes you feel better, we don't know the truth. She might just be stunned. But either way we're for the high jump if your sister thinks we let Rollo get at her, so least said, soonest mended. He didn't chew her, did he?'

'No, I think he was as upset as I was...' Kate peers into the cage at the tiny furry thing and shakes her head. 'She looks perfect. Just as if she's asleep.'

I stifle a giggle. You wouldn't hear the sincerity and sadness in Caffrey's Funeral Parlour.

'Right, so she passed peacefully in her cage, minding her own business, and neither you nor me nor Rollo had hand, act nor part in her sad demise, right?'

'Please tell me you don't do this with human murders.' Kate looks at me with a combination of horror and awe.

'Oh, all the time, Kit Kat, all the time,' I say with a laugh as I lock the cage door, Frankie's body nestled in the fresh straw. 'Now come on. I'll drop you on the way.'

* * *

A FEW DAYS LATER, Sharon calls into the station, wanting me to go for a cuppa, but I'm up to my eyes.

'I can't, Shar,' I murmur as I come out to the public desk. 'It's Wednesday. I've got the council coming in ten minutes.'

'Fine.' She sounds hurt, and I feel guilty for avoiding her so much. It's not like I haven't thought about calling her often. After the restaurant thing with Joel and Róisín, she was the first person I wanted to call to let off some steam about the whole situation, but then I didn't feel able to because I knew she'd be all 'I told you so', which I'd find annoying and frankly hurtful, and I'd end up by telling her to stop behaving like a child.

'It *is* the middle of the working day,' I say in my defence, keeping my voice very low.

'Really, Mags?' She sighs loudly, for everyone to hear. 'Well, you're never available any time, so I thought I'd try you at work. But forget it, it's grand.'

She walks out.

Nicola casts me a glance. Zoë starts to say something, but Nicola nudges her to shut up, and I'm grateful for it. I'm not able for any claptrap today about holding space for hostility and all emotions are welcome and nourishing my inner child.

Five minutes later I'm scanning email from the council for the agenda – road closures next month due to necessary infrastructure maintenance. I told you my life is a roller coaster of excitement, didn't I? At least I can get some movement on the drains if I have someone here.

Nicola comes into my office and hands me a note. 'Sharon came back and left this for you,' she says.

I open it.

Since you're too busy to see me, I have to let you know this way. Kieran was seen yesterday with Róisín Duggan crying in his van. Elsie Flanagan saw them, Róisín getting a bottle of wine in the petrol station and then drinking it in his van, and everyone is talking and it's all over the town now. It's been a source of gossip since the tionól, to be honest, and then with him going in and out of the house. But now it's much, much worse. Thought you should know. S.

I twist the note into a ball and throw it in the bin. I'm so furious. At Sharon, at Kieran, at Róisín, at Elsie bloody Flanagan.

In a fit of temper, I tell Nicola to take the council meeting and march up the town into the boutique that was my mother's since before I was born and now is owned and run by my so-called best friend. She's serving a customer, so I wait, fuming. When the woman leaves and we're alone, I blurt it out.

'What the hell was that supposed to mean?'

She is red in the face under her perfect foundation. 'Exactly what it said, Mags. I've tried about six times to meet you in the last few weeks, and you're always too busy, so I thought as your friend, I should tell you what everyone is saying.'

'And you're taking no personal pleasure in it, are you?' I demand, and I'm surprised at how catty I sound, but I'm so hurt.

'Of course I'm not!' she explodes. 'Why would I?'

'I don't know, but if anyone should know about how it feels to have the whole place talking about your husband being a letch, it would be you, wouldn't it?'

'Mags!' she exclaims, and looks as if I'd slapped her. 'I was trying to do the right thing... I wanted to –'

'Jump to conclusions like everyone in this place is what you did. I'm so disappointed in you, Shar. I thought you knew him and my relationship with him better than that. Róisín is having a hard time. Her father has dementia, so she's upset, and Kieran and I are *both* supporting her.' I swallow. 'Of course I know he was with her, and Elsie Flanagan assuming the worst is one thing, but you...' My face is flushed, and I know this sounds like we're teenagers, not grown women, but honestly, I'm so upset.

'I didn't say he was doing anything. I said that Elsie was putting it around –'

'And instead of shutting it down and saying it was all rubbish, you decided to go writing me notes like a child,' I snap. 'Honestly, Sharon, you'd want to grow up.'

I storm out and feel my face burning. I trust Kieran, of course I do. I put up with the piping, and I suggested the roof myself, and I've been friendly to Róisín every step of the way. So why didn't he tell me about her being in his van? Why did I have to endure that humiliation, and now the knowledge that everyone is talking about us? And when did Sharon become one of the gossips?

This is no good. I refuse to fall out with my best friend since junior infants, since the age of four. I turn around and go back into the shop, where she is writing the sales prices on the clothes on the bargain rail.

'Look, Shar, can we talk and sort this out?'

She keeps writing on the labels, not looking at me.

I lean against the counter, opposite her, waiting. I try very hard not to let the indignation rise again. 'Ah, Shar, talk to me...'

Still, she says nothing. She can sulk; it is the one thing about her that drives me mad. She is the one in the wrong here, yet here I am with the olive branch.

'So, what? We're not talking, like a pair of teenagers now, is that it?' I demand, and hear the dismissal in my voice.

'You're the one coming over here and shouting the odds, Mags, not me,' she says, still not looking at me.

'I'm not shouting any odds, for God's sake. I'm trying to fix this, whatever it is.'

'An apology might be a good place to start,' she says archly, and I feel my blood boil.

'I might apologise to you?' I can hardly believe this.

'Well, you were the one that came barging into my shop, calling me childish and a gossip and all the rest when all I was doing is looking out for you.'

'By writing a stupid note? What are you, eleven?' I explode now. 'Forget it, Sharon. I thought we could be grownups about this, but clearly you can't. So just forget it.'

I don't give her a minute to reply, and I stalk back out of the shop.

* * *

I ASK HIM THAT EVENING, after dinner, while the girls are watching TV and we are having a cup of tea in the kitchen. I don't want to tell him about Sharon; I'm still too hurt to think about it. And I'm even undecided whether to say anything about Róisín crying and drinking wine in his van, but I decide it is stupid not to.

'Have you seen Róisín lately?' I ask, faux casual.

He holds my eyes for a second longer than I expect and then turns his head away. 'I have actually.'

'And?' I keep on looking at him, even though he's not looking at me. 'Are you going to tell me?'

'She's signed up for lessons with Gobnait.'

Oh, has she. I know she was talking about it in the restaurant, but still… 'And you gave her a lift there and back in your van?' I feel a bit weird. We don't check up on each other like this, but something about the way he's reacting makes me want to go deeper.

'Not on the way there. I didn't even know she was coming. But after the lesson, she was sitting in her car waiting for me, and I realised she was a bit drunk. It was odd – she was slurring, and there was an empty bottle of wine in the driver's door. So I said to her to leave the car and I'd bring her home and run her out again in the morning, early, because she didn't want Joel to know she'd had to leave the car. It was awkward and embarrassing. She was a bit of a mess, to be honest with you, but she said her parents are driving her nuts and she's having a hard time with Joel, and she insisted on getting another bottle in the garage because they're open until eleven.'

Phillip O'Flaherty in the petrol station shouldn't be selling wine after ten o'clock at night – he's in breach of the liquor licencing laws – but I choose to ignore this piece of information. I'm too busy staying calm.

'Why didn't you tell me all this?' I ask, and my hand shakes as I pour myself another cup of tea.

A beat. Then another. 'I should have.' He sounds odd. I can't put my finger on it.

'Am I missing something here?' I rake his face. We never lie to each other, but he is definitely shifty now. There's something big he's not telling me.

'No...of course you aren't. I... Look, I do still feel sort of bad how I broke it off with her years ago, and then the crying...and she'd had a good few drinks, I'd say. God, Mags, I don't know how to say this. You're going to go mental...' He looks desperate. What has happened between him and Róisín?

'OK,' I say, 'first things first. I trust you completely, so don't be worrying I think there's something going on. I don't and I never did.'

'I know, but...' He still looks panicky.

'Kieran,' I say, 'just tell me what you did.' I'm not sure I want to know, though.

He takes a huge breath. 'I kind of told her we'd mind the dog if she and Joel split up again,' he blurts out.

'*What?*' I stare at him, dazed.

'If she and Joel split, and it's looking likely, she'll move into her parents' place, but her mother is allergic to dogs, so she can't bring the dog with her. She was wailing about it, and the dog is like a child to her, so I kind of said we'd mind her, because she couldn't bear to abandon her to Joel, who doesn't really care about her and...' His voice trails off guiltily.

'Ah, Kieran, seriously?' I don't know whether to laugh or cry. 'No. I'm sorry but no. I don't want any animals, as you well know, but so far now we have Knickers, Rollo and Meatloaf, and now you're telling me we're to have another dog?'

Yes, you heard that right. We now have a guinea pig called Meatloaf.

Kate was able to pull off the lie, so the story of Frankie Velcro's tragic passing was swallowed by Ellie, thanks be to God, and a funeral was duly held, with tea and sandwiches of course, and Frankie laid out in a matchbox. The twins came, and Goosey and Carrot, and to ease Ellie's pain, Goosey gave her a fat guinea pig with long silky hair called Meatloaf, who stinks to high heaven. He looks depressingly robust, so he's here for the duration, I'd say.

I'm tempted to encourage Rollo to bark at him; we got away with it once. But only a fool would try the same stunt twice. The prisons of the world are full of people who thought they were onto a good thing, so Meatloaf will have to survive. Unfortunately. What was it Oscar Wilde said? 'To lose one parent...may be regarded as a misfortune; to lose both looks like carelessness.' Something like that, but with members of the rat family.

'Ah, she'll be company for Rollo...' Kieran says hopefully.

'Rollo doesn't need company, he needs counselling, or strong tran-quillisers, or a shovel to the back of the head. He has Dympna the Postwoman convinced I'm battering him every day, the way he sidles along the wall, giving me that eye like he's scared witless of me. He has her eating out of his paw.'

'He loves you, I know he does...' Kieran knows no such thing.

'He hates me, and I'm not his biggest fan either, so let's cut that crap for starters. And that dog of Róisín's is like some kind of pedi-gree prize-winning thing, isn't she? We'll probably poison her or mess up her perfect fur or something. Please, Kieran, you can drive around the countryside with your ex sobbing in your arms if you want, but please, for the love of all that's holy, do not land another four-legged creature on me.'

He laughs now. He's always found me hilarious. 'You are a strange woman, Mags Munroe,' he says, relieved I'm only pleading and not losing the plot entirely. 'Fabulous, but very strange.'

Because he has relaxed, I do too. I've been so tense since Sharon and her note. I open my mouth to tell Kieran about it, but the words stick in my throat. I guess I'm even more upset than I'm willing to admit. Honestly, though, what kind of a woman behaves so imma-turely? I thought I knew Sharon, I thought I could trust her, but clearly I got it all wrong. I look out the window into the black night. It's raining.

'So,' Kieran says eventually, 'are you going to tell me, or am I going to have to guess?'

'What?' I ask.

'Whatever it is that's still upsetting you about this,' he says gently.

I sigh, and to my surprise, tears prick my eyes. I'm angry, not sad, but once I start, the tears won't stop. He takes my hand.

'Ah, Mags, what is it? Tell me.'

Then it all comes out, Elsie Flanagan, the whole place talking right back to when Róisín came to the tionól, Sharon and the note...

He lets me finish the tale and then exhales. 'This is my fault. I should never have gone near her. I should have known the jungle drums would put two and two together to make nine.'

'No, it's Sharon's fault. She said everyone was talking. And I know it's stupid and I shouldn't care, and I don't, not really, but I'm so hurt that Sharon thinks it's true. She's supposed to be my best friend, and she loves you, so that she'd believe that...'

'But she didn't say she believed it, did she?' he asks, not unreasonably. 'She just wanted to put you wise to the gossip. She didn't say that she thought I was having an affair, did she?'

'No, but...' I begin, while wiping my eyes on my sleeve.

'No,' he says quietly. 'So fair's fair.'

'Yeah, but it's a bit primary school, isn't it? Like could she not have just said it to me, like a normal adult?'

'She said she tried but you were too busy to meet her, though, isn't that what she said?'

I can't do this. Now it feels like he's on her side. 'Yeah. Look, I'm tired. Let's just go to bed.'

As I am brushing my teeth, he comes up behind me. 'I'm so sorry about the gossip. I didn't know Elsie Flanagan saw Róisín crying in the van. But you know I would never look at another woman, don't you?'

I meet his eyes in the mirror as I rinse the toothbrush under the tap. 'I do, love, but we will have to come up with a strategy. Ballycarrick is a small place, and I can do without the lips flapping.'

'The truth is the best strategy,' he says, pulling off his t-shirt. He's handsome, my husband. He doesn't know it, but he is. No wonder everyone thinks the polished Róisín has him wrapped around her finger. 'I'll tell Róisín straight that there's been gossip and we have to put a stop to it.'

'Really?' I say, turning and wrapping my arms around his waist.

'Yep,' he says, holding me close. 'I'll tell her that it's not fair on you, and that I love you, and that we don't need to be giving anyone reasons to be gossiping. She's not thick. She knows what this place is like. There's a different set of piping lessons starting up on Thursdays, and I'll ask her to go to that one instead of Tuesdays.'

'Your battle-axe missus keeping an eagle eye on you, is it?' I smile.

'No, not that, but I won't have my beautiful wife upset. Not for Róisín Duggan or anyone else. I won't go over there again. The roof is done now, and I'll send one of the lads if needs be. I won't see her in person at all. I'll just ring her and say that I'm not the right person for her to be confiding in, that it isn't fair on you or the girls, and though there is nothing in it, I don't want you to be the subject of gossip, and I'll ask her not to contact me.'

I don't know how to feel about that. 'I don't want to stop you seeing her...'

'You're not. You're the most understanding, kind person I know, but it's not right.' He kisses me then, and I relax against the bulk of him. Whatever else feels wrong, Kieran is my home.

'What about the girls?' I wonder. 'Ellie likes her too. They might think it strange if you stop seeing her altogether.'

'If they raise it, we'll sit both of them down, tell them the truth and explain how I put you in an awkward position, and that's just the way it is.'

'OK... And the dog?' I ask tentatively.

'Is not our dog.' He smiles down at me.

'Well, at least that,' I say, and give him a watery grin.

CHAPTER 17

'Well? What do you think?' Kieran asks me as I gaze out of the window of the beautiful hotel across verdant lawns, smooth as a billiard table, and though the flowers and hedges are bare, being winter, the heathers are in bloom and the lights they've put up for Christmas make the place look beautiful.

'I can't believe it,' I say, turning and smiling at him. 'And I had no idea whatsoever.'

'I know.' He grins, wrapping his arms around my waist. 'Orla said she'd be happy to have the girls, and I rang Nicola and she made sure you were off. You said when we came here to meet Oilibhéar that time that you'd love to stay here, so here we are.' He kisses my lips gently. 'God knows, Mags, it's been a lot lately – you deserve a treat.'

I look at the bag on the huge four-poster bed in the luxurious turret bedroom. 'Please tell me someone other than you packed for me?' I ask with a worried laugh. Once, years ago, a friend of ours died and he packed me an outfit for the funeral that consisted of jogging bottoms, a knitted cardigan and no shoes.

He looks sheepish and says nothing.

'Oh, dear God.' I go to the bag. My husband hasn't an iota of a clue about clothes. He is not allowed to shop alone, and any unsupervised fashion choices generally have me and the girls screaming in horror or hilarity or both. With my heart in my mouth, I unzip and raise the lid…and let out a sigh of relief. He has packed a dress I rarely wear. Sharon bought it for me for my birthday, but it's more her than me honestly. It's rust-coloured with a bishop's collar and ruched at the waist, so to give it its due, it hides a multitude of sins, but the back is cutaway, and though it has an inbuilt bra thing, I've never quite trusted it. He's also packed the pair of gold high slingbacks she made me buy to go with the dress. They are made of recycled razor blades that have the wearer begging for mercy within nanoseconds of wedging their feet into them, but I suppose they are just to go downstairs.

'Great. Well done. The clothes are perfect.' I walk over and kiss him. 'I really appreciate this. A weekend all to ourselves. I can't believe it.'

'Well, dinner is booked for seven and it's only five now so…' he murmurs into my hair, and I feel his hands on my back. I've been so uptight recently, work, Sharon, the Róisín situation, I've not really been in the mood, but now that I'm here and there are no distractions, I find myself responding to him.

Afterwards, as we lie on the huge bed with far more pillows, cushions, bolsters and covers than any person could ever want or need, I feel myself fully relax for the first time in what seems like ages. Kieran gets up and closes the heavy curtains and makes me a cup of coffee in the fancy machine supplied. I pull his shirt on and sit up in bed with him beside me.

'So, my lovely wife, are you doing OK?' he asks gently.

I let it all out: that the McGoverns seem to no longer trust me – I saw Jerome and Dora in the street yesterday, and they crossed the road pretending not to see me; the sadness over the fight with Sharon; how there's a new project on at work, and I'm going to have to put up with Duckie being involved; Kieran's mother and her frostiness over the horrible dresses… It just goes on and on.

He lets me talk and never interrupts.

When I've finished, I collapse back against the pillows, and he puts his arm around me.

'Well, let's go through this. The McGoverns are just a bit nose out of joint. Well, I doubt the rest of them care, but Jerome is probably getting it in the neck from Dora – she was always much more wary of you than he was, and her sister is losing money because this pair in the Lodge seem to be having some degree of success, so that's really nothing to do with you. It's a fortune teller turf war, and you're just caught in the crossfire, that's all.' He laughs, and I remember how much I love that sound.

'As to the stuff with Sharon –' he continues.

'I honestly don't know what's got into her,' I interrupt miserably. 'I mean, I could even overlook the childish note, and as you say, she didn't say she thought you were messing around with Róisín but that other people were saying you were. But I went back into the shop to try and talk things out, and she just wouldn't. We've never had a row like this, I hate it...'

He squeezes my shoulder. 'Shar loves you, Mags, she always has and always will. It's going to be grand, just give it some time.'

'I hope you're right,' I say, not sharing his confidence.

'Look, I wasn't going to tell you this,' he confesses, looking sheepish again, 'but with your mam away, I texted Sharon, and she came over and packed for you. I knew I'd make a dog's dinner of it, and if I let Ellie do it, you'd be dressed like a pole dancer.'

I stare at him, taken aback. So that explains the dress and the shoes. 'Seriously? She agreed to do that?'

'I hope you don't mind...'

He looks really anxious, and I'm not sure what I think about this, him asking her when he knows I'm still mad at her, but to be fair, Sharon hasn't taken advantage by packing anything she knows no longer fits me, so I suppose that's kind of an olive branch from her. And I'm touched that Kieran cares and wants to fix the rift between us.

'No, I don't mind. It's a bit weird, but I don't mind.' I'm not going to let anything spoil this weekend. I relax and sip my coffee; it's delicious.

'On the subject of the eejit Duckie, I know you can't tell me police business, but I'm sure you're the one the top brass trusts, not that clown. And as for my mother, Mags, you know what she's like. Don't let her get under your skin, just ignore her…'

'Like you do, is it?' I ask, stung. Easy for him to say; he's not the one she attacks. She adores him and thinks I'm not good enough; that has always been the crux of the problem.

'Well, yeah.' He shrugs. 'Look, Mags, she's a basket case, always was, always will be. She's got some gripe against you, but it was to you she came when she thought her life was about to implode over Ollie, right?' He lifts my chin and looks me in the eyes. 'So you are the one with the power here, not her, so don't let her wind you up. I'll back you completely every single time, and she knows that, so she's only playing mind games. Don't give it another thought.' He kisses me then, and everything seems better.

'So…dinner?' I say with a smile.

'You're a woman of insatiable appetites, Mrs Munroe.' He grins and kisses my neck.

'Well, I'm starving, if that's what you mean.' I slap him playfully and get up. 'Why don't you go down and have a pint and I'll join you?'

Kieran laughs. 'One day you have to let me see the ritual.'

'I don't know what you're on about,' I retort, but of course I do. After all these years of marriage, I have never let him see me wriggle into shapewear, or lie on a bed to get my zip up. How do those women do it? You know, the ones that one hairpin is pulled and their shiny locks tumble beautifully, or they slide out of the satin dress to reveal a tiny lace thong, no control panels, and a bra made out of wispy lace with no steel wires. Even before I had kids, that was never an option, and since then…well, the 'natural look' is created using all manner of strong fabric and elastic and Lycra and wire.

My husband pulls on his jeans and a clean white shirt, and he looks so handsome. Effortlessly so. I shoo him out before the pulling and dragging begins. I watched a programme once about deep-sea fishermen, hauling nets aboard, and it reminded me of nothing so much as me trying to get into those contraptions that hold your bits and limit wobbling. Men wouldn't dream of it.

I pray to God Sharon has put in some industrial underwear, because that dress takes no prisoners, and I find she has. Another olive branch, which I grudgingly accept.

Bodysuit wriggled into, push-up bra doing Trojan work against all the odds, I finally pull the dress on and tie it with tiny fiddly buttons at the neck. It takes me about ten minutes – I'm all fingers and thumbs – but eventually I manage it. Who designs these things? I squeeze my feet, accustomed to the very practical but as unsexy as it's possible to be Garda shoes, into the implements of podiatric torture.

I look in the mirror and have to concede it's all not too bad, especially if I don't breathe out. I don't look like a sausage roll in the dress, I don't think, and I wonder if Delia was in on this, because she insisted that I get my hair blow-dried by Gerry during my lunch break, who had, amazingly, a rare twenty minutes. You can't ever get an appointment, but I just breezed in on the off-chance and he fit me in.

I'm growing my hair a bit longer. I used to have it in a bob, but one day Ellie told me I reminded her of Dora the Explorer, so that put paid to that style. It's shoulder-length now, with a side parting. I wear it in a ponytail for work mostly, but it looks nice tonight, dyed of course. I'm a silver fox naturally. Works for George Clooney but not for me, I'm afraid, so Gerry does his stuff with a bottle of dye every few weeks.

I don't wear make-up at all usually, but Sharon has put some in as well, so I do a light foundation and a bit of mascara and blush. I don't wear lipstick ever. I feel vaguely ridiculous in make-up, like I'm in a play or something, and lipstick makes me look a bit mental, I always think. Sharon's always trying to plaster me in something – she's a divil for the stuff – but I resist.

Sharon. I miss her so much. I pick up my phone to text her thanks for packing my bag, but I just don't know what to say that wouldn't be a bit cringy. And I imagine her reading it, maybe mockingly aloud to Trevor, and I stop myself.

CHAPTER 18

*D*inner is amazing, really delicious. We have a sharing board to start with, smoked mackerel pate, smoked salmon, crab claws in garlic butter and mussels in white wine and cream. For the main course, I have monkfish and mango salsa cooked to perfection, with sauteed broccolini and gratin potatoes, and Kieran has prawn and chorizo kebabs. We refuse desserts as we can't squeeze in another bite, but then the owner, the gorgeous man I remember from the last visit, approaches the table.

'Kieran and Mags, isn't it?' He smiles, and I wonder if anyone could resist this man. In his hand is an ice bucket with a bottle of Moët chilling inside. His wife is in the restaurant as well, chatting with a big group. She is very beautiful too, but not in the way you'd expect. If you saw this man, Conor O'Shea is his name, you'd imagine him with some kind of Eva Longoria type or Claudia Schiffer, but his wife is tiny and styles her blond hair in a pixie cut. She is wearing a hippie-looking dress, beautiful burgundy velvet that goes almost to her ankles, and on her feet, she has Doc Martens boots. Her ears are pierced several times, as is her nose; a tiny diamond sparkles there. He, on the other hand, looks so polished, with his definitely hand-made suit, leather shoes and expertly cut hair. He could be a politician or an actor or something, and she looks like she might have walked out of Woodstock this morning.

'That's right. Nice to meet you again, Conor.' Kieran stands and shakes his hand.

'And you.' Conor smiles warmly, and his blue eyes twinkle in his handsome face; I hear the lilt of Cork in his accent. 'Ollie said you were coming and sent this. I should have got here before you started eating, apologies, but our daughter Lily needed to be collected from a friend's house, so I had to duck out.'

'Oh, we've a pair ourselves, and myself and Mags would be worth a fortune if they were paying mileage.' Kieran chuckles as Conor expertly pops the champagne.

'You know the story of my life so. My twins are just driving, and that's terrifying too, so you can't win, can you? Would you like to have this in the library?' he offers. 'The fire is lit, and I think you'll have it to yourselves, if you've finished eating?'

'That sounds lovely,' I say and stand, sucking in the belly that is definitely protruding now after the huge meal, defying even the most diligent of constricting undergarments.

'Great, follow me so.' He walks out and we follow him. Imagine owning this place, I think as I look around. The reception is a circular stone area, with a large desk of some kind of polished wood, and behind it is a door, which is Conor's office presumably. The whole place is spectacular and so beautiful but has a slight touch of shabbiness as well. The rugs are antique for sure, and the books on the shelves look ancient. The stairs are worn down in the centre from thousands of feet over hundreds of years, and wax clings to the giant wrought-iron candleholders either side of the main door.

The library was where we first met Ollie and Muireann last year, and I remember the room well. It is, like our hotel bedroom, in the base of a turret, octagonal in shape, and the floor-to-ceiling bookshelves are full. A huge fireplace is set into one wall, and a full ring of an old tree burns merrily in it. Dotted all around are various chairs, leather, upholstered, polished wood, as well as side tables and coffee tables. The whole effect is charming.

'A bit less tense than the last time, I suppose?' Conor says, pouring champagne into two flutes and setting the bucket down on a three-legged barley twist table.

'That's for sure. Thanks,' Kieran says, accepting the glass and handing me the other.

'I'm so delighted it all worked out. I had lunch with Ollie in Dublin a few weeks ago, and he was telling me all about the family and how he felt instantly at home.'

'It's the strangest thing. He's absolutely one of the family, and it was kind of effortless in the end – he just fits in,' Kieran agrees.

'Your mother must be delighted?'

'Well' – my husband gives a rueful sigh – 'my mother isn't the world's easiest woman, and it took a while to bring her round to the idea of meeting Ollie. Mags was wonderful for persuading her. But now that he's found, she's very happy to have him in her life.'

Conor nods, his hands in his pockets. 'It's good to bring family together. I didn't see my own father for decades. He left my mam when me and my brother were only small lads. My brother is dead now, and so is Mam, and I had no interest in meeting my father when he resurfaced a few years ago. But Ana kind of got around me – she's the only one that can. I'm desperate stubborn when I get an idea in my head, but she kind of forced a reconciliation. So we only really know each other in the last few years, and we get on fine. God knows he can be a cantankerous auld goat sometimes, but Ana has the patience of a saint, and he'll do anything for her. He even gave me the money to get this place up and running again after the fire.'

'A fire? That's awful. What happened?' I haven't heard this story.

He shrugs. 'A disgruntled ex of my former business partner torched the place out of spite. It was pretty catastrophic, but it could have been so much worse.'

I'm surprised how relaxed he seems about it all. 'Worse in what way?'

'Well, my boys, Joe and Artie, they were only small, they were up on the third floor, and by the time the fire was noticed, it would have been too late to save them if someone wasn't looking out for us that night... And is still looking out for us, I think.' His smile is enigmatic.

'Who was it?' I'm intrigued, sensing a mystery.

Conor thinks for a moment, as if debating saying anything. Then he decides to tell us. 'Years ago, I came into a bit of money unexpectedly. I was just a tour bus driver, but I got a legacy in a will, and along with a friend of mine, an American woman, we bought this place – it had fallen into dereliction – and turned it into a hotel. There was a room upstairs, an old nursery, with all sorts of old toys up there, and my boys loved playing there. They used to talk about another little boy who lived in the turret, who owned the toys, but we just put that down to imagination.'

He shakes his head, remembering. Kieran and I are hanging on his every word. 'Well, that night, the fella that torched the place hit me a clout with something very hard across the back of the head and knocked me out cold. Everyone else was in a marquee we had set up in the garden. There was a big launch party going on, music and everything, so nobody knew what was happening, nobody had noticed the fire. But someone woke me up, a little boy in Edwardian clothes, and told me to go and get my boys, that they were in the nursery. I managed to do it, and they're alive today because of it.'

'And who was the boy, and why was he dressed that way?' Kieran asks, fascinated.

Conor shrugs. 'After the fire, I did some digging into the history of the place. This castle was once the home of the King family, very well-to-do, as you can imagine, but in the twenties, during the War of Independence, the place was burnt by rebels, seeing it as a symbol of British imperialism. The family got out, but one little boy, Grenville King, didn't. He died in his nursery. Over the years people said the place was haunted, and I took all that with a pinch of salt, but we could never heat that room, no matter what we did. And that night... look, I don't know, but a little lad in old-fashioned clothes woke me up and told me to go and get Joe and Artie – they were his friends, you see – and I can't think of any other explanation.'

A silence falls over all three of us then. Conor is not the kind of man to make something like that up; I just instinctively know he isn't.

'That's an amazing story. Thanks for telling us,' I say eventually.

He nods. 'We keep that room empty – well, not empty, the old toys are still there, and it's still hard to heat, honestly, but nothing strange like that has happened since, so...' He shrugs again. 'Who really knows? Was it Grenville who came to get me? Was I concussed? Did I imagine what I saw? I don't know, but I do know that if I hadn't gone in, Ana and I would have lost our boys. So whoever it was, or whatever it was, will always have our gratitude.'

I find myself thinking about the witch and warlock, and Jerome's sister-in-law, and all the mysteries I tend to dismiss as nonsense in my practical way.

'And do you believe his ghost haunts the castle?' Kieran asks, no trace of mockery in his tone. He is very open-minded on the subject of the supernatural. Surprising for such a practical man.

'Well, I don't give it much space in my head, to be honest with you, but I can't explain that stuff, and so I just accept it and get on with my life.'

'"There are more things in heaven and earth, Horatio, than are dreamt of in your philosophy,"' I murmur.

'*Hamlet*, isn't it?' Conor asks, and looks pleased when I nod. 'Now I'll be murdered if I don't get back to work, so enjoy the rest of your evening.'

'We will. Thanks, Conor,' I say as he leaves.

Kieran and I chat about the story for a while, both coming to the same conclusion as William Shakespeare. We have no idea, but there would appear to be more to this earth than anyone understands.

As I sit on a lovely pink-silk wingback and Kieran relaxes opposite me in a leather chesterfield armchair, the fire crackling between us, I debate bringing up the Róisín thing and asking did he speak to her yet. We're so happy here in this beautiful place, the champagne giving everything a rosy glow, that I'm reluctant to break the spell.

Before I can make up my mind, he says, 'I've told Róisín I can't be her shoulder to cry on any more. Her mother rang me afterwards.

Róisín is very upset I've ended our friendship, she says, but I told her the same thing I told Róisín, that I'm not the one to help her. She's drinking an awful lot, I think, and maybe she should get help for that, but that's up to her.'

I find myself exhaling in relief. 'So now what?' I ask.

'Now, nothing.' He reaches over and takes my hand. 'Mags, you and the girls are my priority, nobody else. I made my choice years ago, and it was the best decision I ever made. You're the greatest thing to ever happen to me, and I wouldn't risk our marriage for anyone or anything.' He swallows. 'Look, I booked this to say sorry, really, for putting you in that position. I know you trust me and you believe me when I tell you there is nothing to worry about, but it's very hard for anyone, let alone the local sergeant, to have the whole place whispering behind their hands when you go by, and for that I'm so, so sorry.'

He looks so crestfallen, so genuinely contrite, that my heart goes out to him. 'This isn't your fault, love. You did what anyone would do when a friend is in trouble. She reached out to you, and you tried to support her. You weren't to know it was going to become the story of the week. But look, let's put it behind us. They'll find some other scandal next week for sure.'

He relaxes back against the chair, placing the empty glass on the side table, and just stares at me.

'What?' I ask.

'I'm a very lucky man,' he replies simply.

CHAPTER 19

I've just finished up all of the court depositions for the following week, and I need a break.

I've the weekly debrief with the team at 2 p.m. at the shift change, and Duckie has announced he's arriving to 'update me' at four. He's part of Operation Greengage now, and he texted me earlier, summoning me to a meeting in Dublin next Tuesday about increased surveillance in the Galway Bay area. I haven't texted him back yet. I already know about the Dublin meeting; Ronan rang me. Operation Greengage is a multifaceted investigation, it would seem, with each component part only vaguely aware of the other parts, at least up to now. But because there has been an increase in Russian activity in our territorial waters, everyone is being brought together to report back and share information. Nothing particularly unusual or interesting has happened in the Ballycarrick area, though – well, not Russian-related anyway, not as far as I can see – so I'll have nothing to say.

I wonder if Duckie knows I was at that meeting with Ronan and John Greene, and so his coming down here to 'update' me is just him flexing his muscles, poking his nose in and lording it over me as usual. I will be collegial and professional and hope it's over quickly.

I leave through the public office, where Zoë manages to say, 'Morning, Sarge,' instead of 'Slay, Queen,' which is progress.

Ellie showed me last week a post Zoë put on Instagram, with a picture of me in uniform, and the caption 'My boss, my mentor, my guru. She makes me a better person. Forever grateful.'

Ellie thought it was sweet. I'm inclined towards unhinged, but she means well. I pretend I never saw it, though several people mentioned it to me.

As I walk up Main Street to the café, Nicola comes the other way in the squad car, and I wave to her to stop and hop into the passenger seat. 'So how did it go with Caelan?' I ask.

She shakes her head, depressed. Young Caelan Cronin is depressing all of us. I really thought after Mike Cantillon got sent back to prison, he would settle down again, but he is still knocking around with the Carmodys and was seen at the site of a break-in on Saturday night. I had to phone Liam and tell him. The poor man is at the end of his rope with that boy. Nicola has just been to question him at his house.

'He denied everything, Sarge, but I told him there's CCTV footage, so he's snookered, and then he just acted like he didn't care and wouldn't say anything. So I said I would come back later with another officer to bring him into the station to make a formal statement, and I explained that as he's a minor, he has to have an adult with him when he's being questioned and we can provide him with a solicitor.'

'How did that go?'

She checks her notes. 'His father said he'd act as the presiding adult, but Caelan's exact words to him and me were "Get Angela. You can piss off."'

Angela Casey is the social worker who's been working with the family since Caelan's mother got knocked down by a drunken Mike Cantillon. It seems it isn't only Trish's life that's been destroyed, but also that of her beautiful, once sweet-natured son.

Nicola looks so fed up, I suggest she take the car back to the station and join me for lunch in Teresa's, which she agrees to with enthusiasm.

In the café, Nora is sitting in the far corner with Orla, Kieran's sister, and I wave at them but keep well away, taking the table in the window. I should probably go over and thank Orla again for minding the girls while we were at Castle Dysert, but they're almost finished and I know Orla will stop at my table on the way out. I don't know about Nora. She is still in a huff over the dresses, so we've not had the Sunday lunch summons for three weeks. It's nearly worth falling out with her to get off the hook.

I sit looking out of the window while I wait for Nicola to join me.

Minnie passes by on the street outside just as Tatiana comes marching in the other direction, and they get into a brief stand-off. Tatiana is not very good at giving way, and it seems neither is Minnie; they both wait for the other to step aside so they can proceed without having to navigate the flooded half of the pavement. The council still hasn't sent anyone to fix our drains.

The window over my head is slightly open – it's a warmish day for November – and they're near enough for me to hear what happens next.

'Your aura is very dark, Tatiana,' says Minnie. 'Perhaps you should come to see Neil for a good clearing.'

I wait for Tatiana to say something hilariously brutal and scathing in return, but instead a strange expression passes over her face. She says nothing, just looks at Minnie closely.

Ballycarrick's white witch meets her gaze, then takes a step back and lowers her head to fumble in her bag. 'Never mind the aura cleanse. Maybe black is its natural colour. Just bring this, and I will give you a free reading.' She hands Tatiana a card. 'I can see there is a spirit that wishes to talk to you. Your mother perhaps.'

Tatiana takes the card, scans it and hands it back. 'No. You born. You die. End. I have no time for this. Too busy living.'

'Well, if you change your mind...' Minnie refuses the card.

'Not possible.'

'Very well.' Flushed with annoyance but with nothing further to say, the white witch eases her way around Tatiana, the hem of her flowing black skirt getting wet in the flood.

A moment later Tatiana stalks in through the door of the café.

'Is everything OK, Tatiana?' I ask as she passes my table.

'All OK.' But then she sees who's asking and stops. 'That woman is… I don't know.' She stares out of the window at the diminutive figure of Minnie Melodie disappearing down the street.

'What don't you know?' I ask. Tatiana gives very little away about herself, but it's not like her to be anything but totally forthright in her views on other people.

'Mm…' Tatiana looks uncharacteristically unsure of herself, and I can't decipher what's going on in her head; she is hard to read. But you don't spend thirty years as a police officer and not get a feel for when people are hiding something.

'Is something wrong?'

'Nothing, I was just…' Then she shrugs. 'Nothing. Here, you have.' She hands me the card Minnie gave her. The print is very small, so I get out my reading glasses; I'm starting to struggle with fine print, so I bought a pair from Julie Dullea in the chemist's the other day. The card is covered in stars and moons and says *I can tell someone wishes to speak to you. Free reading. Valid until March.*

'You need new lenses for eyes,' Tatiana tells me.

'I know they're not very stylish' – I smile – 'but they work fine.' Tatiana's frames are always very *a la mode*; she is very particular about her appearance.

'Lenses for *eyes*,' she says, very distinctly, raising her voice to get the message through my thick skull. 'Operation. Very expensive but worth it to stay young and beautiful. I have operation next week. No more glasses. Ten years off age.'

'Oh, I see…' Mam had that operation last year in Galway hospital, because she had a cataract, and she's been reading the newspaper without glasses since. 'Where are you having it?'

I'm not really expecting an answer because, as I say, she's not very forthcoming about her movements, ever. Maybe it's being brought up as a child under the Soviet regime, or maybe it's just her. In lots of ways, Tatiana reminds me of Ireland long ago, where people kept secrets routinely for fear of poking the bear of moral outrage. Kieran always jokes that even if you ask her something about the menu in the Samovar, she exudes a 'why do you want to know' vibe.

But to my surprise, she tells me. 'Optizone clinic, Dublin, Tuesday.'

'That's great. How are you getting there?' I know from when Mam had it done that everything can be blurry for a while after, and I hope Tatiana's got someone to drive her, though I don't want to ask her straight out. I'm a guard, so most people panic if I ask them anything about driving, even if they've never had so much as a parking ticket.

'I get train.'

That also bothers me, the idea of Tatiana making her way back to the train station half blind. She's so bad at giving way to anyone, she'll probably walk in front of a bus. 'Well, I'm going up on Tuesday. I could take you if you like?' I offer. 'I need to be at a meeting at ten, so leaving about seven, and I'd imagine it should be over around three or four if that's any good to you?'

She looks surprised and maybe a tiny bit relieved. 'You do that?'

'No bother at all. I'll collect you.'

'Mags, you are good friend.' She actually smiles this time. 'Appointment at three, so I will have many hours to get Victor's birthday present. I think a fishing jacket.'

Nicola comes in as Tatiana leaves, and we organise ourselves, ham salad sandwiches and coffees, and try to talk about anything but poor Caelan Cronin. She asks me how the uilleann piping is coming on, and she comforts me by telling me how her boyfriend stays up late at night to watch videos online of Indian bus drivers navigating cliffs and ravines and other deadly looking terrain. We laughingly debate which hobby is worse. Men. They are a mystery.

'Mags, hi!' As I knew she would, Orla has stopped at my table on the way out. She looks immaculate as always, in a camel-coloured coat, chocolate-brown polo-necked dress and gorgeous knee-length leather boots, not a hair astray and make-up perfectly applied. How do women like that do it? I'll never know. Nora too looks elegant, her grey hair in a bun at the base of her neck, pearls at throat and ears, perfect for clutching in horror... I know, I know. I should be kinder, but honestly, she's a head wreck. We've not spoken since the dress business.

'I saw the picture of Kate with the cup on the school Facebook page – amazing,' Orla gushes. Clearly she doesn't know, or doesn't want to know, about the latest feud.

Orla's daughter, Evie, isn't going to the local school, much to her and Kate's misery, as they are best friends. But Orla's husband, Fergus, thought their kids should go to a private school fifteen miles away. Tom, their son, is a computer genius, so he loves the techy school, but Evie would be much happier in Ballycarrick. But it's not my business. I like Orla a lot, but she's hard to really get to know. She's a lovely auntie to the girls, but you don't really get to have real conversations with her. It's all very surface, which is fine, but I would never tell her anything personal.

'Yeah, she was over the moon,' I say. 'She trained really hard, so it's great when it works out for them.' Kate won gold in the hundred metres in the provincial athletics competition.

'Tell her we'll celebrate her great success on Sunday,' Nora says, all sweetness and light.

'Sunday?' I ask, also sweetly and lightly.

'Lunch. I said it to Kieran?' She smiles.

'He didn't mention it, but he's had a lot to think about of late.' I smile back.

'Yes, poor Róisín, I heard.' Nora tuts and shakes her head. 'That poor girl... Frances was only saying at bridge the other day how upset she is that you've stopped Kieran going round to fix her roof, just because that Sharon Joyce said something nasty, or that's what I heard. That girl really needs to grow up.'

Don't react, Mags. Do. Not. React. She's trying to wind you up. I repeat the words like a mantra.

'I didn't stop Kieran going to Róisín's house, Nora. The job was done.'

'Well, that's not what I heard. Poor Róisín, she's very upset all round. I suppose she really never got over my Kie –'

Orla speaks across her. 'Mum, we'd better be going.' She shoots me an apologetic look and ushers Nora out. 'See you Sunday, Mags. Bye, er, Garda Holland.'

'Yikes, your mother-in-law is a bit of a weapon,' Nicola says quietly after the door has tinkled shut behind them.

'She certainly is,' I reply.

'How do you put up with it, Sarge?'

'I have no idea.'

On the way back to the station, I send Nicola on ahead and pop into the post office to buy a card. I didn't like Nora's nasty little dig about Sharon. I haven't plucked up the courage yet to thank my annoying old friend for packing my clothes, but as Facebook reminded me this morning, it's her birthday tomorrow.

The card is a funny one that says *I would walk through fire for you. Well, not actual fire because that's very dangerous. But a very humid room, but not too humid because, you know, my hair.*

Sharon, with her poker-straight sleek hair, is in a permanent one-woman war against humidity.

I scribble inside before I have time to change my mind.

Happy birthday, Shar, and thanks for packing my stuff, and I miss you. M x

I seal it, and instead of walking down the sideroad to her shop, like a grown-up woman, I buy a stamp and drop it in the postbox. For a person who isn't afraid of criminals, I'm a right baby sometimes.

CHAPTER 20

I finish around five and arrive home to find the house empty and in darkness. Confused for a moment, because it's not Tuesday, I then remember that Kieran is at a piping gig and the girls are at something in the community centre, a youth club course that Zoë is running as part of the community liaison team about 'becoming your best self', which the girls and their friends seem to like. I'm hoping their best selves will be better at picking their clothes off the floor, but no sign of that yet. Still, early days.

Anyway, Zoë has offered to drop them off on her way home; she lives with her parents about a mile up the road from us.

I go upstairs, flick on the heat and take a shower. Then I put on my fleece pyjamas that won't be featured in any lingerie catalogues but are so cosy and a pair of fluffy socks that Kate bought me last Christmas. They feature a dog not unlike Rollo and say 'Madra Mad'. 'Madra' is Irish for dog. She's determined to make me a dog person. Specifically, a Rollo person.

I get out the dog biscuits to feed him, and as usual he looks like I'm about to kick him into next week, sidling up to the wall, his eyes rolling and him whimpering in terror.

'What is wrong with you?' I ask, filling his bowl. 'I've never laid a

164

hand on you, but you act like you're scared witless of me?' I pat his head, and he cowers and yelps. I wish I could talk to Jerome about this, and about Caelan Cronin as well, for that matter, who also acts like I'm deliberately out to persecute him and hurt him when all I want is for him to keep out of trouble. If things were better, I'd ask Jerome to keep the Carmodys away from young Cronin. They are not his family, but he has influence. Everything seems harder without Jerome. I think briefly of asking Delia to act as a bridge between me and her father, but she has her own difficulties with her parents right now, what with her and Darren moving into the new house together.

Meatloaf is in his cage, munching some stalks of cabbage that Kate put in there this morning, and hopefully Knickers is in his enclosure in the utility room. A few days ago, he was in the cupboard under the sink when I bent down to get the bleach, and I nearly killed myself leaping backwards and crashing over a kitchen chair with an almighty roar of fear and then pain, while Rollo – terrified of us both – peed on the floor with fright.

I light the fire in the sitting room and heat some soup from the fridge. I got a new book from the library a few days ago, and I'm looking forward to starting it. It's called *Tomorrow, and Tomorrow, and Tomorrow*, something about two friends who connect through a video game or something, I'm not too sure.

I finish my soup and curl up on the couch to start my book, enjoying the peace and quiet. Rollo comes into the sitting room, realises I'm there and flees back to the kitchen in horror.

I ignore him. The book is actually really good, and it captures my attention from the first page. I used to be the kind of person who had to read a book all the way to the end even if I hated it because I'd started it, but not any more. If it doesn't grip me after a few chapters, I abandon it nowadays. Life is too short.

After a while, Zoë texts to say she is dropping the girls and they'll be there in ten minutes. I close the book and get up to wash my cup. That's all that needs doing because it's Wednesday, only the day after Klara's cleaning day, so it's still pretty spotless. I hear the tyres on the gravel outside and go to let the girls in and thank Zoë for driving them, but as I approach the front door, through the glass either side, I see there are two sets of headlights. Another car has driven up behind the first. Maybe Kieran is home early?

I open the door to see Zoë and Kate and Ellie getting out of the first car, then turn to stare in horror at a very drunk Róisín Duggan, who is climbing out of the second.

'Mags!' she yells. 'Mags…' She's slurring her words, and she's definitely far too intoxicated to have been driving.

'Come on, girls…' Zoë and I immediately try to get the girls into the house, but Róisín makes a mad rush and gets between them and the front door.

'No…no, no, no, no, no, no… They must hear this. I'm sorry, girls… I know you love him… I'm so sorry…so sorry about your dad…'

An ice-cold hand of fear grips my throat. I step forward and take her by the arm, moving her aside. 'Zoë, bring the girls inside please, and stay with them.'

Róisín starts laughing then, a borderline hysterical laugh. Kate looks terrified and Ellie is as white as a sheet as Zoë escorts them in.

'Róisín, where's Kieran?' I ask as soon as the door has closed behind them.

'Mags… I…I schorry…' she slurs. The smell of booze is strong from her, and she has an almost empty bottle of wine in her hand.

'Róisín, where's Kieran?'

'It's not just me who knows it…everyone…Joel…Minnie Melodie… She said it, Mags…she knows.' She points an ineffectual finger into my chest. She is normally so polished and chic, but now she looks a mess. Her leggings are stained with something, and her hair is wet and pulled into a bedraggled ponytail; loose strands have escaped and are sticking to her face.

'Róisín, where is Kieran?' I ask again. I am trying to keep my voice calm, but I'm terrified of the answer. I have seen people go to pieces like this when they've just committed awful violence in the name of love. Her next words make me weak with relief.

'I don't know, Mags… I texted him and rang him, and texted him and rang him but...but...but...' More finger-pointing. 'Minnie knows where he should be. The spirits say it. He's my true love, Mags, and I'm so, so, so shorry to take him off you and the girls but...even sh...sh...she said it. She said she shaw me and my first love reunited.'

'So you don't know where Kieran is?' Right now that's all I care about, not this awful scene in front of a work colleague and my daughters, not the state of Róisín and her scary declaration that Kieran loves her, but whether something terrible has happened to my husband.

'You have to let him go, Mags. It's tearing him apart, this...' She is mumbling now, swaying, ready to fall. She slugs the last of the wine by the neck, then waves the empty bottle around. 'Mus' go find him...'

'Right.' I make a decision to leave her there while I run in for my phone.

Nicola answers.

'Nicola, radio whoever is on patrol and send them to my house please. Female, forties, driving under the influence of alcohol, to be taken into custody.'

I end the call and think about using my cuffs, which are hanging on my police belt – it's thrown over the foot of the banister, behind my jacket – but it seems like an excessive use of force for someone who can hardly stand.

I go back out to find her swaying around, blinking vaguely. 'I know you're angry, Mags. I don't...don't blame...' Tears flow down her face, mascara all over her cheeks. 'But you stole him from me, remember? He was never yours. And Minnie said he was shupposed –'

'Róisín Duggan.' I sigh, hating having to do this, but Zoë saw everything, and even if she hadn't, I can't let someone off for an offence like this, I just can't. I represent the law in this town, and Róisín could have killed someone and still might if she gets back in that car. 'I'm arresting you on suspicion of driving a vehicle while under the influence of intoxicating liquor. You do not have to say anything, but anything you do say will be recorded, and it may harm your defence if you do not mention something when questioned that you later rely on in court.'

'What?' She's shrill now. 'Oh no...no way, Mags... You can't abuse...abushe... You can't do this just because you're a guard...'

And before I know what's happening, I'm on the flat of my back on the gravel and she's standing over me, screaming, brandishing the bottle in my face. She must have walloped me over the head with it, as it's broken now. I try to get up, but I can't just yet...

'Just let him go, you thief!' she roars. 'He was never yours! He's mine, always was and always will be, and even Minnie Melodie said it. She said it, Mags. You have to let him go...'

Again I try to get up. And then the front door flies open and it's Kate, tears streaming down her little face. 'Get away from us! And get away from my dad! He doesn't love you – it's all lies. You just want everyone to think he's your boyfriend, when he's Mam's husband and our dad and he's nothing to you...'

'Kate, come back.' Zoë tries to stop my daughter from escaping, but Kate slips from her grip and lunges at Róisín. Róisín whips around with the bottle, and thank God she misses Kate's face with the jagged glass, but she gets her with her elbow. Kate screams, blood pumping from her nose, and Róisín goes for me again, this time kicking me with her pointed boots as I struggle to my knees. Ellie and Zoë pull Kate back into the house, and as Róisín draws back her foot to kick me again, Rollo launches out from the hallway and buries his teeth in her ankle. She howls and tries to get him off her but to no avail. And then Zoë rushes back out of the house. She's not in uniform because of the youth club, but she's found my cuffs on the stairs, and while Rollo clings to Róisín's leg, she snaps them onto Róisín's wrists and forces her to the ground, knee between her shoulder blades. And this is the scene that greets Darren and Michael as they pull into my driveway.

Róisín is in the back of the squad car in seconds, and Michael stays with her while Zoë and Darren get me to my feet. Ellie is holding a towel to Kate's nose, but Kate leaves her and runs to me, blood and tears combining on her face. 'Mam…are you all right? Did she hurt you?'

'I'm fine, pet,' I reassure her, and gently hold her by the shoulders and move her back a little so I can see what damage that madwoman has done to my child. I'm furious, so angry I could tear Róisín limb from limb, but my priority now is Kate. 'I think it's OK, Kit Kat. You'll have a bruised nose tomorrow, but it doesn't look broken.'

'I just want Daddy,' she sobs into my chest, a child much younger than her years again.

'Call Dad please, Ellie, and tell him to come home at once,' I say to my oldest daughter, and she's on her phone before I've finished the sentence, being wonderfully calm and in control and her best self.

'Should I call an ambulance, Sarge?' Zoë takes out her own phone.

I think for a second. It might be no harm to get some medical attention, and it will be evidence as well. 'No, but get Dr Harrison,' I say. 'I want him to check Kate's nose, but I'm fine.'

'You're not fine, Sarge. Your head is bleeding,' she points out.

'Is it?' I hadn't realised. I rub my hand over the back of my head. It's sore, and my hair is sticky. 'Well, get Dr Harrison first anyway, just to check us both over. He can say whether we need to go to A & E or not. Tell him I'll need him to document our injuries.'

'OK, Sarge.' She turns away to make the phone call. It's nice to see her being serious, responsive and efficient, and the way she cuffed and subdued Róisín was impressive; she didn't make any rookie mistakes like she did with Cantillon.

'Dad's on his way,' says Ellie, coming over to put her arms around me and Kate in a group hug. 'And Mam, didn't Rollo do well? He was so brave, protecting Kate, and you as well. He must love you after all.'

'Rollo did very well,' I say, and I wave and smile at the dog, who is hanging around in the doorway. When he sees me looking, he whimpers with fright and rushes back into the house with his tail between his legs. I'm obviously still a lot more scary than a drunken Róisín armed with a broken bottle.

Darren appears; he's left Michael in the car with Róisín. 'What do you want us to do now, Sarge?'

169

'Take her to the station and throw the book at her. Make sure you get blood and urine, and do every single thing to the letter of the law. She's a barrister, and I do not want her to wriggle out of this.'

He nods. 'Absolutely, Sarge. Every I dotted, every T crossed. She's not getting away with this. Anything else?'

'Yes, bag up that broken bottle and any other glass as evidence of the assault.'

'I'll help you.' Zoë has finished her phone call. 'Is there an evidence bag in the car, Darren?'

'Yep.' He nods. 'And gloves.' They walk back to the squad car to get the kit. Róisín is looking mutinous in the back seat, with Michael beside her, and I lead my daughters back into the house, leaving my three fine young officers to do their jobs.

* * *

I CLEAN KATE UP, but her nose is beginning to swell. Kieran arrives, and he is more upset than I've seen him in years and absolutely furious at Róisín, but he also blames himself for having had anything to do with her at all and not realising what was going on in her head. He apologises again and again to me and the girls for being so blind, and says how it was stupid of him to allow himself to be in such a position but that nothing and nobody will ever come between him and us. It ends with hugs and tears and everyone feeling a bit better.

Then Dr Harrison arrives, and we do have to go to A & E. I need two stitches at the back of my head, and I'm mildly concussed and need to not drive for a couple of days, but after that I'm good to go. Kate has an X-ray of her nose, which thankfully isn't broken, but the experience has rattled her badly and she clings to me a lot.

News travels fast in Ballycarrick, and within five minutes of us being back home again, all patched up and on painkillers, Luigi delivers pizza to the house and Teresa sends up a cream Swiss roll, and then there's yet another ring on the doorbell. Kieran goes to answer it, and he comes back to me and says there's someone who wants to talk to me. Gingerly I get off the couch and go into the hall.

It's hard to see who it is because she's hiding behind such a big bunch of flowers from Violetta's flower shop, but I recognise the long legs and painted nails and the sleek blond top of her head. It's Sharon. I burst into tears and so does she, and I'm so glad I posted the birthday card; she'll get it tomorrow and know it was already sent.

CHAPTER 21

J'm sitting in my car outside the St Ita's Addiction Centre in Claregalway, and I'm in two minds whether to drive away.

Róisín is facing court next week. She was kept overnight in the station, then charged with DUI – her blood alcohol levels were off the charts – and also assault of a member of An Garda Síochána and of a minor. She was released but had to surrender her passport to make sure she didn't shoot off back to New York.

Kieran and I got a letter from her the next day, saying she was mortified and that she remembered very little of the night but that she wanted to offer us a total and complete abject apology.

When I read the letter, I felt a bit sorry for her, to be honest. She'll definitely lose her driving licence and will face a hefty fine as well as probable community service. There's even a small risk of a custodial sentence. Not a great look for a lawyer setting up a new business. And this is just gossip gold for a place like Ballycarrick. Already the story has got legs: she broke Kate's arm, she had a knife, she was pregnant by Kieran... Why people make up this stuff is beyond me, but they do.

Kieran doesn't feel at all sorry for her; he is only delighted the book is being thrown at her. When the letter arrived, he contacted Alberto Ramos, a solicitor in Galway, and had him write to Róisín, warning her to stay away from him and his family and to make no further contact, and telling her that if she did try, we would seek a barring order.

But today I got a second letter from her, addressed to me at the station, which I suppose crossed with the solicitor's letter. She must have known Kieran was likely to throw the first one in the bin.

Mags, I'm so very, very sorry. I'm so ashamed, and I really want to apologise to you in person. I can't believe I hurt you and Kate. I can't sleep thinking about it. Today I checked myself into St Ita's Addiction Centre while I'm awaiting trial. I'm determined to get sober and make amends. I'm an alcoholic. And that's not just since coming home, it's a long time coming, but that's the unvarnished truth. If you could visit, and I know it's a big ask, I would be so grateful to you. If you don't want to, I totally understand.

Róisín.

And now I'm here, sitting in my car outside the centre, because I think I'm entitled to an apology in person and I think it will do her good to make one.

At the same time, though, there's another big part of me that thinks Róisín checking herself in here before she's ordered to get treatment by the court is a smart legal ploy to show ahead of her trial that she's taking steps to improve herself and to convince the judge she will never offend again. And maybe apologising to me in person is another way of getting ahead of what's coming down the tracks at her. She's shrewd, and this is exactly what she would advise a client in a similar bind to do.

I should drive away.

Kieran would definitely want me to drive away. If he knew I was here, he'd go mad.

But I'm here now.

Also, there has to be a path to redemption for us all, otherwise what's the point? Especially the world I'm in, people do wrong, but if they can and they genuinely want to straighten up and be a force for good in the world, then we should at least afford them the opportunity, shouldn't we? You can't give up all hope in people.

I get out and walk across to the reception of the old hospital. You see these fabulous drying-out places on TV, with swimming pools and yoga studios and manicured gardens – St Ita's is nothing like that. It's a concrete two-storey place, very 1970s industrial-looking, with a tarmacked car park and a big statue of a saint outside, presumably Ita herself. Inside it's clean and warm and has that institutional smell all places like this seem to have, a mixture of overcooked vegetables and disinfectant. The reception is in front, in a sort of entrance hall, and the door from there to the main building is locked.

'Mags Munroe to see Róisín Duggan,' I say to the harassed-looking man behind the desk. He checks his computer screen and presses a button. A loud buzz and the door to my right opens.

'First on left. Take a seat. Someone will be with you,' he says, while answering another call.

I follow the instructions and go into a small room with a few torn magazines on a side table. There are a few tired-looking toys, and one of those tables with wriggly bits of metal that kids can play with. I take a seat. A few minutes later, a stocky woman in her sixties with vermillion hair pulled back in a ponytail sticks her head round the other door in the room.

'Mags Munroe?' She checks her clipboard.

'Yes,' I say. I'm wearing a hoodie over my uniform, so hopefully I don't look official.

'Follow me please.' She leads me down a corridor with a pervasive smell of boiled turnips and indicates I should enter another room. There are two easy chairs covered in mustard leatherette – one has a tear and the stuffing is protruding – and a small glass table with a jug of water and two glasses. There is also a box of tissues.

'Would you rather someone stayed for the meeting, or are you happy to meet with Róisín alone?' she asks.

'I'm fine to meet her alone,' I say. I'm guessing she hasn't got an empty wine bottle on her at this stage.

'Right. Just hold on here, and I'll bring her down.'

Five minutes later Róisín appears, and I can hardly believe the change in her in a few days. She's wearing black leggings and runners and a navy zip-up sweatshirt. Her hair looks limp and in need of a wash and blow-dry, and I realise I've never seen her before without a full face of make-up.

She doesn't speak, just stands there looking at me.

'Hi, Róisín,' I say eventually, to break the ice.

She just nods and inhales deeply through her nose, then out through her mouth as if to steady herself. 'Thanks for coming. I really hoped you would. I suppose Kieran didn't want to see me? I don't blame him.'

'He doesn't, and he doesn't know I'm here,' I say truthfully.

'Oh…right.' She swallows. 'I don't want to cause any more trouble between you.'

'You won't.' I smile. 'And for the record, you never did.'

'Well, I just…' She looks a bit rattled. 'Do you want to sit down?'

I sit, and she takes the seat opposite me, inhaling another deep breath and launches into her apology.

'I need to tell you to your face how sorry I am, Mags. I've been told what I did, though I don't remember coming to your house. I was blackout drunk after two bottles of Sauvignon Blanc and most of a bottle of vodka. But I chose to drink that much, just like I chose to lie to Joel so many times about my drinking.'

She speaks quite fast and in a curiously flat voice, and it all sounds rehearsed. I err on the side of forgiveness; she knew I'd show up, and she's been practising what to say.

'It was my choice to blame Joel for the difficulties in our relationship,' she carries on, 'even though I was impossible to live with after our final round of IVF failed. The hormones I had to take affected my thinking, but it was my choice to take them. It was also my choice to tell you Joel had an affair, though he always denied it, and I think now maybe that was just in my head. And it was my choice to tell you his affair was the reason we came to Ireland, when in fact we came because I promised if we did, I would be happier and stop drinking. And, well, I meant it at the time, but it didn't work.'

I could have told her it wouldn't work. As Hemingway says, travelling won't ever help you to get rid of your problems; you can't run away from yourself.

She carries on in the same fast, flat voice. 'It was my decision to chase after Kieran, to try to re-create what we had together. I went to your house, I drove my car drunk out of my mind, when I could have killed someone, and physically assaulted you and Kate. Those were my choices, and I'm not blaming drink or Kieran leaving me in New York or Joel or circumstances or anything. It was all me.'

She pauses, waiting for me to respond. I say nothing. She flushes slightly and continues. 'Seeing Kieran again brought back all my sadness about his leaving me and my not having children, and when Minnie told me that the love of my life was in Ballycarrick, and his name began with a K, well, I thought...' She's getting more emotional now, and her voice has started to rise; she catches herself and lowers it again. 'I wanted to believe Minnie was talking about Kieran. And in my pathetic self-pitying state, I decided a witch knew best, and that if I could turn the clock back, then everything would be fine, and Kieran and I could be together, and I could even share the girls with you...'

The hackles rise on the back of my neck, but I clench my teeth and say nothing.

'But honestly, Mags, I'm not trying to blame my instability on the hormones or on alcohol. I know it was my decision to do what I did, even if I don't remember it. I take full responsibility for my actions. It was all me.'

Again she stops and looks at me, as if hoping for me to disagree or try to brush it off.

I don't, because she's right – it is all her. And also I think she has a lot more work to do before she genuinely believes that instead of just parroting stuff about personal responsibility from her therapy sessions. For instance I notice she hasn't owned flat-out lying about Joel having an affair; she only said the affair was maybe just in her head. It makes me wonder if it was all her idea, not Joel's, to suddenly try for a child after putting it off too long. And she's still implying everything went wrong because Kieran left her all those years ago. Nor is she mentioning her efforts to cosy up to me while planning to take my husband off me and 'share' my daughters. And on top of all that, she hasn't said a single word about Sharon.

I decide to help her along. 'You told Sharon I didn't like her.'

Róisín drops her eyes, which are tired and lined without make-up. 'I'm sorry.'

I wait.

She says, still with her eyes lowered, 'She came up to me in the street and accused me of trying to get my hooks into Kieran, and she said you were too soft and trusting to realise the truth about me, and so I got angry and defensive.'

I sit in silence.

Róisín inhales, exhales. 'OK, I said you'd told me you were trying to shake her off for ages, that you were such a nice person, you didn't want to be cruel, but that your friendship with her was just one that had gone on for years and you didn't know how to get out of it.'

I nod, finally satisfied she's telling the truth, because I've already heard it from Sharon.

Sharon told me about it while we were separating the huge bunch of flowers she'd brought me into three vases and two water jugs. 'You knew she was lying, though, didn't you?' I asked in horror.

'Ah, Mags, like you're so smart, reading all those books that I couldn't get through in a month of Sundays, and rising up in the cops and everything, and sure I just sell dresses for a living and only read gossip magazines... I thought maybe...' She was on the brink of tears telling me, and I walked around the kitchen table to hug her.

'Ah, would you have a shred of sense! We're best friends since we were four. Do you seriously think I was only putting up with you for nearly fifty years?'

'But you were always so busy, then she said that, and then we had the big fight over the note. I never thought Kieran was with Róisín, of course I didn't. I just wanted you to know what people were saying. I wasn't stirring, I swear. I was just trying to look out for you.'

'I know, and I'm so sorry, Shar.'

Now, remembering Sharon's pain, I meet Róisín's eyes and say,

'You didn't just try to take my husband and attack my little girl. You made my oldest and dearest friend very, very sad.'

Her face drops, and for the first time, she gets tearful. 'I'm so sorry. I'm a selfish, manipulative cow who is only happy when everyone is as miserable as me.' And then she bursts into floods.

I sit for a while, watching her as she sobs, and I can see she genuinely feels wretched. Yet in many ways, she's a very lucky woman.

I think of Mike Cantillon back in prison, having to live with the fact that Trish Cronin isn't here to raise her kids, how as a result of his actions, young Caelan is going off the rails and poor Liam can't grieve for his wife because he's trying to be mother and father to two heart-broken children. Cantillon's the villain of the piece, I know, but even he is not an evil man; he's an alcoholic who can't or won't stop. But the guilt and self-hatred behind his eyes is there. No doubt about it.

'OK, here's the thing, Róisín,' I say at last as she mops her face with a handful of tissues. 'Nobody died. It wasn't your finest hour, fair enough, but it's over now, and there's no permanent harm done. I'm fine, Kate is fine, you didn't kill anyone with the car, though you could have, and you've now got to a point where you realise you need to make some radical changes to your life. So maybe, in a horrible way, this is a good thing. Bad enough to give you the wake-up call you needed, not so bad as to have caused lifelong damage to yourself or anyone else.'

She nods slowly, wiping her eyes. 'At least that, I suppose. And I'm so sorry.'

'I know you are.' I stand. 'Now I've to go back to work, but I'm happy to see you're here and you're going to sort yourself out. Kieran might forgive you eventually, but he's very angry for now, so I wouldn't write any more letters. He needs time to get over this.'

On my way back to my car, I get a text from Ronan.

Want to travel to Dublin together tomorrow? I'm in Galway today and staying tonight. I'll drive. R

I text back. *No, it's fine, thanks. I'm giving my friend Tatiana a lift.*

I'm quite relieved to have Tatiana as an excuse. It's always nice to catch up with Ronan, but at the same time, it feels a bit complicated. I know Ronan has a bit of a thing for me, never spoken or acknowledged but we both know it. I don't know why, but I'm the kind of woman he can relate to or something. But he likes me, and I like him, and I don't want him ever to say anything to me that would jeopardise our friendship.

CHAPTER 22

*K*ieran is in the kitchen when I arrive home, and there's a lovely aroma of cooking dinner. The heat is on, and the girls and the twins, Catriona and Trish O'Leary, are playing on their Switches. They have this ridiculous game called Stardew Valley where they need to farm and have kids and get married and buy supplies, and it absorbs them. It sounds like life to me. It's nice to see them laughing and joking together.

'Anne came to collect them, but there was a mutiny,' Kieran says as he kisses me hello, then he holds me for a while. He's still so shaken by the Róisín thing, he didn't even want me to go back to work this morning. 'Apparently the livestock are angry at them for not feeding them, so production is at an all-time low, Ellie has two coops of very irate chickens, and Catriona has given Kate a stone instead of a proper present, so that's an issue as well.'

I laugh. Overhearing the conversations of this game has become one of our favourite things to do. I know screens are bad and all of that, but this is a fun game and they spend loads of time socialising and playing sports and acting and all sorts, so I don't mind really. And it's great to see them happy and relaxed after the terrible fright they got from Róisín. Kate's nose looks normal again, and she's laughing her head off.

'I said we'd feed the twins and I'll drop them back after. Is that OK?' he asks.

'Ah, yeah, it's fine. What's in the oven?'

'Ah…pass…' He grins. 'Something your mother left in the freezer before she went that says heat on 180 for forty minutes?'

'A surprise, great.' I laugh. The kids would probably have scurvy if it wasn't for my mam. I really miss her. She'll be back in a week, thank goodness; the freezer is getting very empty.

I look around and the place is tidy despite it being a Monday and Klara not due till tomorrow. 'You've been cleaning up?'

He shakes his head. 'Nope, not me, the girls. I'm only in a half an hour. The church roof is leaking again, so Father Doyle was onto me. I spent the day down there, but' – he looks out at the torrential rain – 'I might pop down in an hour or so to check the sealant is holding. The whole thing needs to be replaced – I can't keep sealing it – but there's no money, it seems.'

'Thanks for tidying, girls,' I call.

'The twins helped us,' Kate calls back.

'Thank you, Catriona and Trish!'

'It's no problem, Mags, we're happy to help. And thanks for letting us stay for dinner,' Catriona tends to be the spokesperson of the pair.

'And the laundry is folded and a new load on,' says Kate.

'And we made an apple crumble for dessert,' Ellie is wiping down the countertops. 'It's all about being our best selves, see, Mam. Zoë the new guard has been teaching us at the youth club how it's important to be grateful and open and show the people you love in your lives how much you care, and then karma means the universe will reflect it back to you, though of course that's not why you do it in the first place. It has to come from the heart.'

I'm astonished, on so many different levels. Zoë is teaching our teenagers to be civilised human beings? The girls have made my favourite dessert? I focus on the easy thing. 'How do you know how to make an apple crumble?'

'We looked it up on YouTube. There was frozen apple in the freezer, and we followed the recipe,' Catriona says with a smile. 'You said before it was your favourite.'

'It is. Thanks girls, that was really sweet of ye.'

They go back to their game, and Kieran checks the timer on the oven. 'This will be another twenty minutes, and I've the fire lit inside – will we go in and have a small break?'

'Lovely,' I say. 'Let me just change, and I'll be down in a few minutes.'

I strip off my uniform and pull on leggings, a hoodie and a pair of fluffy socks. I realise after I've put them on that they're not the leggings with a phone pocket, so I pop the phone in the side of my bra, something I do if I'm out walking and have nowhere to store it, and come back down to join my husband, who has also changed out of his work clothes and is in a pair of jeans and his beloved old green jumper with the holes.

The sitting room is warm and cosy. Kieran has pulled the curtains against the horrible night, and he's standing by the sideboard holding a bottle of rioja, looking at me with a question on his face.

I settle on the sofa. 'Only half a glass. I have to drive up to Dublin in the morning.'

Immediately he's anxious. 'Do you have to? It seems a bit early after the concussion.'

'I do, and the doctors said I'm fine to drive after a couple of days, and it's been five, and it's just for a meeting. I'll be back by teatime,' I tell him firmly, and he hears me and nods. He's inclined to be anxious, and we don't want to go down that road again.

He pours me half a glass of the rioja and a glass of elderflower cordial for himself, because he has to bring the twins home, and comes and sits beside me on the couch. I sip my rioja and it's delicious. I can feel it relaxing my aching body and mind. It always strikes me as very unfair that some people like me can enjoy a drink now and again – I'm not a slave to it; weeks go by and I don't drink at all, and when I do, it's never more than a glass or two at the most – but for some others, it gets a grip of them and won't let go, so they can't have this pleasure.

'I went to see Róisín today,' I tell him. 'She's in St Ita's.'

He stiffens slightly but says nothing.

'Are you annoyed with me?'

'Not with you, Mags. It's her I'm angry with. And I don't like the idea of you being in the same room as her, even somewhere safe like that.' He sighs and draws me closer to him. 'I'm still so furious with myself for allowing all this to happen.'

'You were just being a friend. You couldn't have known.'

'Sharon knew.'

'Yes, and she kept telling me, but I wouldn't listen, so it wasn't just you.'

'And that's another thing that makes me so angry,' he says. 'Her pretending to be your friend, and trying to suck up to Ellie as well, and...' He stops and takes a deep breath. 'What did she say to you anyway?'

I lean against him. 'I don't think she's fully faced up to things, to be honest. She's very contrite and low in herself, but a lot of it is just self-pity. I told her she's lucky that her rock bottom, the thing that will make her turn her life around, which she will hopefully do, hasn't had any long-term impact. Not like Mike Cantillon killing Trish Cronin, ruining his own life and all her family's lives as well. That poor lad Caelan is going from bad to worse – he's never away from the Carmodys.'

'Yeah, you're right, at least nobody died.' He sits a moment, then adds, 'It's really hurt her mother, though. I met her and Martin coming out of Mass when I was trying to sort the leaks earlier.'

'Did they speak to you about Róisín?'

'Frances did. She's in a terrible way about it. But then Martin started talking over her, and it got even more awkward. His dementia is advancing quickly. He thought I was my father, and he asked after me and Róisín, how were we doing in New York and all that...'

I sigh. 'Poor Martin. And he's not the only one living in the past. I met your mother the other day. She was all sympathy for Róisín, saying she never got over losing you. I wonder if she'll change her tune now?'

'God only knows. My mother is so deluded on so many subjects, this is just one.' He sips his glass of elderflower. 'She told Enrico that Ollie would probably have RTÉ cameras at his wedding to Gearoid, which sent him into a spin because half his family in Spain doesn't even know he's gay, and he's set to inherit some money or something from his grandfather, who is homophobic, and Enrico wants the cash, so he's freaking out. Gearoid rang me today.'

'Why would Ollie have cameras at the wedding?' I'm confused.

'Of course he won't, but you know Mam…' He rolls his eyes and sighs. 'Oh, and Gearoid wants to invite Trevor and Sharon to the wedding.'

I laugh. 'That will be fun. Your father thinks Sharon is mad, since she had a full-scale conversation with him after a party in your house wearing only a bra and knickers. It might have been thirty years ago but he's still not over it. And your mother will have a stroke when she hears Trevor of Tequila Mockingbird will be at her high-society wedding. Sharon might have tidied him up, but not enough for Nora.'

'Mam, Dad, we've dished up, come on,' Ellie calls, and we exchange a look. This new and improved domesticity in our kids is unexpected but great.

'They're after something,' we say to each other simultaneously.

Dinner is lovely, a beef casserole with mashed potatoes, and the crumble is perfect. The girls are all chat about a match that's coming up on Sunday; Kate's soccer team is in the Western Challenge Shield Final in Tuam.

'Let's all go. All the lads from St Colm's are going because the Under 16s are playing the semis before the kids' match,' Ellie says.

'We're not kids. It's Under 13s.' Kate is indignant.

Ellie dismisses her. 'You know what I mean. We want to meet hot lads, and none of them are going to be at a kids' soccer game. Oh, and Mam, Cat and Trish's parents are busy, so they can come with us, can't they?'

'Well, I can only fit five people...' I say.

'But Dad can drive too, then we've two cars.' Ellie has an answer for everything. Clearly she is willing to give the universe a helping hand when it comes to karma.

Before this can go any further, the landline rings and Kate goes to answer it.

'Hello... Oh, hi, Father Doyle... Yeah, just one sec, he's finishing his dinner. It's for you, Dad, it's Father Doyle,' she says, holding out the receiver.

Kieran gets up to take it. 'Hi, Father...? Right. Right. Right.'

I know by his face something bad has happened. The leak is worse, or the ceiling's come in or something; either way it will mean Kieran going out again.

'Right... You make sure Tessie is all right, and I'll be down there in twenty minutes.' He hangs up. 'The leak is after spreading, and there was water pouring down onto the statue of poor St Teresa, so Tessie decided to move her.' Tessie is the sacristan of the church and a formidable lady. 'Anyway, she dropped the statue – it must weigh a hundred kilos – on her foot, so he's getting her down to Galway now for an X-ray. I better go down and see where the leak is coming from now that it's showed up.' He bends and kisses my cheek, then goes for his raincoat. 'Twins, come with me,' he calls. 'I'll drop you on the way. Mags, take your book in by the fire, leave the girls to tidy up. I won't be long hopefully.'

He gathers his phone and keys, and the twins get their stuff, and they head out into a squally wet night.

I have a moment of unease, seeing him go. I know he is always careful; he won't do anything daft like go on the roof of the church in the dark. But I'll be relieved when he's home. I've been acting as calm as possible, not to send my husband into another spiral of anxiety, but the incident with Róisín has unnerved me more than I like to admit.

The girls load the dishwasher and feed Knickers in the utility room, and Meatloaf, whose cage is now on top of the tumble dryer, and the brave yet cringing Rollo, then head up the stairs to their rooms while I retreat to the sitting room.

Before long I'm involved in *Middlemarch* by George Eliot, and I wonder as it describes provincial life in England around 1830 how much different life really is now. Vastly in some ways but not so much in others.

I'm deep in the story when there's a ring on the front doorbell. Who on earth could be out in this weather? It's thunder and lightning now. I wonder for a second if I should answer it but realise it's ridiculous to be afraid of answering the door in my own home, and I get up and go into the hall.

I can see through the glass at the side that the visitor is tall and slender. I open the door, and it's a man, muffled up against the weather, the hood of his jacket pulled up. 'Mags?' The smooth, cultured New York accent is instantly recognisable.

'Joel, what are you doing here?' I'm a bit shocked by him showing up out of the blue, but he's getting soaked out there, so I step back into the hall, letting him in.

'I wanted to speak to you and Kieran, face to face. I hope you don't mind me calling...' He's shivering and dripping all over the hall.

'Kieran isn't here. What can I do for you?' I keep my voice official. I'm not about to have a social chat.

'It's Róisín,' he says, pushing back his hood, and his eyes are sad and dark. 'Look, I know this is not your problem, and the last thing you want is to be dragged into this, but –'

'Joel, I'm sorry, but Róisín really isn't my business any more.'

'Please, hear me out. I'm not trying to get you on my side, and I totally respect your right to stay out of it, but...but the truth is, Róisín isn't well. She's been under a lot of strain. She decided to try for a baby, and I said OK, if it made her happy, but nothing has worked, so she's in mourning for that. And then her father, and it's hard trying to set up a new business from scratch, and I suppose she's destroyed all hope of that now. She called me this afternoon from St Ita's, and she is so upset, and I could hardly make out what she was saying – it was all garbled. But basically she says she thinks she's worthless, and she's threatening to end it all...'

I suppress a sigh. I need this like a hole in the head. I can't help feeling sorry for her, but bloody Róisín Duggan needs to get herself and her drama out of my life. 'Have you told them at St Ita's that she's having suicidal ideation?'

'I have, and they're moving her to a psychiatric facility in Galway to have her mental state assessed.'

'Well, I suppose that's the best place for her then,' I say, still being cool and official. But it's hard. All my instincts are to bring him in for a nice cup of tea, let him dry off and say comforting things about the future.

At the same time, I can't help thinking a psychiatric diagnosis is a handy thing to have if you've been charged with the assault of a police officer and a child.

Oh, well. Either way, this isn't Joel's fault, especially if Róisín is as manipulative and persuasive as I suspect she is, and I relent. 'Why don't you come in and dry off and have a cup of tea,' I say, and I lead the way into the kitchen and pull out a chair for him at the kitchen table, which the girls have wiped down.

He keeps on talking as he follows me, and there's misery in his voice. 'She's complicated, Mags, and troubled and very sensitive, and that so-called white witch played her like a violin. It was awful.'

'Mm...' I flick the kettle on and get down two mugs.

'That woman kept filling Róisín's head with delusions about Kieran and saying how you were keeping him under lock and key, and that the baby they should have had was somewhere out there in the ether. It was awful. My heart broke for her. She wasn't herself, and she was drinking more and more. I think this whole thing has been a psychotic episode – I hope they diagnose her properly.'

It amazes me how forgiving he is being, but if he genuinely believes the Kieran fixation was not about the real Róisín but about mental illness, I suppose I can understand. Just about.

'It doesn't excuse her attacking you, but I don't know, with this on her record, I don't see how she's ever going to practise law again.' He has his elbows on the table now, his head in his hands, clutching his glossy black hair. 'And I can't even be here for her. I have to go back to the States for...' He hesitates, then says in a rush, 'Something bad has happened there as well. I'm maybe going to get prosecuted myself.'

I suppress another deep sigh as I bring the mugs and milk to the table. So Joel has his own legal problems. I really don't want to ask him what it's all about; I'm sure it's nothing I can help him with.

'It's about that phone Róisín was on about in the restaurant,' he says. I have no idea why he thinks I'm the right person to talk to about his troubles, but he's clearly wound himself up to this point and now he's determined to spill everything, so I sit down patiently to listen. 'It was my work phone. It was full of important stuff, very important. I was supposed to surrender it with all the other documents when I left the Senate job, but I completely forgot, and then when I was unpacking the boxes in Ireland, I found it...'

So the phone with the Daffy Duck cover was his work phone. I'd thought it was a kid's phone, but maybe it was supposed to look that way, cheap and childish, to hide its importance.

'And that was bad enough. It's full of classified information, and I knew I'd have to confess and bring it back again and get interviewed by the FBI and all sorts about where it had been, but then I put it down somewhere and couldn't find it again. And now they think I've stolen it or sold it to the Russians or something, and I swear I haven't. I've even walked up and down the beach a million times, because that bloody witch said it's lost beside a body of water...'

'You put it on the shelf under the VELUX window,' I say.

He stares at me. 'I'm sorry? What?'

'We came into the room where you were, me and Róisín, and you had the phone in your hand, and you stood up and put it there, like you wanted to hide it or just get it out of the way. It's a very narrow shelf, but maybe there's a gap behind it and it slipped down? Or something else got put on top of it?'

I'm not being clever; I'm saying the obvious. I'm telling him that what he's lost is where he last had it but under something or behind something. It's what psychics always say, according to that podcast on cold reading, and apparently nine times out of ten, they're right.

The effect on Joel is electric. Leaving his tea, he pulls his wet coat back on and leaves, hardly even saying goodbye.

Half an hour later, a text. *Not there. But thanks for listening.*

Seems I won't be giving Minnie a run for her money just yet.

CHAPTER 23

*A*s promised, I pick Tatiana up at seven in the morning from outside the Samovar, where she is already waiting, wrapped in a fur jacket and fur hat. She's not wearing make-up, and I realise it's the first time I've seen her without her dark eyeliner and heavy mascara. We drive on up to Dublin, me for my meeting about Russian agents and her for her new eyes.

She asks me where I think is the best place to buy Victor's fishing jacket, and while we're mulling over the possibilities, a strange thought pops into my head. Victor. I assume he's Russian. And he spends all that time on Ballyloughane Strand…

OK, I've actually eaten the evidence of what he's doing; he's definitely fishing for sea trout. But suppose he's up to something else as well? Like letting the Russians know where the cable comes ashore? Maybe he's wearing a tracker to show them? And another worrying thing – Joel said he's walked that beach a million times, because Minnie said to Róisín about losing his phone near a big body of water. What if she's right somehow, and Joel did lose the phone on the beach, and now Victor has all his classified information? There might even be something about digital cables – the one that comes ashore on Ballyloughane Strand is directly connected to New York…

I shake my head. I'm letting my imagination run away with me. None of that makes any sense. Anyway, Tatiana hates Putin; she would never date a Russian agent. Though I suppose Russian agents don't exactly go around announcing themselves. Ronan said they always try and blend in, act ordinary, so maybe working as a chef is the perfect cover. I feel a bit silly, but I have to ask.

'When did Victor come over from Russia?'

Tatiana stares at me, astonished. 'Why you think Russian? His accent not Russian.'

'Oh...?' You could have fooled me.

'Is Moldovan.'

'Ah...OK. Sorry.' Well, that's a relief. If Russia wins in Ukraine, Moldova will be fearful they'd be next, so Victor will hardly be Putin's greatest fan.

Tatiana is still shaking her head over the fact I can't distinguish between a Russian and Moldovan accent, and it strikes me that if anyone can spot a Russian in Ballycarrick, even one with hardly any accent at all, it will be her. I should have thought of this before.

'Are there any Russians in Ballycarrick apart from yourself, Tatiana?' I ask. 'Like, any new arrivals?'

'Only Minnie and Neil,' she says.

I nearly crash the car. 'What? Ah, hang on, Tatiana. They're from the North of England...'

'No. Russian.'

'But –'

'You hear the way that witch call me Tatiana? Not Tatiana, as Irish do. Tatiana, as Russians do.'

I can't hear any difference at all in the two ways Tatiana says her own name, but I take her word for it. But still, this can't be true... 'Maybe she did Russian at college or something and that's how she knows how to pronounce your name properly?'

'Is true her English accent very good, but not that good. Other words sometimes. Like Samovar. When she come in and order tea, and ask me do I own Samovar.'

'But that could be the same thing, she did it at college?'

191

'Tea is other thing, always black with lemon and sugar,' says Tatiana, ignoring my suggestion.

'But lots of people –'

'And she not bang cup with spoon when she stir like Irish do. She stir in middle of cup, like a Russian – they don't touch sides of cup with teaspoon. And when she scald her mouth on tea, she say "oy", not "ow".'

'That's a *thing*?'

'Russian thing. And he, the husband, I see him one day in butcher's shop, and he counts number of sausages he wants on his fingers, in right way.'

'There's a right way?' I'm really struggling with this.

'Of course, Russian way. Irish do it like...' I glance over as she makes a fist and counts off by extending first her thumb and then each finger in turn. 'One, two, three... In Russia we start with open hand and fold each finger.' She demonstrates. 'All Russians do this way, and so does he.'

'But –'

'Victor agree. He see them at beach a lot, and he say they in car in car park few days ago. They planning journey, he says, and they looking at a map, not GPS. He know Russians don't trust GPS, is joke about when they invade.'

'But if they are...' I can't get my head around it. If Minnie and Neil are Russian, why would they lie about it? Unless...

No. Just no. There's absolutely nothing about a witch and a warlock that could be said to blend into the general population, especially ones that writhe around together naked on the beach by the light of a bonfire.

'Victor don't like them. They disturb fish, always light fire and make noise. He has to go different beach now, not as good.'

'That must be very annoying,' I say, my mind in a whirl and my eyes fixed on the road as I overtake a tractor.

'Yes, less fresh fish.' She tilts back her head and closes her eyes, and the next minute, she is asleep. Tatiana is a great believer in power naps; it's how she keeps going.

I drive on, trying to talk myself down but also thinking about how a bonfire might be a good way to show a boat far away in the dark exactly where a very important digital cable comes ashore. It's true a witch and a warlock don't 'blend in', but at the same time, who on earth would suspect them of being spies? And it would be a clever way of getting all the information they need, about everything. There must be hardly anyone in the town who hasn't been to Minnie and told her, consciously or not, all about themselves. And about their family members.

Suddenly the floodgates open in my mind. Why did Minnie offer Róisín a free reading? Maybe it's because, thanks to Nora, everyone in Ballycarrick knows Joel is 'very high up in the American government'. Nora probably told Minnie herself; she was talking about going to the witch for a reading the last time we went for Sunday lunch. And Róisín used the free reading…and somehow Minnie picked up that Joel had lost his phone, and guessed it was important, because Róisín told her straight out that Joel was so worried about it.

And then both of them, Minnie and Neil, went to the house, using their so-called powers to find the phone, and found it exactly where I'd told Joel to look for it. Róisín was with me when Joel put it away on the shelf under the VELUX window. She must have forgotten, or not consciously noticed him doing it, but Minnie would still have been able to find out the last room Joel was in when he still had the phone, because cold readers can get information out of someone without that person knowing they're giving it away…

That 'it's near a body of water' thing was just to convince Róisín that Joel had lost it somewhere else, outside.

I think about calling Ronan and running my theory past him, but I have Tatiana in the car, so I can't. And anyway, when I imagine putting what I'm thinking into words, it sounds totally far-fetched.

Then, thinking about the free reading, I remember Minnie offered one to Tatiana as well, and I get a shiver. If Minnie is a Russian spy, I can see why she wanted to get her hooks into Róisín, but why Tatiana? To find out if the Russian woman had rumbled her? And then what? Get rid of her?

I tell myself sternly to stop coming up with wild theories. Maybe Minnie gives out free cards to everyone the first time, as a way of getting them hooked. I have nothing to go on here but Tatiana noticing a few idiosyncrasies these people could have picked up anywhere; maybe one of them had a Russian grandmother or something. I'm letting my imagination run away with me.

I drop Tatiana at a fishing tackle shop on the north side and arrange to pick her up from the Optizone clinic on Grafton Street, then make my way to the Westbury hotel. It's the second time the meeting is in a hotel, so it's presumably a security measure. It seems a bit outlandish, but maybe they think the Garda Headquarters are being watched.

I pass several armed detectives on the landing, and just outside the door of room 436 is an airport-style scanner that I have to pass through. My pockets and clothing are searched, a uniformed officer runs a wand over my entire body, and my hat is taken and examined, as are my shoes, before he hands me the usual bag for my phone.

There's a young man in naval uniform behind me going through the same procedure, and I smile at him as I pop my phone into the plastic bag. 'Hi, I'm Sergeant Mags Munroe. I don't think I've met you before?'

The lad blushes. He seems a bit overwhelmed. 'No...I... It's my first time at this sort of meeting. I'm Lieutenant Commander Richard Boyle.'

We shake hands before going in. There are about sixteen people already in the room, sitting at a large rectangular meeting table. Ronan is at the far end, next to John Greene, who I met before in Galway. John nods and smiles at me, and I smile back while looking around for somewhere to sit. My heart sinks when I realise the only seats still available are on either side of Duckie. When I take the chair on his left, I realise why no one else is sitting beside him; the scent of his cologne is so overpowering, it actually stings the back of my throat.

'Hi, Mags, how are things in Ballygobackwards?' He chuckles, and I see Ronan shoot him a look that could kill. Duckie really is a total eejit, but he is very well connected and somehow always manages to weasel himself into things.

'Hi, Duckie,' I say cheerfully. People only ever call him Duckie behind his back, but now that Zoë has started calling him Duckie to his face, like it's his real name, the secret is out, so I think I'll start doing it as well every time he says something stupid. At the top of the table, I see Ronan's mouth twitching; he must have overheard.

Duckie glares furiously, then turns to Richard, who has taken the chair on his other side. 'The name's Detective Inspector Donal Cassidy,' he snaps to the naval officer.

'Lieutenant Commander Richard Boyle,' says Richard to Duckie, clearing his throat and coughing. 'Nice to meet you.' He moves his chair slightly further to the right; the cologne is clearly getting to him.

At the head of the table, Ronan rises to his feet. 'Thank you all for coming here today,' he starts, before going around the table, intro-ducing people by name and rank, beginning with Lieutenant Commander Richard Boyle. As well as the navy, we seem to have representatives from the Irish Coast Guard, the Irish Army, the head of Galway Council and also several international bodies, including a Swedish woman called Brigitta Jannsen from Europol, and three Americans, from Interpol, NATO and the CIA respectively. He intro-duces me as Sergeant Mags Munroe, 'our ear to the ground in Bally-carrick', and then Duckie as 'another colleague from the west, Detective Inspector Du...Donal Cassidy...' and sits down hastily, no doubt hoping Duckie didn't notice his near slip of the tongue. I think Duckie did, though, as he's fuming; with his shaved head, he looks like a purple boiled egg.

John Greene gets to his feet, beaming at everyone in his congenial way before fiddling with the projector in front of him, which is pointed at a white pull-down screen on the wall. 'You all know why we're here, so I'll get straight to the point. As some of you are aware, our defence forces have monitored and observed four commercial and military Russian vessels in Irish waters in the last week alone. One such ship' – he puts up a slide of a warship – 'is the *Admiral Bogorovich*, which was used to attack Ukraine with cruise missiles last year. So we have stepped up our surveillance all around the coastline, especially where the digital cables come ashore' – he puts up another slide showing all the landing points, including Ballyloughane Strand – 'and we hope you can each play a part in making sure we maintain the security of the island of Ireland, not just for ourselves but on behalf of the entire democratic world. This might well, ladies and gentlemen, be the most important thing you ever do.'

Everyone gives him their undivided attention, even Duckie.

'What will happen now is we will break into three smaller groups and debrief and formulate plans going forward. Each group has an area to work on. Agendas are on the table, so as per these groupings' – he points to a list on the wall – 'please disperse. We'll break for lunch, which will be served here for security reasons. The door here' – he gestures behind him – 'will lead you to the various meeting rooms. Given the nature of our discussions, discretion and security are of the upmost importance, so we have taken all manner of necessary precautions. As you are all aware, these discussions are totally confidential, the highest level of security, so it goes without saying that what happens here stays inside these walls.'

Did I imagine it, or did he look directly at Duckie as he said this last bit? Maybe Ronan has warned him our colleague from the west is a bit of a blabbermouth. Duckie doesn't even notice, though; he's busy eying up the Europol representative, who is a tall, gorgeous blonde.

'So if you go to your assigned meeting, then we'll reconvene here at 1 p.m., and after lunch we'll all report back from our groups and we'll wrap up then.'

Brigitta turns out to be in our group, which is me, Duckie, Ronan, Richard from the navy, a woman called Ester Osbridge from Scotland, who is some kind of tech engineer, and the leader of Galway Council, Padraig McCarthy. As soon as we have located and settled in our separate meeting room, Duckie sits down next to Brigitta and starts trying to ingratiate himself in his oily way, while she fishes out a handkerchief and presses it to her mouth. By the look on her face, she finds the scent of cologne horrifying and its wearer both repugnant and bewildering. Got it in one, Brigitta, I think.

We go around the table, giving updates on what we've been doing. Ronan asks the Lieutenant Commander to start. Richard looks nervous, but I shoot him an encouraging look, which is returned with a small smile. Once he starts speaking, he is very articulate and clear, explaining how the NATO military alliance has highlighted the benefit of increased partnership with Ireland in protecting digital cables coming across the North Atlantic. 'As a neutral state and not a member of NATO, we must tread carefully, but NATO believe Irish maritime security is a top priority.'

Padraig speaks next and says that Galway Council have been given extra funding to secure the works offices for the submarine cables, and he asks me to advise them how to go about ensuring their operations centre is adequately protected, which I promise to do. Ester Osbridge, the no-nonsense Scotswoman, also agrees to meet with us in Galway. She has a thorough understanding of how to protect digital systems from hackers.

Brigitta reports on a Russian spy who was in Sweden for a while, calling himself Peter Berg. 'We have reason to believe he is in fact Vassili Morozov, a Russian agent once attached to the Russian embassy in Budapest, and we think he entered Ireland in August.' She passes around a very grainy still of a man caught on CCTV at Dublin Airport. He's lanky and thin, and I try to work out if he could be Neil, but it's impossible to tell.

Duckie pontificates at length without actually contributing anything. He's trying to impress Brigitta by making out he knows things he's not saying, which, given the nature of this meeting, is ridiculous.

Ronan cuts across Duckie's stream of drivel to ask me if I've seen any strange comings and goings around Ballyloughane Strand, and I'm faced with a decision I do not relish: make myself look a complete fool by talking about a witch and a warlock who perform satanic rituals on the beach, and who I think might be Russian agents...or keep my mouth shut and preserve my dignity and pride.

I opt to make myself look a complete fool. 'I know this sounds outlandish, but the brief is to reveal everything, so...'

I've barely got as far as the way Minnie stirs her tea before Duckie is spluttering and nudging Brigitta with his elbow. 'We've been told to look out for people trying to blend in,' he chortles. 'And in Ballygob-ackwards, that's a witch and a warlock, signed up to the KGB.'

'The KGB were disbanded in 1991,' Brigitta says coolly, and that shuts him up for a bit while I explain about Oscar asking me to inves-tigate what Minnie and Neil were doing on the beach. I don't go into the gory details, just the bonfire, but I can feel myself going red in the face. Everyone is looking at me with a combination of fascination and horror, and it all sounds ridiculous, even to my own ears.

When I've finished, no one speaks for a bit. Duckie snickers loudly, and even Ronan looks very uncomfortable. 'Um...so...mm...Mags...' he manages, and I can tell he wants to help me out of this hole I've dug for myself but doesn't know how. 'Your local pub owner thinks these...um...these...'

'Yes, as I said, Tatiana is Russian by birth and emigrated to Ireland seven years ago – that's how she identified the idiosyncrasies that make her think –'

'Oh, you mean that Russki ball-breaker barmaid in the Samovar?' Duckie roars with laughter. 'Sure, she's having ya on, Mags. You'd be better off investigating her. She's come on to me a few times, and me a married man... I'd say she's on the game.'

I don't care what it does to my career – it's time someone put this creep in his place for once and for all. 'My *friend* Tatiana is not, nor has she ever been, a prostitute, which is why she consistently rejects your advances. Neither is she a supporter of communism, or whatever you meant by the remark. She married an Irishman, and the relation-ship unfortunately broke down. She now is the proprietor of the Samovar pub and restaurant in Ballycarrick, not the barmaid, and a better-run licenced premises would be hard to find. She tolerates no drunken behaviour, her taxes are paid on time and in full, and she has never served a minute past the licencing hours or to anyone under the legal age. So please, Detective Inspector Cassidy, I'd thank you to keep your ill-informed and frankly vulgar and nasty remarks to yourself.'

Duckie goes pale, then bright red, then dark red. He swallows and opens his mouth, but before he has a chance to reply, Ronan jumps in, saying smoothly, 'It's important to remember, Donal, there are many Russian citizens in this country, and the vast majority are decent, hard-working people who feel tremendous loyalty to Ireland. I'm sure Tatiana was only trying to be helpful to Sergeant Munroe. And Mags, I want you to go on keeping your ear to the ground in Ballycarrick and don't be afraid to report back on anything unusual, even if it does seem, as you say, outlandish.'

Duckie glowers at me but I don't care. He's an eejit. Always was and always will be. I still feel a bit mortified by having made a report about a witch and a warlock of all things, but I'm fifty-two, not twelve, and I'll get over it.

At one, we break for lunch, served at the table in the original room, and it's delicious, rare roast beef with all the trimmings. Ronan takes the seat beside me, which has Duckie glaring at me again. He hates that Ronan and I are close; it drives him distracted.

'So how's it all going?' Ronan asks, tucking in.

'Grand, I think. Look, I know it sounds ridiculous about Minnie and Neil, but in for a penny, in for a pound...' And I tell him about Joel and the Daffy Duck phone.

He listens politely, but when I ask him what he thinks, he says kindly, 'You know, Mags, I'm no fan of that man there...' He doesn't move his eyes, but we both know who he means. Duckie, who is currently sniggering under his breath to his companion, Richard, whose face is stony. 'But he is right about Russian spies not wanting to be flamboyant or stand out in any way. By all means keep an eye on this pair if you think you should, but it's certainly not the usual modus operandi of undercover agents.'

'Sure, I'll do that.' I'm a bit disappointed in him but can see his point, so I try not to let it show.

'Anyway,' he says, 'what I was actually asking is, how's it going with *you.*'

'Me? Ah, I'm fine...' I feel that familiar discomfort when Ronan and I speak personally.

He lowers his voice. 'I heard about Kieran's mad ex.' Of course he's heard. Róisín's up in court in Galway next Thursday, and Duckie, I'm sure, couldn't wait to put it all around.

'Yes, well, hopefully that's all behind us now.'

'Is it true she assaulted you and your daughter?'

'She floored me with a bottle, and she elbowed Kate in the nose. But Kate's OK. It was dramatic but it's over. To be honest, I'm thinking of asking the judge to be lenient.' It's true. I have been mulling this over, ever since that visit from Joel; the poor man looked so broken. It's never just the perpetrator who suffers, it's their family too. Frances Duggan as well, having to cope with Martin's rapidly advancing dementia.

He looks incredulous. 'I hope you aren't thinking of letting her off the hook because Kieran –'

I cut him off. 'If it was up to my husband, she'd do time. It's me who feels sorry for her.' I know Ronan likes Kieran, but I also know he has a bit of a thing for me, and I don't want him to imagine there's even the slightest rift between me and my husband over this.

'Well, I hope the judge doesn't listen to you,' he says darkly, not buying into my benevolent attitude. 'She sounds like she's out of control. People have their hearts broken every day of the week – it doesn't mean you can go around assaulting people, especially kids, for God's sake.'

'We'll be fine, trust me.' I smile.

We finish our meal, and on the dot of two, Ronan calls the full meeting to order once more.

Brigitta Jannsen gives the report back from our group. She explains that I and Ester Osbridge will be advising Galway Council how to secure the works offices for the submarine cables both physically and digitally, and she mentions Peter Berg, aka Vassili Morozov, and passes the grainy picture around again. But she doesn't say anything about the witch and the warlock – she clearly thinks that would be hanging me out to dry – and to be honest, I'm grateful.

After the other two reports, marine surveillance and border control operations, John wraps up the session. 'Operation Greengage has been ongoing on several fronts, both here and across Europe, and what really needs to happen now is we need to step up our efforts and watch like hawks for anyone like this Peter Berg, or any others.'

After a few more comments, he wishes us all good luck in our endeavours. Ronan stands up then, thanks everyone for coming and reiterates the importance of what we're doing. 'This is not merely an Irish issue. Potential Russian interference with infrastructure has ramifications for economic safety for all of Europe and indeed further afield.' He nods slightly in the direction of the Americans. 'Respectful cooperation is critical between all of us, from the ground up.' And he looks meaningfully at Duckie, then smiles very slightly at me.

CHAPTER 24

When I pick Tatiana up from the Optizone clinic on Grafton Street, she needs me to lead her to the car as she is as blind as a bat. But by the time we pass the Drumlish halting site, she's seeing everything from a mile off; it's like having an eagle in the car.

For instance, she recognises Jerome when he's still a good three hundred yards ahead of us, while all I can see is the vague outline of a tall man walking along in the dark. He really shouldn't be out on the road at all, particularly in his old black coat; someone might knock him down. Plus it's starting to rain and it's cold now – four degrees, the car says.

I slow down and open the window. 'Hi, Jerome, all OK?' I ask, ready for him to ignore me. But he doesn't, though he keeps on walking.

'My van won't start,' he says as I drive along slowly beside him. 'I don't know what's wrong with it. Dora needs a prescription filled, so I rang Julie and she's going to stay open for me.'

'Well, why don't you jump in. I'll drop you in and back out when you've got it,' I offer.

'Ah, you're grand, Mags, thanks. I'm happy enough to walk.'

'But it's going to lash any minute, and you should really have a hi-vis for this road – it's dangerous.'

He looks at me then, and I sense renewed hostility. The Travellers dislike intensely being told what to do by anyone. The wearing of hi-vis vests, however sensible, would be something they would hate.

'Walking on the road's a crime now, is it?' he asks, and though his tone isn't exactly antagonistic, it's not friendly banter either.

'Course not, but I'll have you in town in a few minutes, and Dora will get the medicine into her sooner?'

He sighs. 'Grand.' And when I stop, he reluctantly opens the back door and sits in. His black leather coat is soaked, and his dark pelt of hair is brushed back and sheens with rain.

'You know Tatiana, from the Samovar?' I ask as I pull off again.

'I do.' He thaws a bit when he realises who my passenger is in the front seat. 'Hi, Tatiana.' He likes her; she's one of those rare publicans who let Travellers drink in her pub.

'Hi, Jerome.' She turns and smiles. She likes him too; he supplies her restaurant with free-range eggs and organic vegetables.

They chat about how the hens are laying less now that it's getting cold, and then we're in Ballycarrick and I drop Tatiana and carry on to Dullea's with Jerome still in the back.

'I'll wait,' I say as he gets out.

'There's no call to. I'll manage away myself.' He crosses the road to the pharmacy, which still has the light on, though it's almost 7 p.m. Julie Dullea inherited the shop from her father and is a great asset to the town. She knows as much as Dr Harrison, everyone says. I remember Elsie telling me she is seeing a man now, and I'm delighted for her. She had a tragedy young in life; her boyfriend was killed in a motorcycle accident.

I turn the car and wait anyway, and I can see Julie handing Jerome the bag with whatever medication Dora needs. It's hammering rain now.

My phone pings. Kieran. *You OK? Got a lasagne in Bertie's, ready in 30 mins. Will we wait for you?*

I'm just replying when he texts again. *I got salad too before you give out!*

I smile. If I didn't force the issue, my husband and children would never eat a green thing.

Home at 7:30, see you then, xx, I text back.

Jerome comes out, sees me there, hesitates, then gets into the car. 'Thanks,' he mutters.

'No bother,' I say, pulling out into the street and going back the way I came. 'I hope Dora's OK?'

'Era, she has a bad chest, coughin' all the week...' he answers gruffly, and I know he's hiding his concern. Dora may be the diminutive wife of a large and physically intimidating man, but he adores her and, according to Delia anyway, is a bit afraid of her too. She rules the roost behind the scenes.

I might not get a chance again, so I decide to try to make things good with him again. 'I'm sorry about the thing with the couple in the Lodge, Jerome. I don't like falling out with you.' Honesty is the best policy, I find, in almost everything.

'They are a pair of gangsters, Mags. You *do* know that, don't ya?' he replies.

'Maybe they are.' I don't tell him I've been coming around to that way of thinking myself, for a very different reason.

'They're leavin' tonight anyway,' he adds with certainty. 'Things aren't goin' well for them here. Their electricity line is down, their kitchen flooded, ten slates came off the roof, a window blew in, and more is coming.'

'What on earth happened? I didn't think the storm was that bad?' I'm especially alarmed about the slates. Kieran did a load of work on that roof, and I know it cost Minnie and Neil a fortune, so I'm as much worried for my husband's reputation as anything.

'Kathleen lit the black candle for them.'

I exhale. 'Jerome, it's very important that nobody from your family, or the Carmodys, does anything to harm the two of them. If you do, there's nothing I'll be able to do to protect you.'

'And is it a crime to light a candle now?' he asks. 'We never went next nor near them.'

'No, but…well, it's not good, is it?'

'I thought you don't really go in for that kind of stuff,' he retorts.

'I don't, but…' I need him to understand that anything that could be construed as harassment is illegal.

'So Kathleen is dealing with it her own way. No member of my family, not the Carmodys either, I'd say, would lay a hand on them. But mark my words, they'll be gone soon enough if not tonight.'

I sigh and give up. 'Fair enough.' I've enough to do sorting out real crimes without worrying about spells and hexes.

We drive in silence for a minute or two.

'Delia says she's getting properly married now, in the Church. At least that, I suppose,' he says, and I smile. I'm glad she's told him. 'She said 'twas you put the idea in her head.'

Delia and I had talked about it, and I gently said there were some things they could do to appease their parents without compromising what they both wanted. So she and Darren recently had an in-depth discussion about it all and agreed that for both families, a proper diamond ring and a traditional wedding in a church with the bride in white and the groom in a three-piece suit and a big reception after-wards would make the unusual union a bit easier for their parents to explain to their friends. And though the two young people still don't see the point of it, they've decided to do it anyway.

'I didn't, not really. They were thinking they were saving you all a lot of money and hassle, and I just said maybe it was up to you to decide if you wanted the expense and hassle of it all,' I say. 'And she loves him and he her, but the wedding is for you and Dora, and his parents as well. She doesn't want any of you to feel ashamed of her, she told me so.'

'Well, we have been ashamed of her, her letting him into her bed before getting married, living like a man with his wife. And what was to stop him getting what he wanted off my daughter and doing a legger?'

I laugh. 'If anyone holds all the cards in that relationship, it is your daughter, Jerome. Darren wouldn't leave her if his life depended on it. Come on, you know that.'

I can tell from his reaction that he suspects it but is glad to hear it articulated.

'I should never have let my mother talk me into letting her join the guards. That's where all the trouble started,' he grumbles for the hundredth time.

His big bulk takes up most of the passenger space of my car, and I nudge him playfully. 'Go away outta that, Jerome McGovern. The trouble with that one started the day she came into the world. Neither you nor Dora, nor Dacie when she was alive, God be good to her, nor me nor anyone else can get in the way of Delia McGovern when she gets an idea in her head. You know that as well as I do.'

'She's a right bold strap. Maybe I was too soft on her…' he mutters.

'She's not and you know it. She's a fabulous girl, and she's clever as a fox, and she was never going to marry one of the Carmodys and have a tribe of kids in a caravan and be happy with that. You know it and I know it.'

'I wouldn't have let one of the Carmodys have her…' he says wistfully. Jerome loves all his children, I know, but Delia is the light of his life, and it grieves him and makes him proud in equal measure that she's so independent.

'She's going to marry the man she chose, and he's a good man, Jerome, I promise you that. I know him well. He loves her, but he respects her too, you know? He's who she needs, not some fella who'll expect her to take orders and do as she's told or take the consequences.'

'Like a Traveller man, you mean?'

'Not all of them. You're not like that, but a lot of them are, you must admit it.' Domestic violence is a feature of the Traveller life, no point in saying otherwise. 'And she couldn't stick it. She'd be miserable, and she'd up and leave him, and if a man raised his hand to her, she'd knock him into next week, you know she would. So letting her do it her way, even if it's not how you'd like it done, is better in the long run.'

He sighs so deeply, his whole frame rises and falls, and again we drive in silence.

As we pull up at the halting site, he says, 'Thanks for the spin. Will you come in for the tea?'

I beam at him, delighted at being asked. 'I would but I can't. Kieran has the dinner made at home.'

He chuckles. 'Ye women won't be happy till ye have fools made of us all.'

'Go on outta that, Jerome McGovern. Yourself and Kieran Munroe are lucky ducks with the women you got. You are minded like prize pigs.' I laugh, and I know things are fine between us again. It's a massive relief. More than I care to admit to anyone, being held in Jerome McGovern's high esteem matters to me.

'Oh, and bring me that dog of yours,' he adds. 'We'll see can we sort him out.'

'Thank you, Jerome, I will,' I say as he opens the passenger door, and then I chance my arm. 'And there's one other thing…'

He half-closes the door again and sits looking at me.

'Caelan Cronin…' I begin, and pause as I think how to put this. But it's fine; he knows exactly what I'm talking about.

'You want me to tell Patrick and Kenneth to stay away from him?'

'If you wouldn't mind, Jerome. He's breaking his father's heart, the trouble he's getting into.'

'Consider it done,' he says. He climbs out of the car into the rainy dark and is gone.

CHAPTER 25

The Gate Lodge looks kind of spooky, all lit up on the wild windy night, with the old ruin looming behind and the black arms of trees flailing. Lanterns powered by solar but reminiscent of the old gas lamps line the driveway, and every arched window sheds an eery, yellow, flickering light. Candles, I suppose.

Both Neil's van and Minnie's car are parked neatly beside each other on the gravel, and I can see boxes piled on the back seats. So it looks like Jerome isn't wrong about them leaving, even if it's just temporary while the electricity and stuff get fixed.

I park my car on the roadside and get out. The rain has stopped but not the wind. I stand there, wondering about knocking on the Lodge door. I would like to see the lie of the land, but I can't just barge in for no reason.

I have a card in my wallet for a free reading. It's the one Minnie gave to Tatiana in the street outside the café.

Before I've made up my mind to act, the door opens abruptly, and there's Minnie, in her embroidered coat with the pointed hood, carrying another cardboard box. I think we both get a bit of a fright, but then she recovers and shouts over her shoulder into the house, 'Neil! Guess who's here, and we were only just talking about her!'

CLOSER THAN YOU THINK

I can't really now get back in my car and drive off again, so I walk up the short drive between the solar lanterns. Minnie greets me, smiling apologetically. 'We must have manifested you by accident, Mags. I'm so, so sorry for dragging you out on a night like this.'

'That's OK. I came of my own free will this time,' I say as I take out my wallet. 'I have a card for a free reading, and I heard you were leaving for a while anyway and wanted to use it before you went.' I get out the card and give it to her, and she studies it with a frown.

'Is this urgent, Mags? We're only going away for a day or so, while the electricity gets fixed, and we had a window blow in and several slates off. I was going to call Kieran...'

'Well, not urgent exactly, but I have this missing-person case I'm finding very hard to solve and I was hoping you might help me?'

'Do you now.' She looks at me closely, but I'm used to keeping a straight face in lots of circumstances; as a guard you have to play your cards close to your chest. Then she looks over my shoulder into the wet night, and at my car parked out on the roadside. 'It's just you here, by yourself?' she asks.

'Just me, Minnie.'

'Well...' It's started to rain again, and she's standing on the gravel getting wet, but I have my fabulously waterproof Garda jacket on.

'Do you want help with that, Minnie? Will I open the car boot for you?'

'No, no, it's fine.' She puts her head to one side, birdlike. 'Look, why don't you come in?' She goes back into the house and leaves the box down in the hall, which is stacked with more boxes, some still open and filled with odds and ends, books, CDs. They're definitely going away for more than a couple of days.

Or maybe I'm letting my imagination run away with me. Maybe they're worried with slates off the roof that more will go and they'll get water damage, especially with a window out as well, so they're putting stuff in storage until everything is fixed. The electricity is still off; there are lots of candles burning on the empty shelves in the hallway.

She goes to the foot of the stairs and calls up. 'Neil? Mags has come for a reading! I'm going to give her twenty minutes. Can you keep her company while I just put this box in the car?'

A muffled agreement from upstairs, where much thumping and crashing is going on, and then Neil descends the stairs, carrying yet another cardboard box.

'Just wait here a minute,' Minnie says to me. 'I need to prepare the room, burn some sage and clear the space.' And she goes off deeper into the house, leaving me with Neil in the hall.

'So you've come for a reading?' he asks as he sets his box down on the pile. He takes up a reel of Sellotape from on top of another box and scratches his fingernail along it, looking for the end. 'Why tonight?'

'Missing person,' I say casually. 'Well, not officially missing yet, but her husband is worried.'

'Oh?' He stands looking at me, a torn-off piece of Sellotape stuck to his thumb.

'And I've heard Minnie is great at finding all sorts of things.'

He looks pleased and nods, stroking his straggly beard, getting the piece of Sellotape stuck to it and having to pull it off again with a wince. 'She is very good, so prepare to be surprised. A relative of yours who has passed over might come through and tell you what you want to know. It often happens, so don't get too much of a fright.'

'I'll try not to.' I smile.

He turns back to the box, but then there's a massive blast of wind outside. All the candles gutter spookily, and there's a crash as a tree falls, followed by another almighty smash from one of the rooms off the hall – this one sounds like a window breaking. Neil goes white, drops the Sellotape and rushes into the front room, cursing and swearing, clearly forgetting he is supposed to be keeping me company.

I take the opportunity to have a quick look along the line of boxes. The one he was about to fix is still open and full of plastic baggies, herbs and weird-looking mushrooms, all dried, and what seems suspiciously like a dead frog and some worms. God knows what they've been brewing in their cauldron or whatever witches cook in these days. I shudder, feeling a bit sick. And then I see it. The Daffy Duck phone. It's not in with the dead frog; it's in the box beside it, which is thoroughly Sellotaped but the cardboard flaps don't quite meet. I would never have seen it if it hadn't been so on my mind. As it is, just the black and white corner peeks out under a tangle of wires and other electrical stuff, but it's enough for me to know what it is.

I step away as Neil rushes out of the room behind me and then out of the front door, roaring like a true warlock, 'If that's you, Oscar O'Leary, breaking our windows, I'll put such a curse on you, you'll be dead in a week like Desmond Dunne!'

If I really thought it was Oscar out there, I'd follow, but I don't. Oscar is way too scared of our witch and warlock now. Could Kathleen and the black candle be causing all of this? I mentally shake myself. It's an old building, and it's blowing a gale out there. Kieran said it was renovated shoddily in the first place; no wonder with all this wind and rain, it is coming apart at the seams.

I estimate I have maybe three seconds. I slit the Sellotape with my car keys, take out the phone, undo the top button of my jacket, stuff the phone with one quick practised movement under my shirt and hoodie into my bra and put the box with the dead frog on top of the now-open box of wires.

'Where's Neil gone?' gasps Minnie, appearing around the corner of the stairs.

I smile blandly at her. 'He ran outside – he was looking for someone. Sorry for snooping. I just was fascinated by your cooking ingredients. I love cooking.' If she can't tell that's a lie, then she's definitely not a witch. I hold up the dead frog. 'I was trying to work out what this was?'

She rushes to take it off me. 'Put that back!' she hisses. 'It's a very valuable ingredient.'

And then Neil appears in the hall again, extremely ruffled. 'There's another window smashed, Minnie. I thought maybe it was Oscar, but it looks like a small tree fell and the top branch hit it.'

'This bloody house… Did you see anyone?' she asks me.

'Well, you said to wait here, so no… I was just waiting for you to do my reading, but I can see it's not a good time,' I say, but even as the words come out of my mouth, I know I've made a mistake, because something happens between me and Minnie. It's subtle and almost imperceptible, but I'm positive she knows I'm lying. This woman is a genius at reading people's characters, and of course I'm not one to stand around doing nothing just because she's told me to. That's why she called Neil down to watch me in the first place.

'What shall we do, Minnie?' bleats Neil, looking into the front room again.

She dismisses him. 'Oh, just sweep the glass aside and staple the curtains together.' But then she adds in a more patient voice, 'We'll get someone in to fix it while we're away for the next few days.'

I'm sure that last bit is for my benefit. I don't think they have any intention of coming back. Whatever they needed to do here is done. Bonfires lit, maps drawn. The work phone of the assistant to a New York senator is just a bonus, not part of the plan – and it's been their undoing. It's the one tangible piece of proof I have of them not being who they say they are, and right now it's tucked into my bra.

'Now, come on along, Mags. I have the room set up for you.' With a sudden bright smile, like she's made her decision, she's back to her smiling self once more and holds out her hand to me. Neil moves beside me. 'Why don't you take off that big jacket and leave it here. Oh, and your phone – I need you to turn off any recording devices you might have – they disrupt the ether.'

I smile back at her, just as brightly. 'You've reminded me, Minnie, my phone is in the car. I better get it before I turn it off – I need to let Kieran know I'll be a bit later than I thought.' I go to the door, which Neil has left open, but before I can step out, I feel something hard stick into my back and I hear Neil's soft voice in my ear, his straggly beard brushing my neck.

'Close the door and turn around now. Nothing bad will happen if you do as I say, right now.'

Has he a gun to my back? Surely not. But it feels like one. I turn and he turns with me, keeping behind me, like guards are trained to do. Minnie is still there by the stairs, smiling, holding out her hand.

'Minnie, Neil,' I begin, calmly. 'What on earth is that about? I came here to get a reading, and suddenly you're acting as if I'm your enemy. I don't understand...'

'Oh, Mags, I think you do,' purrs Minnie. 'In fact I'd say you're in the wrong job, the way you're sniffing around us. You know something, you sense something. Maybe you should have been a psychic – you'd earn a lot more money and people would respect you more.'

'What do you mean?' I try to look bewildered. 'I don't know anything except you're a white witch and a white warlock, and I've come here for your help...'

'Don't try to fool the likes of me, Mags, it can't be done. I'm still not sure what you're doing here. I have to admit, you're not easy to read, not like most people. But what I do know is, there's something going on in your head, and I'm afraid tonight's operation is too important to allow a bumbling country sergeant to go clumping around all over it in her hobnailed boots.'

'It is an offence to obstruct an officer of the law in her duties –'

'Neil, bring her.'

'Please do as I say, Sergeant Munroe,' says Neil in his soft, soothing tones. 'I don't want to hurt you, but if you won't comply, I don't have a choice. Now just walk in front of me, follow Minnie there, past the stairs, past the kitchen, to the door at the back.'

The door they lead me to is painted gold and covered in silver stars and moons, and when Minnie opens it and Neil prods me in with what I assume is the gun, it's just as Kieran described the room where Minnie does her readings: windowless and painted black, with weird crimson symbols painted on the walls. There's a pack of tarot cards laid out on the board, and even an actual crystal ball.

'Hand me your phone and jacket please,' says the white witch. 'And I know you have it, so no more of that claptrap about it being in the car.'

I'm not going to argue. There's no point. She knows I know something, even if not the extent of it. I hand her my phone and the jacket. She checks all the pockets, then comes towards me and frisks me like an expert. Joel's phone is in my bra, but the garment is an industrial piece of engineering designed to keep my breasts from falling around all over the place when I run, so she doesn't notice.

'Now' – she hands me my own phone back again – 'I want you to text your husband and tell him you're at the station working on the missing-person case.' She realises something then and looks annoyed with herself. 'There isn't a missing-person case, is there, Mags?'

'No, there isn't,' I say, rather proud of myself for getting that one past her.

'Then tell him you're held up with paperwork,' she says silkily. 'And say you're going to put your phone on silent.'

With Neil pointing what I can now see is definitely a gun at me, I have no choice but to text the following to Kieran. *Went into the station, and now I'm stuck filling out some bloody forms that need to be in by tomorrow. I'll be a bit late, so go ahead and make the dinner. So sorry. I'm going to put my phone on silent for an hour. Xxxxxx*

I show the text to Minnie, and she nods. I hit send.

Then I grin at her. 'You know what's going to happen now, don't you?' I say tauntingly. 'He's going to phone the station to ask me what on earth to make for dinner, and then Delia, who's on duty, will tell him I'm not there.'

She looks at me, her eyes narrowed, trying to assess whether I'm telling the truth.

'Come on, Minnie,' I say contemptuously. 'You know what men are like. You've made a big mistake. So if I were you, I'd let me walk out of here now before you get into even worse trouble.'

Neil looks steely, and the hand with the gun is steady, but Minnie just rolls her eyes and takes my phone and calls Ballycarrick Garda station. When Delia's voice answers, giving her name, she ends the call and hands the phone back to me. 'Fine, it is her, so text her and tell her that if your husband rings, she needs to tell him you can't be disturbed, and say you'll explain later.'

'And what if I refuse?' I reply.

'Then instead of just being locked up in here alive until someone finds you, Neil will shoot you and we'll set the house on fire, and you'll be found in here dead.'

She means it.

I rack my brain...and then I remember.

I take the phone and text Delia. *Hi, Delia. It's complicated, but if Kieran phones the station looking for me, tell him I can't be disturbed. Sarge.* And I add the woman officer emoji.

I show it to Minnie, she nods, and I hit send. Then she takes my phone and puts it in her pocket. The two of them back out of the room side by side, the door closes behind me, and I hear a key turn.

Immediately I look around the room to see if there's anything spying on me. The only candidate is what looks like a smoke detector on the wall. I climb onto the table to reach it and remove the cover. I'm not sure exactly, but it looks like some kind of device. Maybe it's the innards of a smoke detector, but either way I pull the wires and break them and disconnect the battery.

As soon as I'm satisfied I can't be seen, I reach into my bra. I hope they've charged Joel's phone in order to try and hack it, and they have, but it's down to one percent battery and I have to make a quick decision. Mercifully they have removed any passcode lock and the phone is an old one, so I can open the main screen.

Ronan Brady first. I have memorised his mobile number, a precaution since the night of the people traffickers.

This is Mags. Greengage, Ballyloughane Strand. Attack tonight. Send everyone. Whatever big operation is going on that Minnie and Neil don't want me to trample over in my hobnailed boots, that's my top priority.

I watch as the two blue ticks appear. Ronan's seen it, and I hope he has too much sense to call me; I can't see how to put this thing on silent.

I text Kieran. *I'm in the Lodge. Neil has a gun. I'm safe, just locked in the inner room. Wait until they've left before you come –*

Before I can send, the screen goes dead, and my lifeline is gone.

In a fit of exasperation, I go to the door and shove it with my shoulder. Pointless exercise. There is no keyhole on this side of the door, just a steel disc, not that I have anything to hand with which to pick a lock, just a pack of tarot cards and a crystal ball. I decide not to waste my breath shouting to be let out. I go back to the table and sit down to wait for rescue. I wonder how long I'll be stuck here. Not too long, I hope. My only worry is that the cavalry will turn up too soon, while Neil is still here with his gun. Hopefully not.

Kieran won't call the station; he knows not to disturb me at work. But Delia will hopefully know by the emergency code Zoë invented – the word 'Sarge', followed by the woman cop emoji – that something is amiss, and I just have to pray that she'll get onto everyone, including Ronan, though I'd say his phone will be hopping, so it might take a while for her to get through to him.

Ronan knows I gave a lift to Tatiana, so if I'm lucky, after talking to Ronan, Delia will call Tatiana, and she'll tell Delia I left Jerome home, and Delia will call her father, and Jerome will say I've gone, and hopefully if she drives the route from the halting site to my house, she'll see my car...

Unless they've moved it; the keys are in the pocket of my jacket.

Long minutes pass in dead silence. Maybe they've left the house already? I get up and press my ear to the jamb of the door, but it's a tight fit. All I can hear is a very soft roaring sound. The wind probably.

And then a loud bang in the distance, like something heavy falling – another tree?

And then another much fainter sound, a sort of crackling, followed by another loud bang, this time more like an explosion, and the roaring sound is louder now... My eyes go to the bottom of the door. It's undeniable. Smoke.

I'd thought even if I had all night to wait, someone would turn up eventually. But they've set the house on fire with me in it, not dead but alive.

CHAPTER 26

*T*wenty minutes pass, then half an hour. I have my hoodie rolled up along the bottom of the door, and I've rammed tarot cards all around the frame to seal it, anything to stop the smoke coming in…

I kneel to push the hoodie harder against the door. The smoke is leaking through now, and I try to talk myself out of panicking. Someone will see the fire; the fire brigade must be on its way. And yes, Minnie and Neil might have moved my car off the road but only to the back of the house, so the firefighters will see it and know I'm in here. Maybe the text to Kieran delivered even though Joel's phone was dead? I'm grasping at straws and I know it.

Even if they do see the fire, how will they get in through the blaze? How will they find me in this sealed room?

I take a deep breath to calm myself. Big mistake. Despite my best efforts, the smoke is pouring in under the door. I inhale it and start to cough, painfully, and stagger to my feet.

Is that sirens, or wishful thinking? Either way, I've realised now, it's too late. Yes, they might find the car. Yes, they might decide I'm still here. Someone might even call Kieran, who understands the layout of the house, having roofed it all. He even knows about the windowless room. But it makes no difference. There's no way to get me out other than through the internal door, which leads to a house in flames.

The strands of acrid smoke are swirling at chest height now, and I can't stop coughing; I'm finding it difficult to breathe. I lie on the ground – the lower down I am, the better – but I know it's just postponing the inevitable. The smoke inhalation will kill me before the fire. I try to relax my mind. I say goodbye to the girls and Kieran in my mind, blinking back tears, with love in my heart.

And then I hear it.

A dull thudding crunch coming from the outside wall. Over and over.

The thudding is rhythmic, which suggests a machine, and the plaster cracks. Another thud, and a huge chunk of plaster falls off the wall. I'm watching from the top of the table. There are stone blocks behind the plaster, and the cement between them seems to be crumbling. Then I see it as well as hear it – the tip of the carbide blade that is grinding through the stone.

The consaw stops, is withdrawn and returns in a different direction, then a third; whoever it is, is cutting out a square. It's getting harder and harder to breathe. My throat is raw and my eyes are streaming; I can't see now for the smoke. Then the saw stops again, and there's a loud creaking crash. A section of wall is forced through, then another and another, and even standing on the table, I'm hit on the legs and body by the debris being battered out of the hole. I'm feeling very woozy, my throat is burning, I'm fighting to breathe, and I'm struggling not to fall.

A face appears through the hole, ghostly in the swirling smoke... 'Another few blows, love, and we'll have you out. Just stay back.'

It's Kieran. Kieran. Thank God.

Hurry, I gasp, but nothing comes out of my dried-up throat.

The thudding continues, and a sledgehammer smashes through the ever-growing hole. It's still not big enough for a person to fit through, but then I see something else, hard to make out what, coming through, a hook of some kind. And then a terrible tearing sound and a huge chunk of the wall comes away.

The world goes grey, and I fall to my knees on the table, then slide to the floor. I am as weak as water, but I crawl to the pile of rubble, and strong hands reach in and pull me through. The cold night air mingles with the smoky fumes. I suck in a big gulp. And then I feel more hands. I'm being dragged, then carried, and there are voices and blue lights, and it's very cold, but it's so much better than that horrible small room…

I'm on a stretcher, and Kieran is beside me.

'Mags, I thought… Oh God… I…' His face is covered in dust and dirt. I reach out to hold his hand. I can't speak, and the pain in my chest is horrible. Someone puts a mask on my face, and I'm strapped onto a trolley and rolled into an ambulance.

'Ballyloughane Strand…' I'm trying to get the mask off. 'It's happening tonight! They're going to attack the –'

'Just relax now, Sergeant Munroe. We're taking you to hospital, but just try to relax,' says a woman whose voice I don't recognise.

Kieran tries to get in the ambulance, but they say no, that he can follow in a car.

'Kieran, I need Kieran…' I try to get the mask off again, but strong hands push me back down.

The doors of the ambulance close, and the siren is on as we drive at speed. I want to take the mask off, to tell them, but I'm strapped down. Is this really an ambulance, I wonder. What if it's the Russians… A peculiar mix of panic and fear mixed with a sense of drifting away overtakes me, and I know no more.

CHAPTER 27

FOUR WEEKS LATER

*a*s I enter the meeting in the Garda Headquarters in Phoenix Park, I am not expecting to hear a standing ovation. I don't even know why I've been summoned. I thought my role in Operation Greengage was over once the attempt to sever the cable at Bally-loughane Strand was thwarted by the combined forces of the coast guard, navy and local guards.

All the same people are in the room as were at the previous Operation Greengage meeting, and as I enter, Ronan stands and so does everyone else, and they clap and smile. Well, all except Duckie, who looks like a bulldog chewing a wasp. I'm so confused. I glance over my shoulder to see who's behind me, but there's no one.

Then I see him, the Garda Commissioner, at the head of the table. He's tall and imposing, a man from Northern Ireland with huge charisma, universally liked in the country. He's brought his dog, a huge Bernese mountain dog that is almost as famous as him, and the animal rests happily at his owner's feet. Ronan comes towards me and leads me gently by the elbow to meet him.

CLOSER THAN YOU THINK

'Your country – and indeed many others – owes you an enormous debt of gratitude, Sergeant Munroe,' the commissioner says as he rises to his feet and shakes my hand. 'If it were possible, you would be awarded a chest full of medals. But the truth is, for reasons you can understand, we cannot publicise your heroics, so it will have to suffice that you know you have my and the government's most sincere gratitude.'

'Thank you,' I say, feeling rather like I did at that first meeting with John Greene, when I was literally convinced it was a dream.

'If I can call everyone to order please,' Ronan says as everyone, including the Garda Commissioner, takes a seat. I sit next to Padraig McCarthy from the council and Ester Osbridge, the Scottish tech engineer, both of whom I've got to know better while reviewing the security of the works offices for the submarine cables. They both lean over to whisper their congratulations, and I thank Padraig for getting the council workers to finally unblock the drains and gutters in Bally-carrick's Main Street.

Ronan remains standing and looks around at our listening faces. 'As you all know, Vassili Morozov, along with his fellow spy, Natalia Petrova, a couple identifying themselves as Neil Jacobson and Minnie Melodie, were arrested, and it was down entirely to the heroic and intelligent actions of our colleague here, Sergeant Munroe. The spies were caught in a pincer operation between the navy and army as they were laying explosives in the car park at Ballyloughane Strand. They are now in custody in Paris, where the case is being handled by Europol.'

He nods to Brigitta, who stands up to take over as he sits down. 'The relevant sections of the international espionage investigation are still piecing it together, but it seems there was a plan to attack the cable simultaneously at several points, putting it out of action for months, and Morozov and Petrova were leading the plot. Having said that, they've not yet revealed any names, but negotiations are ongoing.'

She turns to me with a warm and friendly smile. 'We at Europol have so much gratitude and respect for the work you have done,

Sergeant Munroe – I have been asked to pass that on. And I owe you a personal apology. I was there when you voiced your suspicions about the couple you knew as Neil Jacobson and Minnie Melodie, but I was unable to think outside the box. I am so grateful you were brave enough to act and save the day for us all.'

There's another round of applause then, and the young lieutenant from the navy, Richard Boyle, speaks up as well. 'None of us believed her, Brigitta, so it was the ingenuity of Sergeant Munroe alone that led to the apprehension of two people who have been evading international police forces for the last twenty years.'

I exhale. Twenty years? Those two were clearly hard to catch.

'So what happens now?' asks Duckie grumpily. He's clearly sick of hearing about how great I am.

'Well, it's business as usual,' says Ronan. 'The submarine cables are still at risk. The removal of Morozov and Petrova will not have eliminated the risk, only reduced it.'

'So not such a big deal then,' Duckie says sourly under his breath.

Ronan ignores him as he wraps up the meeting, and everyone files past my chair to shake my hand and compliment me. Duckie stalks past, ignoring me, but Ronan hangs back until the room is empty except for us, then takes the seat beside me.

'How are you, Mags? Kieran said there is some lung damage?'

He's been in constant anxious touch since the night of the fire, to the point that Kieran is getting slightly peeved by it.

'Ah, I'm all right,' I say. 'I was in hospital for ten days, and I'm still a bit short of breath at times, but they assure me everything is healing well. Thank God for my husband having that consaw among his tools.'

Delia, who was at the scene, told me she'd never seen anything like it, the way Kieran cut through that wall with the consaw. 'It was two foot thick,' she told me in awe, 'but he just drove that saw through it. He was like something possessed. And then he just let rip with the sledge. I know my dad helped, but Kieran made that first hole himself, just by sheer strength of will.'

'And thank God as well for Jerome bringing the hook and chain,' I say now to Ronan.

'And well done to your staff,' Ronan adds, 'for devising a secret way to communicate danger.'

He's right about that; Zoë's contribution was vital. I'd told her so and she had beamed with pride. She's got the makings of a good officer, that one. And there's room for all sorts.

Delia realised straight away, and she tried to track my phone, but of course it was destroyed by then. It was found in the burnt-out remains, having been smashed with a hammer or something. Then she did as I'd hoped, rang round everyone, including Ronan, and Ronan told her I'd given a lift to Tatiana, and Tatiana told her I'd given a lift to Jerome, and Jerome told her I was already gone. And by that time, she was already out on the road, driving around looking for my car, and it was she who spotted the fire in the Lodge and called the fire brigade. Then on a hunch, she checked around the back, saw my car, called Kieran and then called her father.

Jerome had some kind of metal hook and chains in the four-wheel drive he borrowed from one of his nephews; he brought them with him to the scene of the fire. And after Kieran smashed his way into the room, Jerome helped him jam the hook through the hole and attach the chain to the tow hitch of the jeep, and they dragged the wall down.

'It was Garda Zoë O'Donoghue. She's the one that came up with the "sarge" and the emoji idea,' I say, and I feel so proud of her.

He laughs, resting his elbow on the table as he grins at me, a trace of his old boyishness about him. 'I know that. Delia told me when I went in to congratulate them all. I told Zoë what a brilliant idea it was, then *she* said you were the GOAT and that I was as much of a snack as she'd heard I was. I'd no idea what that meant, but I asked my niece who is nineteen, and apparently a GOAT is the "greatest of all time". My niece just howled laughing when I asked her why Zoë would call me a snack, so maybe I'm better off not knowing that.'

'It means you are delicious,' I say with a weary smile. 'Apparently Kieran is also a snack, which she said in such astonishment that someone as unsnacklike as me could have a snacky husband. She's a good kid really, tries her best, and she certainly saved the day. She'll actually make a decent guard eventually, but she's a lot.'

'Extra?' he asks with a grin.

'Indeed. You've been brushing up on your Gen Z chat, I see.' I laugh, and it's a hoarse, throaty sound still.

'I am. My brother's kids are almost unintelligible to me at this stage. Anyway, Zoë's idea saved your life, so she is the GOAT in my book.' His voice cracks a little, and I see he's moved.

I smile. 'In my book too.' I stand then, as I need to get going. Kieran is outside; he insisted on driving me to Dublin for the meeting.

He also stands, then gives me a hug. 'You're a remarkable woman, Mags Munroe. Infuriating, of course, with all the daft heroics, but remarkable nonetheless.'

'Thanks,' I say. I've already had to put up with Kieran, my mother and even Delia of all people giving out to me for walking in on Minnie and Neil by myself, even though at that point in time, everyone in Operation Greengage – all of them 'very high up', as Nora would put it – thought I had lost the plot for accusing a witch and a warlock of being Russian spies. 'But the only heroic thing I'll be doing in the near future is not killing Duckie Cassidy.'

'Yeah, Duckie's not a happy man.' He grins as we walk to the door together. 'He'll definitely be out there plotting to get one back on you.'

'Not that I can't handle him,' I add.

'Oh, I don't doubt it, not for a second. It would be a foolish man who would underestimate you, Mags Munroe.'

CHAPTER 28

I secretly curse Sharon and Mam for conspiring to get me into this super-tight, curve-hugging outfit; I feel like a trussed-up chicken. But the two of them were insistent that I pull out all the stops for Gearoid's wedding, if for no other reason than to stick it to Nora, who still has her nose out of joint over the girls' dresses.

So after a fierce struggle on the bed, I'm now wearing all the necessary underwear under a dark-purple silk trouser suit with a buttercup-yellow linen top and the same colour shoes, which are cutting off the blood supply as I stand looking at myself in the mirror and wondering if it's all worth it. Sharon did my make-up, although I point-blank refused the false eyelashes, Gerry has blow-dried my hair straight and silky, and I'm wearing the silver earrings Kieran bought me for Christmas. To be fair to my fairy god-torturers, I think I don't look too bad, but what a price to pay.

I take a quick selfie in the mirror and send it to Mam and Sharon. They both text back right away. Mam says,

You look beautiful, love. Have a lovely day – God knows you need it. Don't forget to bring the wrap – it will be cold later. xxx

It's so lovely having Mam back again. It was a big hole in my life not having her. And the girls are so relieved as well not to have to put up with Nana Nora picking them up from school the odd day when I or Kieran couldn't do it, Nora pecking their heads about every little thing. Mam had a fabulous time on her Caribbean cruise, but secretly I'm relieved she still thinks there's no place like Ballycarrick. I realise I was a bit worried she might get used to seeing the sun in the sky every day, might even start thinking that's normal and decide she wants to move to Barbados or something. But no. Apparently she missed the rain.

Sharon sends a GIF of a heart in flames with *You're smoking hot* in the middle. Then another message.

Mags, I'm not getting all soppy, but I'm delighted we're OK again. I can't do life without you. Trev says you are a lasher, btw, and Sean asked who is that? So it works. I'll see you at the reception. And if I get a chance to spill some sauce on Nora's white coat (who wears white to their son's wedding???), will I? Just say the word. Love ya. xxx

I send her a heart back, then walk gingerly down the stairs and into the kitchen, I'm not used to heels, where Kieran is standing at the ironing board bare-chested, fixing his shirt. He looks up, does a double-take, then sets aside the iron and applauds wildly – my second standing ovation in the last while. At this rate I'll start expecting it every time I enter a room. 'You look sensational, my love,' he says, as I try to do a twirl without exploding.

Then my outfit is nearly ruined before I can go over to put the kettle on, because Rollo comes bounding joyfully in from the garden and throws himself upon me, licking me and trying to climb into my arms, and even though I yell and push him away from me, he doesn't care; he just dances around on his hind legs grinning and wagging his tail at me.

It's all Jerome's fault.

He called the day after I came out of hospital, with a bunch of flowers from his own garden, and watched as Rollo slunk around me, whimpering.

'Come here, Jerome. What am I going to do with that dog that thinks I'm about to batter him every time he comes near me? And I've never raised a finger to him,' I said to him as I panted my way over to the kettle to make us some tea. My breathing took ages to come right after the smoke inhalation.

'Ara, someone that looks like you hurt him, I suppose. He's a stray, isn't he?'

'Kieran found him in a builder's yard, no chip, no collar. He was skin and bone.'

Then Jerome picked Rollo up and scratched his ears, and the little dog sighed with pleasure. Still holding the dog, he reached into his coat pocket and said, 'Give him this,' handing me a small round biscuit.

I took it and held it to Rollo's nose, but Rollo looked as he had always done when I offered him anything, dubious at best, cringing in Jerome's arms.

'Break it into pieces and hold your hand flat.'

I did as he said, while Jerome lowered his big head with his mop of oiled black hair and murmured something unintelligible to the dog. Both Rollo's and Jerome's heads were inches from my palm now. Rollo started sniffing my hand and eventually took a piece of the biscuit. Then came back for another and then wolfed the lot.

'Take him,' Jerome said quietly, and handed him to me. I'd never held Rollo before; he'd never let me. But this time he didn't try to get away, and Jerome stayed very close, crooning away in Cant, the Traveller language, one hand scratching Rollo's ears gently, the other digging in his pocket to hand me another biscuit. Rollo gobbled it in one bite and then licked my chin as Jerome laughed at the astonishment on my face. 'Give him a few of them every day, and he'll be your best friend.'

'What brand are they?' I asked him, amazed at how pleased I was by having my hands and face licked by a happy Rollo.

'Oh, you have to make 'em. You can't buy 'em. I'll text you the recipe. It's mostly flour, chicken stock, peanut butter and seeds. Look at him. He's mad about you now. You've the way of it – he was just a bit scared is all.'

And now I've got a dog that barely leaves me alone, and not only that, but one I have to bake biscuits for, when, as Kieran and the girls keep pointing out, I've never baked biscuits for anyone else in this family in my life.

Oh, and did I mention the current animal situation has gone from Rollo, Knickers and Meatloaf to include a very expensive and highly adored Pekingese? Well, we felt bad. Joel is gone back to America and Róisín is in St Ita's, so in a moment of charity, I agreed to have their dog. She's totally appalled by the manner in which we live – she is used to velvet cushions with her name hand embroidered and a blackout blind in her sleeping quarters – I can see it in her bulgy eyes and snub nose, and she looks at Rollo in a manner you could imagine my mother-in-law watching an Ozzy Osbourne gig. But she's still alive and will get used to slumming it. It will be good for her to see how the other half live, the way they send young ones from here to work in Indian orphanages for a week and they come back saying how wasteful we all are.

I'm still brushing myself down after Rollo's joyous assault when Jerome appears at the kitchen door. It's as if I've manifested him just by thinking about him. Maybe Minnie was right and I should be a professional psychic. 'Hi, Jerome, what's up?'

He comes in, looking a little sheepish. 'I know you're off to a weddin' of yer own, but I wanted to give you this.'

He takes a cream envelope out of his jacket and passes it to me. I open the envelope and read aloud the beautiful embossed card.

'Mr and Mrs Jerome McGovern kindly request your presence at the wedding of their daughter, Delia Dacie Bridget McGovern, to Darren James Carney on the 20th of March at 2 p.m. at St Joseph's Church, Ballycarrick, and to a reception afterwards at the Samovar, Ballycarrick.'

'Ah, that's lovely, Jerome. We'd love to come,' Kieran says as he pulls on his freshly ironed shirt.

'Thank you, Jerome, we'd be delighted,' I chime in.

'And the young ones too, bring them as well,' he says gruffly. 'They'll love the style and all of that. And sure you might give us a tune on the pipes, Kieran. I hear you're coming on great.'

'Are you trying to get me divorced, Jerome?' Kieran chuckles.

Well done, Delia, I think. She's done the right thing, and for her parents, this is huge. I can see the pride beaming from Jerome. *He* is paying for his daughter's wedding; he is inviting us. Not Delia, him. And for someone like Jerome, that means an awful lot.

'The girls surely will love it,' I say, suppressing a smile. An Irish Traveller wedding will not be short on outrageous style, no matter what the Carneys might prefer, and it will undoubtedly be a sight to behold. And fair play to Tatiana, a lot of establishments flatly refuse to book Traveller weddings, because they can be a bit, well…boisterous. But they know nobody would dare cause a fight or do any damage when Jerome McGovern is the name on the booking. He'd flatten any young buck with notions he was some kind of a gangster. And if he doesn't, Tatiana will, so it's covered.

Jerome has already warned Patrick and Kenneth away from Caelan Cronin, and I think he might have had a word with Caelan himself. And though I don't know if the poor lad will ever be the same happy-go-lucky boy he was before his mother was killed, he is at least going to school and not vandalising things, and he's stopped the underage drinking.

'Right, I'll let ye at it. Enjoy the day now, let ye,' Jerome says, blushing, as he backs out of the kitchen door. He knows it's a gay wedding we're going to, and for him, wishing us a nice day is a big leap. The world is changing, and I admire people like Jerome, who are traditional and set in their ways but make an effort to at least understand those they find bewildering.

I'd been thinking of having a cup of tea, but then I see the time on the clock, and between Rollo and Jerome, we're running late. I walk out into the hall. 'Girls!' I yell up the stairs. 'Are you ready? We need to go in four minutes flat. Kate! Ellie! I swear to God, if you don't –'

'Would you ever chill?' Ellie says, appearing above on the landing in what can only be described as a black lace body stocking. Her hair is in an elaborate upstyle, and the make-up would not look out of place in a fright show. The worst of it all is that her bra and knickers are clearly visible through the dress. I nearly choke.

'What about the green dress?' I gasp.

'Ah, Mam, I looked like an off-duty nun in that. This is much more my vibe.'

Luckily, before I can reply, my husband materialises at my side. I give out twenty times a week, so they ignore me most of the time, but Kieran never does, so he holds more gravitas.

'Ellie, it will be your Uncle Gearoid's wedding but my and your mother's funeral if Nana Nora sees you in that get-up. Go and change into the green dress now. No debates or whining, just do it.'

There's a moment of silence.

Ellie makes no complaint – she can tell by his voice when there is no wriggle room – just stomps mutinously back into the bedroom.

'I told you.' Kate giggles as Ellie passes her, which prompts Ellie to punch her hard on the shoulder and results in wailing from Kate.

'Enough, both of you,' Kieran says sternly. 'Right, Mags, you and Kate get into the car. I'll wait for Ellie.'

I'm quite glad to have a bit of extra time to get into the car in the high heels, and Kate hovers as I bend cautiously in the middle and ease myself in, then hands me my buttercup-yellow bag once I'm settled. She is wearing a lovely loose-flowing pale-orange dress with flat blue sandals, and I tell her she looks beautiful.

'You look the most beautiful of all, Mam,' she says, and my heart melts because I can tell she really means it.

* * *

IN LINE with Enrico's wishes, the wedding is at Castle Dysert. The ceremony is lovely, flamboyant and dramatic, as would have to be the case with Gearoid and especially Enrico involved, and I'm glad to see them both so happy.

As expected, Conor and his team have done an amazing job. There are sweet trucks and Mr Whippy vans at the drinks reception, and chocolate fountains as well as champagne fountains. They've covered over the sheltered upper garden of the historic castle with a huge candy-striped canvas roof, which makes it feel like we're outside but without the worry of the Irish rain. Though for once the weather is behaving; there's a serious amount of clear blue sky between the scudding white clouds, and the sea sparkles beyond the sloping lawns, on which peacocks and even a pair of flamingos strut around like they own the place.

The girls are gallivanting around with all the cousins, so we won't see them all day. I'm chatting with Kieran's sisters and Sharon and Trevor, all of us marvelling at how spectacular the place is, when Nora wanders up in her starched white outfit and elaborate feathered fascinator. It looks like something is nesting on her head.

'Poor Róisín is still in that St Ita's place...' she says to nobody in particular. 'God love her...that poor girl. Frances was only saying the other day how upset she is... They all are really...'

'Róisín is very lucky she didn't get a custodial sentence. She would have done if Mags had not spoken up for her in court,' Sharon says loudly to Orla, and I feel a wave of gratitude. I know I'm no shrinking violet, but it's nice to have someone stick up for me without me having to do it for myself. She's still the old Sharon I've known for almost fifty years. Whatever dispute we might have, she'll always back me a hundred percent, and I'll back her.

'I was only saying...' Nora's cheeks go pink.

'Well, *don't* only say,' Kieran says firmly, and I'm delighted he's joined us; he's another one who never lets me down. He has come to find me, and he's taken off the jacket of his suit and is just in shirt, tie and trousers. The top button is open, and the tie is pulled down a little; he hates things around his neck. He looks so handsome.

'Doesn't Mags look amazing, everyone?' he says as he puts his arm around me.

'She does,' says Nora, surprisingly. Then, 'That's a very well-cut suit in fairness, hides a multitude of sins.' Ah, there it is, the sting in the tail.

'She has the figure for it, you see, Mam. She could wear a bin bag and look amazing, but today she's a knockout.'

Nora nods reluctantly, but his sisters all agree, and Sharon is particularly loud in her enthusiasm. And then Kieran turns to me. 'Will we go for a stroll before dinner?'

I'm about to reply, 'In these shoes? I don't think so,' when I realise that he's got something behind his back. With a flourish he produces my cruddy old runners, the ones I use for walking the beach. They're wrecked but oh so comfortable.

'They were in the boot. You can put back on those old bench vices after.' He laughs. The idea of deliberately wearing shoes that hurt will forever confound him. 'I brought your walking jacket too. It's breezy out of the shelter of the castle. It's over on the wall.'

Nora looks as though it's a pair of dead rats he's holding up instead of a pair of old shoes, and her horror makes him laugh again.

'Come on, Mrs Munroe.' He gets down on one knee on the billiard-table grass, Cinderella-and-the-prince style, and replaces the yellow sandals with the manky old runners. His sisters are laughing and teasing him and calling him Prince Charming, but he doesn't care. Then he stands up and offers me his arm. 'Shall we?'

We walk over to the wall, and I put on my ancient walking jacket with the broken zip and weird smell, and we stroll on through the arboretum of the castle. The breeze ruffles his shirt, but he doesn't ever feel the cold, which makes it even kinder of him to remember my jacket.

I put my arm in his as we stroll along and chat about this and that. How Nora thought the perfectly respectable green dress Ellie was wearing was a bit revealing, and we laugh at what she'd have thought of the lace see-through bodysuit. Then we come to a little garden glasshouse beside a small waterfall. There is a wood-burning stove lit inside and a comfortable double seat beside it. It looks so cosy and warm, and when we enter, we find a coffee machine with cups and milk and some biscuits and a sign saying *Help yourself.*

'Coffee, madam?' Kieran asks, with a slight bow.

'Lovely.' I smile and curtsey – not very deeply, for the sake of my zips and buttons.

I sit down, and Kieran hands me a steaming coffee, then comes to join me, and his bulk causes the wicker two-seater to creak. After a bit of watching the waterfall while holding my hand, he sets down his own coffee, reaches into his back pocket and extracts an envelope.

'This came this morning as we were going out the door. I recognised the handwriting, and I was inclined to throw it in the bin, but I know you believe in second chances, so...'

I also recognise the writing. Róisín. I'm glad Kieran didn't bin it, though I understand how he feels. He's still so furious with her for hurting me and Kate. He didn't agree with me speaking up for her in court. But he said he respected my decision and that it was up to me.

I nod, take the letter from him and inhale to steady myself. It's been a while since the court case, and I wonder how she's getting on, or whether she's come to any sort of self-awareness. I know Joel went back to New York. There was a huge hoo-ha about the phone. I gave it back to him and left it up to him what to do about it, but he's an honest man and came clean, and hopefully he won't get into too much trouble for losing something that held such classified information. As far as the CIA can tell, the phone wasn't successfully hacked, so at least that. He won't be getting another job in the Senate, though. I wonder, will he come back to Ballycarrick at all?

I pull out a single sheet of rather old-fashioned blue writing paper, which somehow carries with it that pervasive St Ita's smell of boiled turnips.

Dear Mags,

My lawyer told me that I would have been facing a custodial sentence if you hadn't spoken up on my behalf, and for that I'm eternally grateful.

I think I'm coming to understand through therapy how I've lied to myself as well as to you and everyone else.

I want to apologise to you properly, no excuses this time, for trying to take Kieran away from you. It was totally pointless, Mags. He's too in love with you to even look at another woman, but that's no excuse.

I also want to apologise for trying to set Sharon against you. There was no point in that either. That woman is as faithful to you as Kieran in her own way.

It's going to be hard getting my life back on track, but I'm determined to do it, whether here or in New York – that's up to Joel. I feel I have a future now, though I'm not sure what it is yet.

This is a hard one, but thank you for arresting me that day. If you'd let me carry on as I was, something awful would have happened, so much worse than being forced to face up to my own demons here in St Ita's.

You are an amazing woman, Mags.

And for what it's worth, I know Kieran did the right thing all those years ago, staying with you in Ballycarrick.

With gratitude,

Róisín

I read it through once and hand it to Kieran, who reads it then.

'I did do the right thing, staying,' he says when he's finished.

'I think so too.'

He folds it and puts it back in the envelope. 'So will we go back and join the festivities?' he asks gently.

'We will.' I put my empty coffee cup aside and stand.

'Life with you is a lot of things, but boring is never one of them,' he says with a chuckle, draping his arm around my shoulders as we leave the little glass house.

'Oh, that's my shenanigans over now. It's traffic duty and dog licences from here on in. My *Miami Vice* days are behind me.'

He laughs and squeezes me tight until I'm afraid I'll pop. 'I'll believe that when I see it, Mags Munroe.'

THE END

ACKNOWLEDGMENTS

I would like to thank my editing team, the amazing Helen Falconer and Abby Jaworski, without whose expertise, I would fear for your eyes, dear reader.

My advance readers, many of whom have been with me since the start, thank you all. Your support, help, suggestions, broad expanse of knowledge and ongoing encouragement is invaluable.

To Elena for her patience and artistic abilities, you are wonderful.

To my team at Gold Harp Media, Carol O'Donovan and Barbara Dixon, words will never adequately express how much you two mean to me. But I know that you know. I love that we get to do this. To my very precious kids who try their best to help me, by bringing cups of tea and explaining Gen Z speak to this old fossil! And finally to my darling husband Diarmuid, the other half of me. Without whom, there would be no books.

ABOUT THE AUTHOR

Jean Grainger is a USA Today bestselling Irish author. She writes historical and contemporary Irish fiction and her work has very flatteringly been compared to the late great Maeve Binchy.

She lives in a stone cottage in Cork with her lovely husband Diarmuid and the youngest two of her four children. The older two come home for a break when adulting gets too exhausting. There are a variety of animals there too, all led by two cute but clueless micro-dogs called Scrappy and Scoobi.

ALSO BY JEAN GRAINGER

The Tour Series

The Tour

Safe at the Edge of the World

The Story of Grenville King

The Homecoming of Bubbles O'Leary

Finding Billie Romano

Kayla's Trick

The Carmel Sheehan Story

Letters of Freedom

The Future's Not Ours To See

What Will Be

The Robinswood Story

What Once Was True

Return To Robinswood

Trials and Tribulations

The Star and the Shamrock Series

The Star and the Shamrock

The Emerald Horizon

The Hard Way Home

The World Starts Anew

The Queenstown Series

Last Port of Call

The West's Awake

The Harp and the Rose

Roaring Liberty

Standalone Books

So Much Owed

Shadow of a Century

Under Heaven's Shining Stars

Catriona's War

Sisters of the Southern Cross

The Kilteegan Bridge Series

The Trouble with Secrets

What Divides Us

More Harm Than Good

When Irish Eyes Are Lying

A Silent Understanding

The Mags Munroe Story

The Existential Worries of Mags Munroe

Growing Wild in the Shade

Each to their Own

Closer Than You Think

Cullens Celtic Cabaret

For All The World

A Beautiful Ferocity

Rivers of Wrath

The Gem of Ireland's Crown

Made in the USA
Las Vegas, NV
12 April 2024

88617396R00146